My Kind of Love

My Kind of Love

O'BRIEN DENNIS

MY KIND OF LOVE

iUniverse books may be ordered through booksellers or by contacting:

iUniverse
1663 Liberty Drive
Bloomington, IN 47403
www.iuniverse.com
844-349-9409

ISBN: 978-1-6632-2997-7 (sc)
ISBN: 978-1-6632-2996-0 (e)

Library of Congress Control Number: 2021925416

Print information available on the last page.

iUniverse rev. date: 02/28/2022

To SB for coming into my life just at the right moment to teach me some of life's most valuable lessons—the importance of loving myself first and to trust myself enough to make the right decisions. Everything that has happened had to have happened to get us to this point. Everything that must happen cannot be stopped, and that is law. I created My Kind of Love *because of loving you. I am the man I am because I took a risk at loving you, and I am thankful for the experience. I know I have done wrong by you, and this is an open apology of what us could have looked like.*

And to the memory of Dexter Pottinger, a friend who taught me how to live life fearlessly. He has shown me and others how to be accepting of who we are. The star that you shined so brightly will continue with your memories.

Acknowledgment

This has been a long-awaited work, and while fiction, it's a reflection of conversations I have had with friends in the past seven years after publishing *Love on the Wire*. While I have visited several countries in the process of writing this book, it was in Jamaica that I gained the greatest support. I had an opportunity to immerse myself into the local gay culture and got a better understanding of their way of life. While I was born in Jamaica, I was far removed from the culture after living in the United States for twenty-one years.

I would like to acknowledge and express my gratitude to the following people for their unconditional love, support, and helping to guide me on this journey. I have now realized that every incident, every interaction happens for a profound reason. We all have a calling; we can have many different callings. One of my callings is a storyteller and this is my legacy to all the gay men, not only in Jamaica but the African Diaspora who struggle with self-acceptance and self-love.

To all my ex-partners for showing me their kind of love, and for allowing me to get to a point in my life where I can truly define my kind of love.

This couldn't be possible without the tireless support of my young Jamaican tour guides, who took the time to show me around the island. To my Facebook and IG followers for supporting and inspiring me to be my authentic self.

To my Kitchen Cabinet, Nicole, you have always opened your doors to me. Being in Paris is like having breakfast at Tiffany on

New York City's Fifth Avenue. You have always had my back in so many ways. Thank you for your hospitality, encouragements, and our lovely weekend conversations. You are a true sister friend.

To Rushawn, for accepting my friendship and taking a risk in wanting to see the world through a different lens. My trips back home couldn't be as memorable if I didn't have you around. You have shown me so much hospitality and support in going around Jamaica.

To Kadeem, my Jamaican ride or die. I could write a list, however only you would get the gist of the stories. Thank you for teaching me the ropes, for being my eyes when I needed clarity in making some decisions. You have become like a brother. No matter how long since we last saw each other, we play catchup like it was yesterday. Love and respect for all that you have done in helping to get me to a point of feeling safe while in Jamaica.

To Courtney, my true ride or die, you will listen to my bickering no matter what time of day it is. You are and have always been the rock in that hard place and the one person who I know, no matter what, has my back. It's been twenty years of bittersweet friendship and I wouldn't change anything. Thank you for being the brother that I have always wanted.

To Stafford, not just my best friend, but the man whom I call my conscience. I couldn't have asked for a better friend who not only gives solid advice, but listens and says nothing, even when you want to speak. You and Albert have always opened your door. Even on my darkest days, you were just a plane ride away. Thank you for unconditional love and always giving me the space to be vulnerable.

To Sheldon for loving me the way you have. For coming into my life exactly at the right time and for sticking around even when you didn't have to. You have become more than just a lover, you have become a trusted friend, adored by my family. This work reflects our conversations. I met you shortly after publishing *Love on the Wire*, and here you are, sharing with me, my kind of love. Thank you for all that you have given and continue to give. The love wasn't lost.

To my immediate family, thank you for your continued love and support. Both my parents have been my inspiration in wanting to tell the stories that I tell. To everyone who I have encountered in my over forty years, thank you for making an imprint on my life.

Chapter 1

CNN breaking news: An American-born man who'd pledged allegiance to ISIS gunned down forty-nine people early Sunday at a gay nightclub in Orlando, the deadliest mass shooting in the United States and the nation's worst terror attack since 9/11, authorities said.

We got up to one of the most horrific news announcements ever, and it happened on one of the most special days of our lives. We have visited the club at least twice while on vacation in Florida. We have friends who lived there. At least six of our close friends who live in Florida were here to celebrate with us. If they were back home, they may have been killed also. The news didn't give many details. All we can do at this time is just pray for the best.

After 9/11, New York City has increased security. With NYC Gay Pride coming up in a few days, I'm worried that someone may want to copy this attack on our city. My mind was so consumed with the news I just sat there at the edge of the bed watching the footage of the shooting, while he got dressed.

He gave me that look, that deep wondering look, as in, *There is nothing that you can do, and today is our big day, so snap out of it.*

I eventually got up, and I washed my faced, hoping the cold water would make me feel more alive.

"Do you mind helping me with my suspenders?" I sounded rather jaded and nervous, as this was my second time getting married. I also didn't know how to process the shooting, and I felt as though the attack was directed at the entire LGBTQ community.

"You seem tense, Akime. Are you sure this is what you want to do? I am okay with the relationship as is. And no matter what, I am happy and madly in love with you. If you like, I can go downstairs and tell everyone that the wedding is off." It was this level of maturity and frankness that kept reminding me that this was the right decision.

"I'm okay. I'm just remembering the day Nathan and I got married. We had gone to Toronto for the weekend and went down to City Hall with a few of our friends. It was very private, and we had dinner at a Japanese restaurant in Toronto's Chinatown."

As he stood before the mirror trying to fix his black bow tie, he looked like a model right from the cover of GQ's fall magazine. I walked behind him, and while I fixed his shirt collar, I gave him the reassurance that I was okay.

I gently turned him around and kissed him fully on his lips. As he came closer to me, I could feel his bulge growing, and I whispered in his ears, "We will have to leave that until later, baby boi."

He looked at me dead in the eyes and smiled as he grabbed on to my fully erect manhood and ran his moist lips all over my earlobe.

I walked away and stood by the open French windows overlooking the garden and watched the guests as they slowly walked into our yard. So much had happened in the past ten years since Nathan passed away, and this was a big move for me. A great part of me missed him, and I wasn't sure how to deal with those emotions. However, it felt great to finally find love again. I finally got an opportunity at loving. This time around, it felt so surreal. I could now live in my truth, knowing that I wasn't living a lie or dealing with the shame of living with HIV. PrEP had taken over, a new generation of young men were living more responsibly, and the stigma around HIV had lessened significantly.

"If you're having second thoughts, it's okay. And if it means so much to you, I can sign the prenuptial right now."

The previous night, we'd had a huge argument about him not wanting to sign the prenup. I honestly felt that 45 percent of all the shared assets as a couple would be okay. I even offered to give him the house in St. Mary in Jamaica and full support for up to five years if we ever divorced. I got his point; we should be doing this for love and not going into the union with the possibility that the relationship could end prematurely. I questioned myself so often, wondering if this was "my kind of love."

I reassured him that the prenuptial was a no-brainier. If he only knew that I had already signed away the house to my younger brother and given the house in California to my sister. The only shared home would be the brownstone in Brooklyn, the one we'd purchased together in Westchester County, New York, and the house in Westmoreland, Jamaica

The musicians had arrived, and they were playing classical music. The young, attractive waiters were serving food to the guests who had arrived on time. The seven guys who served came from a catering company in Midtown Manhattan. I had asked Shawn if he could cater the wedding for us, and I was extremely specific when it came to the kind of guys I was looking for. I had requested they all stay the night before. And like any bachelors would, my husband-to-be and I sampled some of the young men.

It was like being in a bathhouse in Rome and enjoying the sweets of the city. We mainly watched as they made out. I had too much on my mind to fuck. All I did was watch. And close to my bedtime, I had a healthy nut and went off to bed. It was while getting ready for bed that we'd had the argument about the prenuptial.

The leaves on the tress were already changing, and the view from our bedroom was breathtaking. Next to the bar outside was a lookout point below the garden, which was created with flowers to allow the guests to capture the sunset as they drank and enjoyed the evening's beauty.

There was a soft knock on the door, and it was Warren. He looked as though he was about to get married himself. He wore the navy blue suit he'd worn to his father's funeral, and a white shirt similar to what the other groomsmen were wearing, along with a white rose and handkerchief. Warren was my best man, and I told him that he needed to be on his best behavior to keep me strong. I hugged him as I opened the door and told him that he looked like the groom.

"Bytch, I hope I feel this way when I finally decide to make this big move. By the way, where is he?" His face was furious, and he whispered in my ear, asking if he'd signed the paperwork. Warren was only looking out for my best interest, and he just felt the need to protect me.

"I got this one handled, so you have nothing to be worried about." I felt, deep within myself, that this was the right decision. I had not told Warren that I'd transferred any of my assets prior to this day. That would have been enough ammunition for him to tell me I should just continue to fuck and enjoy my life and call him the live-at-home trade with a degree and no full-time job.

"I won't fight you on your wedding day, but that nigga is playing you for six. If he loves you like he said, he would just sign, as in the end, this shit will last." His anger was too much, and he spoke loudly enough that I pushed him outside. I didn't want an argument between the two of them again.

"We are almost finished; I will meet you outside in a few. You're my best man and I expect you to be on your best *fucking* behavior."

He walked off, smiling and blowing me a kiss. I shut the door with mister staring me dead in my eyes. And all I did was shake my head and say, "You two better know how to fucking live together and work this shit out."

"Is he still holding some grudge that I never fuck him or that you won? I knew our father helped me a lot without the rest of the family knowing who I was. I, however, have a mind of my own. And I desired you the moment I saw you on your return trip to Jamaica. I might have been the yard boi then, but I got a fucking degree. And that is no longer my life." His eyes were teary, and I simply kissed his forehead and reassured him that it was all good.

Warren would always be a *bytch*, and he still held some of the classism that had been instilled in him from childhood. Warren just felt that I had chosen to live a life with the yard boi, the young man who tended to his family garden and took out the trash and that he was beneath me. Warren still hadn't fully accepted the fact that I was marrying his half brother. He was still in his feelings that his younger brother was his family's best kept secret. Warren always believed that *he* was the family's best kept secret because he was gay.

"We have less than thirty minutes to head down and make this happen." I took his hands as we both stood looking through the window. "I know this is a first for you, and I have walked this road before. However, I would not be doing it with anyone else but you. I love you unconditionally and despite all the shit we've endured in the past seven years since you moved to New York. You are the love of my life."

Delaney and her wife, Taylor, were in attendance. Delaney now resided in Belgium with her wife and two kids. Without question, I was the godfather for both children, and I had so wanted to see them during this trip. My sister and her kids and her new husband were both able to make the trip. My brother flew in from Paris the night before, and he was here with his Italian girlfriend who was on child number three.

My mom was somewhere outside. And while she objected to gay marriage, she said she knew how much this meant to me so she couldn't disappoint me by not showing up. Oddly enough, she had a great relationship with Donavan and considered him to be her son. Our relationship had evolved so much, and I was beyond grateful for the support that she had given me.

Nicole and her new husband were seated, and my two godchildren (Nathan's kids) were sitting next to their mother. After Nathan's death they'd become more like my kids.

My relationship with Nicole had improved dramatically, and she was more like a sister from a different mother. The anger I'd had toward her no longer lingered. We'd both come to terms with the fact that we'd fallen in love with the same man, even though I had met him first. We could only treasure the memories, realizing that she was no better woman, and I was no better man. The hurt he'd caused us was real, and we'd just had to move past it. It just went to show that forgiveness could heal all wounds.

I had Shawn send me pictures of his setup in the backyard. The waiters all wore khaki pants, with white shirt, black bow tie, and black suspenders. Green was my favorite color. However, I decided that they should wear orange aprons, as it added a different element of color to what was going on.

Shawn had two incredibly attractive, well-built guys holding silver trays at the entrance to the reception area, with champagne waiting for each guest. Three other attractive, taller, and also well-built guys walked around with finger food. Two other guys carried the specialty drinks for those who had finished their champagne. There was a cold bar with shrimp and fruits, and there was also a cheese-and-cracker section. Right next to the pool house there was a huge water fountain, and it was surrounded by exotic fruits and green orchards. All of the tables were dressed in white tablecloths, and huge silver lanterns were used as the centerpieces.

For those who wanted anything other than what was offered, they had the option to go by the bar and be serviced by a thick muscular man who wore a white T-shirt and a bow tie, with all his muscles showing.

Chapter 2

The week leading up to the wedding, I found myself sitting in my therapist's office telling her about a dream that reoccurred nightly, and I just could not get it out of my mind.

"Do you believe that it's just it's just a case of you getting nervous about getting married all over again and it's bringing you back memories of your past?" My therapist Janet was always so rational. However, I have a great deal of respect and admiration for her. I'd been seeing her for over seven years now, and I'd always felt safe talking to her about anything and everything.

The dreams were getting me scared. I have never had these thoughts before, and no matter how much I tried to get to the end, the dream always left me at a point where I was surrounded by a group of men.

"Last night, I was so close. The tall black guy with the mask had me on all fours. And this time, he wasn't punishing me. He was just standing in a circle with five other guys, and they were all jerking their big black dicks. I offered to give them head, but he alone rejected. It always ends with a kiss and a fight as I try to take his mask off just to reveal his face. Janet, this is some fucked up fantasy. And to be honest, while it turns me on, I'm scared just to think about it."

"Now, Akime, after all the places you've been and the stories you've told me, this could simply be a fantasy that you may want to live out before you get married. Have you had the conversation with your partner about the dream or even told him why you're having sleepless nights?"

This time around I was curled up on her sofa looking through the window at Lady Liberty in all her glory as the sun slowly set and the torch in her hand shone like a light.

I was by no means superstitious. However, I felt as though Nathan was speaking to me in my dreams. And I wasn't sure I wanted to talk to him through that medium. The last time I'd had a dream about him was when I'd ended my relationship with O'Neal. O'Neal was the only man who I fell in love with after Nathan died. And while the relationship was completed, he made me realize all that I was missing out on.

No matter what, I would always have a special place in my heart for Nathan. However, I wasn't sure if I was fully over him.

"How do I let go of him? How do I purge myself of this man?"

The dream seemed so real, and a part of me would want to be in such a setting. The last time I was in a bathhouse, I was in Amsterdam. Tony had flown over from Germany to spend some time with us. The bathhouse was located just a few blocks from Central station, and it was one of the more upscale places in Amsterdam. A friend of ours who lived in London while I was working there and had now migrated to the Netherlands had made the recommendation.

I knew that I had developed an addiction to steam rooms and saunas from going to the gym in New York City. I worked out at least four times per week. I realized that, as I got older and with my hectic work schedule, my metabolism wasn't as fast as it had been when I was in my twenties. I started going to the gym shortly after the accident, and it was recommended that the steam room would help me relax.

It was late one evening when I was at my gym in Midtown Manhattan that I decided to just relax in the steam room. I was unaware of what happened in steam rooms, and I had decided to work out one morning before heading into the office. There were five incredibly attractive guys in the room when I entered. And out of nowhere, I saw the younger black guy in the group start sucking the dick of the tall, toned white guy. I couldn't resist the temptation of joining.

At first, I honestly felt that it was a one-off incident—until I realized over a period of time that most of the men who would usually gather in the steam room after they worked out did so just to get a nut. Because of work, I didn't feel comfortable joining the more exclusive men's health club that carried a steam room and saunas. I felt somewhat comfortable limiting my activities at the gym.

It was, however, while I was working in London that the addiction became more intense, and it became harder for me not to search them out. There was one particular men's club located in Vauxhall in London that I would frequent at least twice a week. I wasn't interested in pursuing a relationship with anyone other than building whatever I could with O'Neal. I never once told O'Neal about my frequenting the bathhouse, as I never really saw it as cheating. After all, I was never interested in penetrative sexual encounters.

That night, I'd told O'Neal I would work out just for a few hours. I went to one particular bathhouse in Amsterdam, and my life took a huge turn. There was just something different about this place. It reminded me a lot of *Queer As Folks*, a very popular gay series on television in the nineties. While I'd been living in Jamaica, the Jamaican government had *Queer As Folks* censored from both cable and any satellite streaming on the island. Most curious minds found some creative way to watch, like I did.

It was summer. Even though it was late at night, the sun was fully erect. I walked in thinking that it would be a regular night. I would just sit in the steam room and jerk off until I nutted.

When I walked in, I was first impressed by the layout. There were two very attractive young men at the front who greeted the guests. They both were shirtless, and they were both very friendly and muscular.

The younger guy asked me a series of questions and told me that there was a smoking section. I was free to smoke; however, drugs were not allowed. He informed me that the cost was twenty-five euros, and upon leaving, I would get five euros for returning the

9

keys. I was also given a gold coin that entitled me to one free specialty drink from the bar.

I paid the twenty-five euros via credit card; I was given a key with the number to my locker. Even though I wasn't insecure about my body, I felt somewhat odd, knowing I was all alone, and it was my first time. I quickly changed and folded the white towel I'd been given in half and wrapped it around my waist. I walked out into the open area, and I immediately saw the smoking section that was enclosed with glass with artificial green foliage in the background.

There was an open lounge area, and all I saw were older white men who seemed drained and exhausted. Some seemed as though they were just looking for a younger man to approach them, and they would gladly open their wallets. To the far right, there was a bar. And I saw, for the first time, a man who was the darkest shade of black I had yet to see in my life, with a rippled chest and green eyes. It was obvious he was mixed based on the texture of his hair.

I needed to take the edge off, and I decided to use the gold coin I'd received for a free drink. The dark-skinned man didn't speak English well; however, he spoke enough so you could understand him. He had tattoos all over his body, and his teeth were white as snow. I handed him the gold coin, and he pointed me to a list and told me to select one. Knowing that I wasn't an avid drinker, I requested something sweet.

My biggest mistake was to have consumed all of the drink all at once. That was how it all started. The liquor gradually snuck up on me, and it hid away some of my biggest inhibitions.

I sat by the bar nervously looking around. A more mature, light-skinned gentleman was sitting three stools from me, and often enough we would make eye contact; however, we never spoke. I saw him stand up, and I was of the assumption that he would be walking away in the direction of the pool. Unfortunately, he was walking in my direction.

"I see that you are here all alone. Would you mind if I offered you a drink?" Before I could even decline, he told the bartender to give me another one of what I had ordered.

As nervous as I was, I yet again took the drink and consumed it all at once. It was sweet, so I didn't feel the effects immediately.

When I dropped the cup hard to the counter, I looked the stranger in his eyes and said, "Thank you so much for the drink. I needed the edge to be taken off."

The man held out his hands and said, "My name is Nicalos. And how is your night?"

I decided to give him a trade name, as I knew I would never ever see him again. "My name is Oliver. It's a pleasure meeting you, and thank you yet again for the drink."

I wasn't sure how to spark up a conversation with Nicalos. At first, we both just stood in silence. "Do you mind walking over to the lounge area so that we can get more aquatinted with each other?"

There wasn't anything better to do, as I wasn't ready to go in the back to see the unexpected as of yet. I was also somewhat embarrassed to be seen.

"So, Nicalos, what brought you here tonight?"

He gave me an odd look that suggested I had asked a redundant question. "I'm actually here with my partner, and he is waiting for me to bring him someone I like."

I wasn't sure what to think or what to say to him. I felt special that he'd selected me, and I also felt that it was honorable of him to be in an open relationship and be so open about it.

"I am only here for the night. I was told about this location by a friend of mine. I have to be back in London by tomorrow evening. So, hey, let's not waste any more time."

We never discussed roles or what he had in mind. I just took a leap of faith and decided to go with the flow. The liquor was already creeping up on me, and my inhibition was slowly kicking in.

There were two swimming pools and a hot tub to the far right as we entered the back section. To our right, a huge shower was separated by a huge wall-to-wall glass, which housed a large sauna. Several men were taking showers, and the men in the sauna could clearly see the men as they showered. There were two young men showering together, and the younger of the two went on his knees, giving the other head. There were several guys in the sauna jerking off, and there were some guys who were sucking dick and eating ass. I just stood in awe, as I had never seen anything like this before in my life.

Nicalos held onto my hands and led me further into the back area. As we got to the back section, the lights became dimmer, and there were small private rooms lining each side of the walkway. There was an open section in the middle, and that room had a huge television with individual beds laid next to each other and a circular leather stool in the middle of the room. In the back section to the far-left side was a lightly dim room with a swing and several booths with open holes for the obvious act.

There were naked men standing fully erect and getting serviced. My interest was sparked. However, this wasn't where Nicalos wanted me to stay.

We walked further through a passage area, and the setting changed as we approached the dim lights. Mask were all over the walls, and all the men who we passed had on something with leather. The room Nicalos brought me into had several silver metal lockers and benches, just like a typical gym.

It felt like Eden as we walked in and saw seven incredibly attractive men standing up and just looking at the both of us. The tallest, more muscular one had his back turned, and his body was covered in oil, glistening before us. A short, thick young man had on a mesh black leather top with a matching jockstrap. The two light-skinned guys were making out and playing with each other's dicks, and they too were fully oiled. The other three guys were slim and well built, with African features. Their complexion was like midnight, and just looking at them gave me a full erection, with all the blood running to the head of my dick and all the veins showing.

"I see you're fully erect now and ready for action?"

I wasn't sure how to respond to him. All I knew was to nod my head as Nicalos whispered in my ear. "I am only here to watch, and hopefully you'll enjoy the party as much as I enjoy watching. You can do anything you so desire."

"There is only one thing I want to know. And that is, who is your lover?" I was excited, hoping that it was one of the darker-skinned guys, as they reminded me of guys from Ghana who had this huge appetite for getting fucked. And I was so in the mood to fuck some Africa ass.

"I saw you looking at him. He is the tall young man with his back turned to us playing with his dick."

That got me even more excited, as I enjoyed fucking taller guys, especially those with big dicks. Nicalos walked over to the young man, and he also whispered into his ears. They both looked good together, and the connection seemed real.

When the young man turned around, my heart immediately stopped beating, and I lost my balance. He was the fucking spitting image of Nathan. He reminded me of the younger Nathan, who'd taught me while I was attending the University of the West Indies (UWI) Mona. I was in so much shock I had to brace myself on the metal lockers, not sure what to do or even how to react.

Chapter 3

I got the call. Judge Mathew was ready for us, and all of the guests were seated. The house had two wraparound staircases in the back leading out to the garden. The guests were seated so that they could see the opening of the French doors. We took to both ends, and walked down slowly to "Conqueror," one of the songs from the soundtrack of *Empire*, the television series on Fox. The song meant a great deal to us because our relationship, leading up to this point, had been a merry-go-round.

I had never truly seen myself getting married to him. I'd chosen to help him make a better life for himself. And while I'd conquered my own personal fears of being alone, he'd become a friend, and we'd fallen in love. He had been very persistent. As tempting as his ass and dick were, I honestly felt that he was just too young for me. Even after he'd moved into the house while attending New York University (NYU), he'd lived in the basement, and I had given him his own space and privacy.

On this day, I stood tall next to him, knowing that he had set me free and we both were conquerors. Mistakes in this life were inevitable, but the universe always had a way of pointing us in the right direction. In this moment, I knew for sure that this was my kind of love. We were exactly where we needed to be.

As we got to the bottom of the staircase, our three bridesmaids and three groomsmen walked out dancing to Jennifer Hudson's "Ain't No One Gonna Love You." We didn't want the traditional walking, so each couple did their own dance to the song as they got to the end. The song was symbolic to us because, when we had broken up for the last time, I had hurt him deeply. We both had felt that there was no turning back. Ironically, we'd both used the song as comfort to the pain we caused each other.

The sun was setting, and the amber of the sunlight was visible in the reflection of the French doors. There was a long silence and stillness as the wedding planner announced our names. My godson, Adam, who was only four and my goddaughter, Layla, came out with two baskets and, with the guidance of the wedding planner and their parents leading them on, started walking out and dropping flowers.

To be honest, this was where it felt real. And I was nervous as *fuck*. I looked him dead in his eyes. And as the tears fell, he held onto my hand tightly and wiped my tears.

As the kids got to the middle of the walkway, our favorite song from *The Best Man Holiday*, "As," started playing. We held hands and walked toward our guests. As we approached the spot where the judge was standing, everyone stood up in unison to the beat of the song. Almost everyone wore white or cream. As they stood up, the whole scene seemed heavenly. I learned then of an arrangement that had taken place without my knowledge. This wasn't a recording; actual singers came out to perform. We both kept our composure as we walked slowly toward our parents, who were standing next to the judge waiting for us.

In that moment, I really didn't care about the prenuptial. I knew deep in my soul, even to my core, that I loved him unconditionally. I could not have asked for anyone else. While the journey leading to this point in my life was painful, I had no regrets. This present moment—this feeling—was priceless, and I felt so loved.

My mother stood next to my father, who looked tall, handsome, and radiant. Just seeing my parents standing in support and unity for our union made me feel beyond special, loved, and appreciated.

My emotions got the best of me as I stood holding the hand of the man I had decided to spend the rest of my life with. The tears just flowed uncontrollably. They sure weren't sad tears; they were happy tears. And I knew for sure that he loved me unconditionally. I know deep in my heart that all the hurt and suffering I had endured had prepared me for this moment. As we got closer to the end, he held onto my hand tightly, and I got that reassuring feeling that it would be okay, and this was love.

As we stood before the judge, we kissed both of our parents. As Judge Matt opened the Holy Bible, I knew that the earth was one, and God was with us both.

The singers stopped singing, and out of nowhere, a young white girl wheeled a huge white-and-gold harp behind the rosebushes and started playing her harp to the tune of "As." This was magical in all forms, and it felt heavenly. The sunset was perfect. The rays of the sun going down reflected on the glasses on the tables surrounding the garden, and rhinestones that embellished the roses that lined the end of each chair just sparkled and gleamed.

As we approached the judge, both sets of our parents sat down. I stood nervously looking at him, asking myself what I was doing and was this what love felt like. He held onto my hands tightly, and he looked back at his mother, who was in tears. The music stopped, and the judge came closer to us.

"We are gathered her today in celebration in the joining of this union. When Akime asked me to officiate his wedding, I was thrilled. I know personally how much he has gone through and what it means to him to finally find love again. As we watch the sunset with all the colors of the sky as it majestically casts a spell on us, please know that God is in our presence." He took out a small black Bible with gold writing on it. He placed the Bible in his left hand and indicated that we should both placed our hands on it. He held onto both our hands with his right hand.

"Shall we all bow our heads and close our eyes? Heavenly Father, we ask for your guidance and blessing as we bring before you these two. And we ask that you anoint them, Holy Father. Dear Father, I ask that you not only bless this union; we ask that you also give them both wisdom and strength to understand the importance of communication and trust in the union. Heavenly Father, I also ask that you teach them both the art of self-love and how to be thankful and grateful for the small things in life. Remind them to seek you first and that a family that prays together stays together."

I found it odd for him to have prayed. But it was his way of doing things, and no one seemed to have objected. The judge asked us both our names and looked me in my eyes. "Are you ready, Akime?

"Do you, Akime, take this man to be your loyal and loving husband?"

He had not quite ended his sentence when I heard a loud *bang* and the sound of crashing glasses. I immediately turned around, suspecting that one of the waiters had fallen. I was now more worried about the safety of the waitstaff than anything else.

Unexpectedly, I heard a commotion and a familiar voice.

"Sir, you cannot go outside. Sir, will you stop please?" The sound of pleading and worry was distinct.

"Don't you dare fucking touch me. It will not go on. He knows that I love him."

The British ascent was distinct and too familiar, but I told myself that this had to be a fucking dream. He would not dare fuck up this day for me after our conversation last night.

"Akime, I know I promised you last night. And I am sorry for all that I did to you. But you cannot do this. I fucked up *big-time*, and I don't want you to go through this. Can we just talk please?"

I turned around and looked at the man who I was about to marry, and I broke down in tears. My brother ran to my rescue, and my dad held onto me. My mother, the woman who should have stood next to me no matter what just because I was her child, chose to go over by him. I didn't even want to fucking see him ever in my life. He'd destroyed my wedding day; he'd fucked up my special day. Why, though, after our conversation last night? Why had I even decided to be friends with him, knowing darn well he could not let me go?

The guests were now whispering as the drunken fool came staggering in my direction. Two of the waitstaff were holding onto him, but he was strong and full of might, and it was a struggle to hold his ass back. All eyes were in his direction. I was filled with shame; rage; hurt; and, most of all, embarrassment. I knew this had to be a fucking dream, as there was no way on earth O'Neal would do this—never.

Two of the security staff who were outside on the open lawn came over and asked me if they should remove him. I was inconsolable at this time.

Out of nowhere, Donavan went over to O'Neal and grabbed him by the neck. I stood still, as I now saw the anger and rage in Donavan. The veins on the side of his neck were fully erect. Just like he lifted the weights in the gym, he was about to drop O'Neal to the ground.

I told the security guys that it was okay. And as always, Warren came to our rescue. He took the mike and apologized to the guests and reassured them that everything was okay.

I asked the waiters to help release Donavan's grip from O'Neal and to take O'Neal inside. I asked the judge to join me as I walked behind my ex and watched his drunken ass stagger into my house. All this time, Jennifer Hudson's "Spotlight" was playing in the background.

Before I entered the patio, I asked the judge to join O'Neal and Donavan in the library adjacent to the kitchen. Mike, who was a licensed therapist, was present. I pointed him out to one of the waiters and asked him to come over. Mike and I had never hooked up, but he went to my gym, and we'd jerked off on a couple of occasions in the steam room. He wouldn't mind a threesome with Donavan; he just insisted that only I fuck him, and Donavan wasn't having any of that.

While I greeted Mike and asked him for his professional assistance, Warren was busy entertaining the guests. Thank heavens, I had live entertainment and the guests were into the music. A part of me was embarrassed and ashamed, as this was my special moment. O'Neal had no fucking right. My parents were just sitting there looking startled, and Donavan's family was whispering among themselves.

By the time I got inside the library, Mike was sitting before O'Neal. Donavan was having a conversation with the judge. O'Neal now had a bottle of water in his hands, and I went over to him and slapped it out of his hand.

"What the fuck are you doing? I am not even fucking upset with your sorry faggot ass, as this is all my fault. The moment I found out about your lies and deception, I should have listened to that voice and backed the fuck away from you. But no, I was so worried about finding love again and even thinking that no one would want to be with me because of my HIV status. Today is the last fucking day I need to see you. And I have a goddamn mind to just fuck your ass up and leave you to the dogs."

The judge came over and rested his hands on my shoulders. "Brother Akime, this isn't the way out of this. It is obvious that he is hurting too, and we have some time to get to the bottom of this. And if you like, we could continue the ceremony."

I looked him dead in the eyes, and I started crying.

Chapter 4

The night I brought O'Neal to my house—it was the day we'd flown to New York together after I had gone to Jamaica to say my goodbyes to Nathan—this was the moment that changed my life. I was hurting. I needed to be loved. I wanted someone just to be my own. I needed validation of self. Most of all, I was in a vulnerable place without fully understanding what vulnerability looked like on the surface. I no longer knew what love was. I had no clue what my purpose was. Money wasn't an issue. I now had enough to sustain myself, and I felt I had no plan. The only thing I thought was missing was a partner, a lover. I yearned for attention and love. I didn't even realize then that, like so many gay men, I too struggled with being alone. I had lost that sense of togetherness when Nathan died. No matter the abuse I'd endured, I did love him. And at one point, he did love me.

The next morning, I got up incredibly early, and I went to the C Town supermarket not far from the house to buy groceries. On my way back to the house, I stopped by the Caribbean market to get yams, green bananas, and plantains. I had left a note next to O'Neal's pillow to tell him that I had gone out for a minute, and I would be back soon to get him breakfast.

When I got back home, the coffee maker was on, and I smelled the scent of vanilla in the air. O'Neal had on white underwear, and he wore no shirt. He looked breathtaking in the kitchen. His ass cheeks were round, and they filled out in his drawers. His legs and arms were well toned, and he looked like a male erotic model in my kitchen. He handled himself as though he lived in the house, and he knew his way around.

As I approached the kitchen area, he came toward me, greeted me, and took the bags from my hands and placed them on the island countertop. As I took my shoes off, he stood before me and kissed me on the lips, saying, "Good morning. I hope you slept well last night."

All I could do was smile. And I held onto his face and whispered in his ear, "It was a perfect night, and it was all I needed. So thank you."

I was realizing now how important it was to acknowledge our partners and just to give them some form of validation.

He sat by the counter and watched me prepare breakfast while, in the background, CNN gave a repeated updated news. It annoyed me how much the news cycle repeated itself and tended to sensationalize the smallest of things. I wanted to learn as much about O'Neal as I possibly could, and I used the time to ask him about life in London.

"So how are the guys in London? And do you mainly date white guys?"

He gave me a side look, and we both laughed at each other. Most of my black friends in Europe tended to have no interest in or desire around dating or marrying a black man. They had no issues engaging them in sexual activities. However, when it came to looking for a future or long-term relationship goals, it was a no-go.

"It's hard dating black guys in Europe, as there is an imbedded stigma that most black men are closeted, and it's too much of a struggle. European black men are exotic, especially those with origins from Africa. I am attracted to black men; however, it seems as though it's just my luck that white guys are bolder to approach me. For the most part, they are actually looking for more than just a quick fuck; most that I have encountered actually find black men attractive." He gave me a questioning look that suggested maybe I was racist, given that I had facial expression that told him I didn't believe him.

"To be honest, I have no issues with them. However, the ones I've encountered in Paris and Italy are just to die for. It's the opposite in America. No matter how it's said, race will always play a factor, as some white gay guys just simply don't understand the struggles of black gay men and the plight of Black America. It's a challenge within itself to be a Black man and survive beyond twenty-five, let alone add being gay to the list. In cases where you see a white guy and a Black guy together, the white guy is usually older and has some wealth."

My hands were filled with the flour batter I was molding to fry dumplings, and I just stood here looking at him.

I saw myself drifting away, remembering one morning a long time ago when Nathan came down to the kitchen. He saw me kneading flour to fry dumplings. Nathan held onto my waist from behind, with his dick throbbing. He gently kissed my neck and slowly licked the center of my back until he got to my boxer brief. He made no haste in removing them, and he instructed me to arch my back and spread my cheeks apart. He used both of his hands to hold firmly to my ass cheeks. He buried his face between my ass crack and used his wet, moist tongue to massage my anal opening. I made soft moans, knowing deep down he was going to fill my ass with his throbbing dick after my ass was left hungry for his nut.

All I heard was O'Neal shouting out my name asking me if I was okay. I was out of it; I was literally back in that moment, and it made me feel so good. I didn't want to hate Nathan; I was still angry at what he had done, but I wasn't ready to let him go. I did give O'Neal the reassurance that I was okay. My mind had just drifted to a happy moment with Nathan.

O'Neal sat attentively watching me cook. At one point, he asked me who taught me how to cook. We spoke at length about my grandmother and how I used to watch her cook on the cold pot in her backyard and how he preferred cooking on an open wood flame. He too shared memories of his grandmother, who had recently passed.

He got a call, and I told him it was okay to use the library in the basement. His call didn't last long; however, he came back with a smile on his face and asked if I would mind if he invited a very close friend of his over to have breakfast with us.

His friend was from Trinidad and, oddly enough, lived across the street from me. His name was Andrew, and O'Neal noted that they'd both gone to the Edna Manley School of Dance in Kingston, Jamaica, and they both were in a local dance group. He gave me a brief history of Andrew and how Andrew was interested in him while at school. However, their friendship evolved into a great bond. I honestly had no issues, and I felt that a new face would lighten my spirit.

O'Neal came over and gave me a kiss on the lips and said, "Thank you." He hugged me from behind, and it felt warm and safe. And in that moment, I missed Nathan and how he would play with me while I cooked for him. For a bit, I drifted away again, and O'Neal saw my changed mood and asked me yet again if I was okay.

"So how will you do this? The house reminds you of him. I realize that you said you changed the layout of the kitchen. Apart from that what else will you do? You can't change the house just to get rid of him." He was still holding onto me and giving me that manly embrace.

I choked up a bit, as I knew deep down that he was speaking the truth. "I am too attached to the house, and I'm not ready to move yet. I haven't even thought about where to move to."

As O'Neal stood and wiped my eyes, I thanked him for just wanting to be there without knowing me and my story.

We heard the doorbell, and I knew it was his friend at the door. Who knew that someone would play with my vulnerability like this? I was in no position to fall in love with anyone. I was only looking for love and comfort. I would have given in to any man who showed me some interest or attention. I was still ashamed to come to terms with the physical and emotional abuse I had endured with Nathan.

I told O'Neal that I would get the door while he put something more appropriate on. O'Neal decided that he would get the door and quickly put on one of my lounge pants. He left me to finish up breakfast.

On their way heading back from the door, I could hear the chatter of both men, and it reminded me so much of Warren and me.

Andrew had a strong Trini accent, and his laughter was infectious. He was wearing close-fitting sweatpants, and it was obvious he was wearing no underwear. And he was an eyeful. He had on a white T-shirt, and all of his muscles were out. He was well toned and had a dark cinnamon complexion that made you think of red dirt in St. Elizabeth. Andrew was an exotic specimen, and his long, flowing, neatly braided hair fell to his back. I had to force myself not to look at him too hard. His ass was firm and round; one could easily hit a tennis ball off it.

"Hey, Akime. How are you doing? I guess I should thank you for snatching this one away from Jamaica and dropping him right in my backyard." We all laughed at the coincidence of Andrew living across from me.

"I figure it's one of those things where it was meant to be. When was the last time you guys met up?" I was finishing up the plantains and breadfruit. Ackee and salt fish couldn't be had without those extra sweet plantains.

O'Neal chimed in. "I think it's about five years now. I had traveled to New York on my way to Jamaica, and I coordinated my stay with Andrew, seeing that we were both attending the wedding of a mutual friend of ours in Central Park." The look he gave Andrew was more than that of a friend. However, it wasn't my place to think more about it, as O'Neal wasn't my man, yet.

We all had breakfast in the den and spoke about life in New York. I got an opportunity to learn more about Andrew, who was a lawyer and ran a nonprofit organization that helped runaway gay youth. I was immediately intrigued with him, and I asked if I could help in any way.

Andrew noted that he wanted to stop practicing law full-time and work as a consultant and focus more on his foundation full-time. He explained that most of his limitations related to funding and the fact that so many of the youths who come into his program struggled with drug addiction, sexual identity, and sexual trauma. He was extremely passionate when talking about the boys and expressed that all they desired was a safe space and someone to love them.

We spoke for hours before deciding to take a walk to Prospect Park. The air was fresh outside, and it was comical for us to just look around and see the trade setting their game into motion. We left Andrew by Grand Army Plaza and took a cab back home.

The moment I got back home, we both took a nap. We didn't even make it to the bedroom. We lay next to each other on the sofa and fell asleep wrapped in each other's arms. This was the level of intimacy I was yearning for. Sex was easy. I lived in New York City, Brooklyn to be exact. Getting boi pussy was like picking up loose change off the streets on Flatbush Avenue, in the heart of the West Indian Community.

Chapter 5

O'Neal left New York three days later, and we made a promise to keep in contact with each other. We both decided we should have no expectations of the friendship, and we should just take it one day at a time. What O'Neal did was simply give me a chance at living again; he made me realize that, even with my HIV status, I could still find love. I so needed that reassurance about finding love and not feeling ashamed about my status and knowing fully well that I alone controlled my happiness.

The Friday after O'Neal left, I picked Warren up from JFK International Airport in Queens. When he got into the car, he not only had a huge smile on his face, he was also glowing; in fact, he was radiating. I decided to not say anything to him and just wait for him to tell me what was going on with him.

"I think I'm in love with him. I know that it's corny, but I can feel it. And this time, it isn't about the sex. I genuinely enjoyed his company, and it was great seeing a familiar face—someone who knew me and wants to be with me for who I am." His eyes were filled with water, and I knew he was in love. I had never seen Warren like this before, and I was so happy for him.

"I am so happy for you, and it shows. So did he fuck your brains out while you were in Jamaica? Did he hit that second hole, so it feels like love?" I was joking, and I said it with a smirk on my face.

"After you guys left, we only had sex twice. I had him spend some time at the hotel with me. We spent more time having conversations and going out. He introduced me to some of his friends, and we just explored Jamaica. We spent a full day at Frenchman's Cove, and it was there that we made love. After spending a day basking in the sun, we agreed to get a room at the local resort. Not only did he lay it good on me, he hit walls and opened up areas in my body I never felt anyone could reach. I came on myself twice as he whispered sweet words into my ear. After he made love to me, he spooned me and held onto me tight, like I was his first love."

He was filled with so much excitement, I got hard just visualizing what he told me. "I am so happy for you. At least the trip was not in vain, and we found happiness."

My statement now led Warren to probe me.

I gave him a *huge* smile and said, "Yes, he did it too, and it wasn't about the sex."

"So we both found love in Jamestown. So what was he like? And what is the next move between the both of you?"

"To be honest, I actually have no set agenda. I go back to work tomorrow, and my life continues. He lives in London. He spends most of his time in Germany, and I live all the way in New York. He has plans to leave London and move to Jamaica. For now, we're going to build on the friendship and see where it leads."

I dropped Warren off at his apartment and decided to spend some time with him before heading back to my place. I helped Warren take his bags up to his walk-up, and we argued about why he couldn't find a more modern building with an elevator. "I know the fucking rent is cheap. But is this shit worth it? You make good money, and my old bones can no longer manage this shit."

We both burst out in laughter.

"Every time you come over, you argue and complain. I know you had no issue fucking Tommy the young white boi who lives two floors above me."

I quickly fired back. "For an ass like that, I would have walked through hell's gate just to get some. He wasn't open. He just had a soft ass, and he just loved getting fuck. And he was a freak at heart."

When we got to the apartment, I dropped the bags at the door and headed for the kitchen.

"I need some water, and I pray that you have bottled water in here. Or else I am going to have a fit." I found several bottles of Poland Spring, and I held a bottle to my head. I never moved it until it was finished.

I turned the TV on to CNN. As always, there was Anderson Cooper talking. "Iran defied a United Nations deadline calling for the Islamic republic to halt its nuclear activities or face sanctions. Tehran insists its program is for peaceful purposes only, and President Mahmoud Ahmadinejad has vowed not to give in to Western interests. But the Bush administration suspects Iran is using its nuclear program to develop weapons, and President Bush has called for worldwide isolation of Iran until it gives up its nuclear ambitions. China and Russia—both veto-wielding members of the Security Council—have been reluctant to sanction Iran, and Moscow proceeded with arms deals with Tehran."

Ironically, I only watch CNN to see Anderson Cooper. He is so hot, and that gray hair is such a huge turn on. I'm not always into short white men, but I would pin him down anyway and give him all my dick. Warren watched me from a distance as I fantasized about Mr. Cooper.

"You know he is out of your league, Mr., and you don't have Vanderbilt money to hold that ass down. So enough of Anderson. What's up with your hot Jamaican man, Mr. O'Neal? You are so fucking lucky." He gave a cynical look, and he forced himself next to me, even though there wasn't enough space between the two of us.

"He is interesting and a great distraction from my current reality, and I can't wait to see him again. I honestly never felt that I could be this open with anyone, especially about my status, and even have the desire for sex again."

Warren held onto my hands in a comforting manner and looked me dead in my eyes. "No matter what, I will always love you and thank you for loving me and giving me so much support."

I was taken aback by his emotions, yet I knew he was telling the truth. "I'm not sure what will happen next. But I'm open to all possibilities, and I wouldn't mind getting to know him. I won't rush another relationship right now. I have so much on my mind. I need to sort out my finances next week. I first need to get the money from the Cayman account. I was wise to have invested all of the money. I really had no plans for it. Investing all of the money in stocks and bonds seems suicidal now. However, I reached out to the banker in the Cayman Island, and I currently have over $1.6 million sitting down there. I plan on having a conversation with Nicole about the kids' future. I am yet to cash Nathan's insurance check. I got $500,000. And I questioned if I should leave my job. But I love it too much to quit now. I could take some more time off, but I keep asking myself, *What would that do?* And I honestly don't think it would be the right thing to do just now."

Two years later

My relationship with O'Neal was long distance, thought it wasn't a serious one. He extended his stay in Europe and spent most of his time in Paris. I was fortunate to travel every three months to see him. My company had started another small investment firm dealing with liquidated properties in central London. With the European Union (EU) so heavily involved in the United Kingdom and the influx of immigrants needing jobs, affordable housing was on the rise.

What my company did was send out several local scouts and have them search out homes that needed repairs or were abandoned. We would go in and make a reasonable offer to the homeowners. Once we acquired the property, we would make repairs, add new fixtures and appliances, and rent the places at market value. My job would be to manage all the properties in Central London.

As the United States housing market crashed, so did the other markets around the globe. My company had several strategic planning meetings and realized that investing in real estate was the way to go. We created an umbrella company so as to not have all assets invested in one entity. I was the project manager, with my office being relocated to Midtown Manhattan. Even though I moved to a different office location, I still had the same boss. The change was needed. I finally got an opportunity to do something different. The old office reminded me so much of Nathan and the fun times we'd had there together.

My boss had assured me that, as soon as the London office was open and functional, I would be relocated to manage the London office. I literally had nothing left in New York but Warren. Warren was contemplating buying a house in Atlanta. Once the move was finalized, I would be left all alone. I was excited about the potential to leave New York, as I would be closer to O'Neal, even though he lived in London. Taking the express Eurostar to Paris from London not only wasn't overly expensive, the entire trip took less than three hours.

It took roughly a year before the transfer came into effect. I had traveled to London at least five times just to get a feel of the environment. I got the opportunity to interview staff and have input in the office layout. I was lucky enough to have gotten first bid in properties. I selected a two-bedroom flat right by Trafalgar Square. It was convenient to all of London shopping and museums and the theater district. O'Neal came over every other weekend, and I went to Paris on the opposite weekends.

On some of the weekends that O'Neal came over, I would have the tub filled with hot water and aromatherapy mint and lined with scented candles. O'Neal usually complained about his feet hurting him after long hours of dance practice. I would gently rub his feet and massage his shoulders for him. I was adamant that he relaxed and reassured him that I was there only to pamper him.

On one evening, he wasn't his usual exhausted self; he seemed more alive. As I massaged his feet, I kept seeing his dick protruding atop the foam in the water. I hadn't had sex in more than two months. I was so preoccupied with other stuff. He saw how excited I was, along with the lust in my eyes, to fuck him.

Just in case the tables got turned, shortly before he arrived, I ensured him that I had prepared myself, as I knew how deep O'Neal liked to go, especially when he has me on my back. I just couldn't resist; I went straight for his throbbing dick, and I could see the excitement in his face. He moved up a bit in the tub, and I could see that all the veins in his dick were filled with blood. It was pulsating in my hands and I gently put my mouth over the head, using my tongue to play with the slit of his dick head. He held onto my head so I would go down further, but I slapped his hands away and gave him a playful look. I used my right hand to hold onto his shaft while I used my left hand to spread his butt cheeks and slightly played with his anal opening.

Without anticipation, I went balls deep and my face went all the way down in the water. I could feel his body move as he tried to put all of his dick in my mouth. I got up gasping for air, and he held onto my neck and plastered a kiss on my lips. He indicated that I should get up. As I stood before him, he pulled my fully erect dick from the side of my briefs, and he spit on my dick and made circular motions as he sucked on my dick. Several times, I pulled my dick out of his mouth and slapped it on his face. I just loved when he spit on my dick and deep throated it up to my balls.

In the back of my head, I wondered who would be fucking who. I don't usually nut when I am flipping. For some odd reason, it's easier in a threesome for me to get fucked and have the other dude suck my dick in order for me to get that good nut out. Other than that, I have to be pounding some ass, and it's always a treat for me to fuck some ass and nut while getting my mouth fucked at the same time.

O'Neal didn't wait for long. He had me stand against the shower, and he went down and ate my ass. My dick pressed hard against the glass of the shower. He tried jerking me off, but the position was too uncomfortable. He instructed me to get inside of the tub. He walked over to the vanity, and I saw him searching for lube. He found the small silver packs and brought five over with him.

O'Neal was very proactive when it came to his health, and when he returned to Paris after our initial meet and greet, he decided to do more research on HIV and undetectable status. There was this new trial pill for couples who wanted to stay with their partners who were positive. The success rate was 98 percent, with the negative partner not contracting the virus.

I believed that honesty was always the best policy in any relationship, and I had decided from the get-go that I would face all of my challenges and rejections head-on. O'Neal decided to get on the little blue pill called PrEP, and I ensured that he got tested regularly.

Like all other nights when I anticipated getting fucked by O'Neal, I knew that I would feel his nut deep inside of me. And as always, I would lay on the bed while he watched his nut drip from my ass. Sometimes he would either lick my butthole or put his dick back inside of me.

I went on my knees in the tub, which was centered in the bathroom with white rocks surrounding the base of the tub. O'Neal made no haste, and he lubed my ass and used his mushroom dickhead to play with the opening of my ass. He did that several times until my anal cavity became hungry for his shaft.

To my surprise, he held onto my neck and whispered in my ears, "Nigga, come fuck me"

I was like, *What dah fuck is he talking about? This was just unexpected, as my ass was twitching so much for his dick deep inside of me.*

I didn't hesitate. I sat on the side of the tub and had him bend over while I ate his ass. It didn't take long for him to start pushing the walls of his anal opening against my lips. That was a clear indication that he was hungry for my dick. I had never seen him like this before.

I literally just poured the lube on the top of my dick head and had him ride my dick. As a dancer, O'Neal was very flexible, and he tiptoed with both hands on my feet as he rode my dick like a champion.

Out of nowhere, he stopped, turned around, and started sucking my dick. I felt like I was about to explode in his mouth. As I felt the nut building up, I instructed him to get on his back. I held onto both legs while I buried my dick deep inside of his anal walls. He was making loud moaning sounds, and I was convinced he could be heard on the streets. I looked him dead in his eyes while I flooded his ass with my load. I pulled out, my dick throbbing with my milky nut still dripping from my dickhead. I scooped both of his ass cheeks and told him to push my babies out. I used my right index finger to play with his hole and lick his now bruised hole.

As he lay on his back jerking his dick, I spit on the head to give him more friction and licked on his nipples. When I realized he was about to climax I slowly went on top of him. I spat on my three right fingers and plastered them on my hole, and I guided his dick inside of me. With just the same force as he rode my dick, I rode him until I saw his eyes rolling. I felt his warm man liquid gushing inside of my guts. I tightened my muscles with the intention of squeezing every bit of nut out of his dick.

We both lay on the floor sex funky and just simply cuddled with each other. We eventually found ourselves sleeping on the floor.

We took a shower together that evening and went out for a late supper in the West End of London. Over dinner, we spoke about my brother moving in and what would that mean for us and the relationship.

My brother had gotten accepted to study engineering at a prestigious school in London. I offered him the opportunity to live with me. He has a fairly decent relationship with our father who lived in Paris, so by living with me he would be closer to him. My younger sister, who lived with my father, and I had never gotten along. My suspicion was that her mother disapproved of my sexuality, and my older sister in Jamaica, for whatever reason, poisoned my sister against me. Usually whenever I was visiting O'Neal in Paris, I would have dinner with my father, just us alone.

O'Neal and I had never really defined our relationship. He had extended his time in Europe and opted out of returning to Jamaica due to the escalating violence on the island. While he had a great deal of passion about going back and teaching at Edna Manley Dance School, O'Neal felt that the crime rate was too large a risk factor.

We were literally in our third year of knowing each other. I was content with how things were going and didn't see the need to define the relationship any further. We would occasionally use the term "partner." O'Neal had, however, made enough statements over several periods in time to let me know that he didn't want a relationship with me. It was a given that we still had casual sex with other guys; however, there was still this huge bond that made us inseparable. It was just an undefined relationship.

After my first year living in London, I had returned to New York briefly for about three months. I was looking into the prospect of subletting my Brooklyn brownstone. Warren would go by occasionally just to open up the windows, and he would also have someone clean at least once a month. I was getting over the city life and felt that I should look into the prospect of purchasing a home in Westchester County. Westchester was nestled right outside of the Bronx, not far from Connecticut and still had the advantage of the suburban lifestyle. The only drawback was the property tax, which was extraordinarily high.

I had proposed the idea to O'Neal, and he seemed interested in moving to the United States. O'Neal had made some connection with a Jamaican dancer who lived in Toronto named Keneel. Keneel had as much passion about dancing and the Afro Caribbean beat within the African diaspora as O'Neal did. There were also several dance schools in New York City that he could partner with. There was one school in Harlem New York that taught inner-city youths dance, and it was privately funded. The youths in the program, if successful, usually got a full or partial college scholarship to dance school, either in the United States or in Europe.

Chapter 6

O'Neal and I had decided to spend Christmas in New York, as the mood in London was very depressing. It had been months since I had seen Warren, and it was long overdue for me to meet up with my friends in New York. We arrived the week before Christmas filled with late-night limes at my house. Warren got me a house boi, as he was adamant that he didn't want me to do any domestic chores around the house. Who knew that he had other plans for me, and that this young attractive man from Brazil would change the dynamics of my relationship with O'Neal?

We decided to be low-keyed for the holiday, and on Christmas Eve, we decided to invite some friends over for a games' night. These weren't my regular work colleagues; these were friends I had either hooked up with or guys I'd met along the way and developed a bond with. Our Brazilian houseboy name's was Luiz, and we asked him if he had any friends who looked as attractive as he did who could be bartenders for the night. Luiz was very comical when we made the request; his English wasn't the best.

"Mr. Akime, do you want him to be light-skinned like me or dark-skinned?"

I actually never had much of a preference for light-skinned guys, so I requested a dark-skinned Brazilian. I told O'Neal that I felt as though I was in an international slave trade, this time seeking an attractive male to work in my house. We all laughed, knowing well that Luiz would come through for us.

At around 5:00 p.m. that evening, Joao Lucas rang the doorbell. Luiz brought him downstairs and made the introductions. I had a huge smile within myself, as Luiz had done an excellent job on his selection. When Joao walked in, he held out his hand and told us his name. I looked over at O'Neal and held onto his legs tightly. I whispered to him, "I can't pronounce this boi's name. I will have to just settle for Lucas and call it a day."

O'Neal just kept laughing.

"Joao." This was O'Neal's failed attempt at pronouncing his name. "How are you doing? How do you feel about us calling you Lucas because it may be a challenge to pronounce your first name?"

"No problem, Mr. Akime and Mr. O'Neal."

His accent was to die for; it sounded so exotic. I knew I had to fuck him before the end of the night, and I hoped he was into threesomes as much as I was.

As the evening lingered, Lucas was able to familiarize himself with the house. I told Luiz that he would be running the show with Lucas for the night.

Around 9:00 p.m., the first guests started arriving. Lucas was literally dressed up, and both O'Neal and I chuckled at him when we first saw him. Our first friend to arrive was Anthony. We used to work out together at the gym in Harlem. He told us that he had invited two of his friends and hoped it wasn't too much of an inconvenience. Knowing my friends, they would all be bringing a bottle of liquor. That made me excited, as that would only add to my existing collection in the basement.

By 10:45 p.m., there were eleven incredibly attractive, well-educated Black men in my living room area discussing politics and gay marriage and playing games. Warren brought with him this guy he was dating name Steve, the new man of his life. Steve lived in Atlanta and owned his own real estate company and had suggested to Warren that they move in together when he purchased his home in Atlanta.

I actually like Steve. But O'Neal insisted he was trouble and too much of a bottom, even though he gave good dick. Warren also didn't like the fact that Steve lived in Atlanta, even though his real estate firm was located in New York City. I wasn't in a position to judge. Finally, my best friend was somewhat stable, and I had to be happy for him. I gave Steve a handshake and hug, and I whisked Warren away to a corner of the living room.

"Yo what do you think of our bartender Lucas? Initially, he treated each of the guys with a glass of champagne, and now he is by the bar." I had turned my back to the bar to not make it too obvious that we were discussing him.

"Nigga please, I saw him the moment I stepped in, and I knew it was Luiz's fine ass who brought his friend over to get some of this good Jamaican dick." Warren actually cupped my balls just for the optics of telling me indirectly not to lie to him.

All I could do was laugh. "To be honest, even though I know you don't believe me, we actually haven't had sex with Luiz as of yet."

Warren gave me his *oh-bythch-please* look.

"Did you hear yourself? You actually said yet, so that means you do have some intentions of fucking him."

I guess I had put my foot up my ass, and there was literally no way for me to argue myself out of this one.

"We are actually hoping that we can get Lucas's attention later tonight and have him join us in bed."

Warren high-fived me. And it was obvious that we were gossiping, as Darren, the queen of all queens from any card deck, who know all the tea in New York City, was on his way over.

"What's up, boys? So I realize your punk ass didn't send me a personal invite, Mr. Akime. Thank God for Derrick, who saved the day and told me that I must come."

Warren and I just looked at each other.

"There was no need to send you an invite, as I knew Derrick would come and, if you were the trade of the month, he would bring you."

"Gurl, you know I don't want no drama up in my house, and this open relationship that you two have is way too extreme for my liking. Kevin is by the kitchen talking to Derrick, and you damn well know he gave Derrick an STD. Derrick's stupid ass came home with an STD and gave it to you. Oh that must be some mother fucking good dick, but there was no way I would have been up in here talking to him like I saw you doing."

Dead silence.

Well I was grown, and that was all behind me now. We'd all worked it out. Kevin apologized, and he actually had no idea he had an STD. It was man of him to have reached out to me to tell me how sorry he was. He also didn't know that Derrick and I were in an open relationship.

"At the end of the day, the two of you have to be happy with whatever arrangements you have." I felt there wasn't a need to prolong the conversation much. So I indicated that I had to go check on the bar.

I left Darren talking to Warren. As I walked over to the bar section, I found something questionable. O'Neal was chatting it up with Lucas, and I just found it to be very odd. It seemed more sexual than anything. In the back of my head, I figured that O'Neal was just ensuring that we had Lucas for a late-night nightcap; and, who knows, maybe we'd have Luiz join in on the action.

The party was very entertaining. We had no more than thirty guys over. All we did was talk about politics and the housing market in the United States. The housing market was more my topic of interest, as I very much wanted the guys in the room to understand the importance of homeownership.

One of my very good friends David was in the back playing cards, and I went to get him to talk more about retirement funds and savings. I had a special bond with David. He used to be our threesome partner when Nathan was alive. He simply didn't want to be in a relationship and felt very comfortable having regular sex with us without the emotional attachment.

David was now happily married to an investment banker on Wall Street. David work for Mutual of America, and he was the ideal person to engage the group in a conversation on investment and retirement. David whispered to me that he didn't want the spotlight to be on him. However, he was pleased to engage the group in conversation.

"Good night, gentlemen. It's a given that too often we have a natural fear about having conversations about death or retirement or even an honest discussion about money. There is one reality that we all cannot ignore, and that is the inevitability of death. All of us here tonight are young, and some of you may even question the rationale for planning your retirement so soon. Because we are unsure of the hour, it's best that we put things in order."

The room was silent for the most part, and some of the younger guys were laughing. Some of the older guys had an odd look on their faces, especially those who knew they had made no plans for their deaths.

"So, how many of you here, outside of the life insurance package offered at your place of employment, actually have private life insurance?"

The response in the room was very dismal at best.

"We have a lot to discuss it seems. Life insurance isn't just planning for your funeral. It's also planning for the future of your partner and family members so that you don't leave this earth and leave an enormous amount of debt on their shoulders. For those of us who are married or even have plans to get married, we need to ensure that we don't leave our partners with any extra financial burden that they shouldn't have to deal with." The conversation became personal, and David now had the attention of all the men in the room.

"You can pay as little as $55 per month or $100 per month depending on the plan that best suits your financial needs. Let's not forget; separate from your will, you all need to have this information stored in a safe place, preferably a lockbox at a bank or a fire-safe box at home."

Joseph, who seemed more eager than anyone else, had to raise his hand to ask a question. "So, what if I have a medical condition? Would that prevent me from getting life insurance?"

"A very good question. Insurance companies are evolving. And with the advent of technology in medical science, more individuals with chronic diseases are living much longer. It's best to seek out an insurance company that doesn't have limits or restrictions on medical conditions."

"Thank you so much. I really needed to ask that." Joseph knew very well that his partner, who was fifty-four years old, wouldn't be dying any time soon. He just needed to get him to put aside as much money as possible.

"So, now on to retirement funds and the best way to go about doing this. There are several types of retirement packages, and that is based on the industry you work in. One of the most important things you need to know about retirement plans is that the funds are taken out before your salary is taxed. That makes it much easier for you to actually invest more. Some companies actually match the amount of money you contribute. You also have the option to invest some of the money you've put aside.

"One of the benefits of setting aside a large amount of money is that you have the option to borrow against your own money. If you're purchasing a home for the first time, you can take funds out without any financial penalties. That was how I was able to purchase my first house. You can also take out a loan for school or during natural disasters, such as heavy winds, flooding, or excessive cold weather that may cause property damages. You can take funds out to make repairs. If you plan to stay with a job for a couple of years, you can withdraw the money when you leave your job."

I went up and stood next to David and thanked him for his wealth of information. "Thank you for taking the time to talk to us. And I do apologize for the short notice. Guys, if any one of you wants a one-on-one with David, please feel free to talk to him. By the way, I didn't mean that kind of one-on-one, as he is happily married."

The guys went off into their little groups and continued their conversations. The liquor was still pouring, and I realized that O'Neal was drinking somewhat too much.

Around 3:00 a.m., the crowd started winding down. Our two lovely waiters seemed to be having a blast serving liquor, and they too were a part of the conversation. Closer to 4:00 a.m., there were four of us left, excluding the waiters. Brandon and Toney seemed to be too wasted to drive, so O'Neal and I offered for them to spend the remainder of the night.

There was a small room in the basement area, and both gentlemen said that they were okay sleeping on the pullout sofa. I didn't feel like going upstairs and asked O'Neal if he felt okay sleeping in the basement. My office also had a pullout bed. Oddly enough, it was more comfortable than the bed in the bedroom.

The area where the gathering was held was already cleared, and I went over and thanked both Luiz and Lucas. I was out of it; I was walking around in my long johns, and O'Neal was in his Calvin Klein white drawers. I approached Lucas and asked him if he wanted to spend the night. I knew it would be too late to either get a cab or take the train back to Washington Heights.

While I was having a conversation with Lucas, O'Neal came over and grabbed me from behind and cupped my balls in his hands. I knew he was literally drunk, and he wanted very much to nut before he went off to bed. I had an idea what he wanted to do. I was hard just from his touch, and O'Neal urged Lucas to come over and hold onto my dick. Lucas seemed more than eager. He didn't just grab onto my dick; he pulled it out and started jerking it off.

Luiz was in a corner wiping the glasses and stacking them on the shelf. I could see his dick print on the side of his pants. I indicated to him to come over. He made no hesitation, and he came over. It appeared he had wanted to touch both O'Neal and me all this time. Luiz wasted no time. He went on his knees, and he started sucking on my dick. I was a bit shocked, as he went down so quickly, and his mouth was already wet and moist. He went balls deep on his first try.

O'Neal was absolutely loving the action. He held onto Luiz's head, forcing him down on my dick while he kissed me passionately. I got the opportunity to have double my pleasure, as Lucas was also down below sucking my dick. Luis was licking on my balls. I felt as though I was in heaven. O'Neal was still behind me and I could feel his dick brick hard in his briefs throbbing against my ass. I put my hands behind my back, and I pulled out his dick and placed it between my ass cheeks.

I could feel my ass getting naturally moist, and I so wanted to have O'Neal fuck me then and there while I got my dick sucked. He actually had other plans, and he too came around in front of me and started sucking on my dick. I felt like I was in fucking heaven. There was no music in the background, just the sound of lips, saliva, and my balls hitting the faces of three incredibly attractive men, including my man.

O'Neal was bent over with his ass arched, and I saw Lucas eying his ass, hungry to eat his ass. I gave him the go-ahead with my eyes. O'Neal seemed as though he was in heaven; he made loud moaning sounds. Luiz was now on his back on the floor, while O'Neal stood over him, jerking off. Meanwhile, Luiz continued to service my fully erect cock as I fed his hungry, watery mouth.

We all went into my office, and I instructed Luiz to get on all fours. I slowly licked his anal opening. He was shivering, but I used both of my hands to hold onto his butt cheeks firmly, giving him that strong grip so that he didn't leave my grasp.

O'Neal had Lucas in the same position as I had Luiz, and his ass seemed hungrier for a dick than it did to be eaten. O'Neal and I switched, and I spat on Lucas's anal opening and buried my face deep inside of his ass. As I tongue fucked Lucas, I used my right hand to jerk his dick, which was dripping with pre-cum.

O'Neal's ass looked wet and hungry for dick and I knew how he got when he was liquored up. He was more relaxed and could take dick for days. While O'Neal was eating away at Lucas's ass, I grabbed the lube from my desk drawer and gently rubbed a small amount on my dickhead. I had him arch his back a bit, as though he was doing yoga and made small circular imprints at his anal opening. I could feel his ass muscles tense up as I slowly inserted my fully throbbing dickhead in his ass. The ring around his anal opening was tight; as I pulled him more toward me, I could feel him gasping for air.

O'Neal was now sucking on Lucas's dick, I guess to get the sensation of two dicks in his open holes at the same time. Luiz went directly over Lucas's face and spread his ass cheeks and sat on his lips.

My mind was in a daze. I felt as though I was living in a dream. I used eye contact to motion Luiz to assume the same position as O'Neal. I went into the drawer for a condom, and I lubed my dick up all the way to the base of my shaft. I wasn't gentle. Luiz had already lubed his ass, and I could see him pushing out his ass lips. I slammed myself balls deep inside of him. The black of his eyeballs rolled back into his head, and he made a gasping sound and surrendered his full body to me. His dick was dripping pre-cum just from the brute force of me fucking him.

O'Neal was still down ass up, and Luiz came behind him and started licking his hole. As he ate my man's ass, he looked up into my face for a sign of approval. I was so fucking turned on by Luiz licking O'Neal's ass juice. As I pounded Lucas, I had my index fingers between O'Neal's ass and Luiz's mouth. He hinted at getting some, and I gave him a smile.

Luiz then stood up with his dick hard and all of the veins running through his dick visible. He was a good nine with a thick mushroom dickhead. He spat in the palm of his hands and massaged the shaft of his dick, and he slowly slid himself inside of the man I had fallen in love with.

O'Neal's legs began to shake, and he arched his back more, lowered his ass, and put both his legs together as Luiz slow fucked him deeply. Luiz's rhythm was in sync with his slow thrust as though he was performing a ritual of some sort. As he fucked my man, I spat on my index finger and inserted it into Luiz's ass. His beat and thrust became more intense.

O'Neal and Lucas now started to kiss. Both men were breathing heavenly; it sounded as though they were making wild animal sounds.

As I saw Luiz slow his thrust, I knew he was about to nut. I whispered in his ears to wait for me. I pulled out and shot my load all over Lucas's ass, while Luiz flooded my man's ass. As he pulled out, his man juice dripped slowly out of O'Neal's ass. O'Neal put his hand behind him and inserted Luiz's dick back in his ass as he released himself.

The dream was now over. As my reality seeped in, I was now filled with rage and anger. O'Neal had never once pushed him out. He never fucking got angry with him for putting his dick inside of him. It was all my fault. Even though I had wanted to watch O'Neal get fucked, I was angry that he had taken Luiz's raw dick. I was even more enraged that O'Neal had gotten flooded and actually wanted more. This motherfucker, how could he do this to me? What the fuck was he thinking?

I slowly drifted away. I found myself heading toward the upstairs bedroom. I felt disgusted and just didn't want to be next to O'Neal anymore. How dah fuck could he have done this? How could he have lost so much self-control and allowed another man to fuck him before me? Was he fucking crazy or something?

I literally cried myself to sleep, telling myself I was still in a dream. Was it all my fault? Was I also caught up in the moment and he'd felt this was what I had wanted? Had he done it just to make me happy?

Chapter 7

I got up the next morning, and he was not in bed lying next to me. Before I opened my eyes, I lay in bed, still, as the sun undressed herself and showed us Mother Nature and her glory. I waited in bed for him to just turn up—to show up in bed next to me—but he just never did.

I was able to process my thoughts. I felt hurt and betrayed. I felt lied to. I felt dishonored that the man I'd fallen in love with had done all that next to me, and it had felt and seemed so normal. I wasn't upset that he'd gotten fucked. I was so fucking pissed that he'd gotten flooded by this hot Brazilian *nigga*. *Fuckkkkkkkk*!

I went downstairs, and he wasn't even in the living room. I went to the kitchen to get a cup of coffee and turned the TV on to CNN. All I kept hearing was "CNN breaking news," but no news anchor was present on the screen.

I waited until the hottest white guy I had ever fallen in love with on television—not to mention who I would definitely date if given the opportunity—Anderson Cooper came on the screen. In that distinct voice, he said, "A Nigerian man on a flight from Amsterdam to Detroit allegedly attempted to ignite an explosive device hidden in his underwear. The explosive device that failed to detonate was a mixture of powder and liquid that did not alert security personnel in the airport. The alleged bomber, Umar Farouk Abdulmutallab, told officials later that he was directed by the terrorist group Al Qaeda."

My body was numb, as this was a young man. I saw my brother's face flashing before me. This young man could have been a family member of mine. What would have allowed him to do this?

I didn't have a hangover or anything. My mind just wasn't clear. I wanted coffee, but I felt that ginger and orange tea would be better. I got my favorite mug. Far in the back in a corner of the cupboard, I spotted Nathan's Mickey Mouse teacup—the one he'd gotten when we went to Disney World with Nicole and the kids. It brought back so many memories. I missed him. I missed his touch, our conversation, the way he would stand next to me in the kitchen and watch me cook. I missed the smell of his dirty clothes, the musky man scent of his drawers. I just missed the way he would make love to me and leave his throbbing dick inside of me after he flooded my ass with his man juice.

I sat on the bar stool just looking through the huge kitchen window overlooking the backyard garden. As I sat in stillness, I asked myself if I was happy and what was it that I was missing. I felt that there was an emptiness within me. I didn't have much time to process what I was thinking, as I heard the house phone ring. It was an odd sound; I didn't normally use my house phone. I believe only five people knew the number. It had to be either one of them or a wrong number.

I picked up, and all I heard was a sobbing sound. At first it wasn't clear who it was.

"Hello. How may I help you?"

The person on the other end just kept on crying.

"Hello. Are you okay? Can I get you some help?"

The sobbing didn't stop, but the caller was trying to talk.

"He's dead. He's dead."

That was all I heard. I was still unable to recognize the voice.

"I am not sure who this is. But who is dead? And do I know you?" I paused for a moment, trying to figure out if the voice was familiar.

"Akime, he's dead. And I didn't get to tell him that I was sorry." The sobbing became louder. I knew that voice. This was Warren. But who had died?

"Warren, is this you? Who's dead? Do you want me to come over?" I had so many questions, but mostly I was baffled as to who had died.

The sobbing calmed down, and he was now breathing very heavily. I was getting scared; I have never heard Warren like this before.

There was an awfully long pause. I knew he was hurting. So all I did was wait for him to talk to me.

"Mummy called me this morning and told me that Daddy died. He was sick for some time, and he didn't want to see me or let me know he was sick. Akime, he was still ashamed of me—too ashamed to even own me as his son." Warren started crying again, and I could hear the hurt in his voice.

"I'm on my way over to you. Hang up. I'm going to get dressed and get a cab. I will call you back on my way. Would you rather me just stay on the line while I get dressed?"

Warren made a very faint yes sound. All that I could do was oblige his request. I put the phone on speaker and ran up to my room.

When I got into the bedroom, I went directly toward my closet. I immediately changed my drawers. It was cold enough outside for me to wear a pair of long johns. I searched for my black Adidas sweatpants. I was wearing briefs so my dick print wouldn't be that visible. It was the holidays, so I picked up that ugly sweater my brother had gotten me last year for Christmas. I got the tan Polo high-top winter boots from the shoe closet. My Burberry coat was by the door, along with my scarf, and that would be it.

"Warren, are you still on the line?" I heard the television in the background, so I knew he was still on. "I'm going to hang up and call you from my cell phone when I get outside." I hung up the phone and headed in the direction of my home office to get my cell phone.

When I got downstairs, I saw O'Neal. He was in his underwear and a white T-shirt. To be frank, I just didn't know how to look at him. I still loved him, but in this very moment, I despised him; and I just didn't want to focus on him right now. He had a hangover, and he wasn't fully conscious of his surroundings either. I got the phone. And on my way to the door, I shouted out goodbye to him out of respect. I just couldn't see myself touching him or even kissing him goodbye.

"Warren is in an emergency, and he needs my help. I am heading over to his apartment. If you need me, just call me. I may be there for most of the day."

I stepped out, walking in the direction of Eastern Parkway and Utica Avenue, hoping I could get a cab. I just hoped that O'Neal would give me some space and not reach out to me for the rest of the today. I hadn't even looked back while walking through the door.

It was my lucky day. I got a cab right by the second light before getting to Utica Avenue. I was so excited that I'd gotten a cab that I jumped right in.

"Nostrand Avenue and Gates Avenue please. I don't remember the exact address, but it's okay to drop me off right at the corner of Gates." I was digging through my pocket to find my cell phone.

When I looked at the screen, I saw that I'd received five text messages from O'Neal. I knew it was Christmas, but I wasn't in the mood to respond at all.

The cab driver was an older Black man. He had an African accent; it sounded like he came from Senegal or some place in West Africa.

"Good morning, sir. How is your morning going? Would you like music? Or do you just desire a calm ride to your destination?" He spoke with so much authority, like a father or a grandfather. He had a manly voice that forced you to respond with a level of respect, even if you weren't in the mood to respond.

"I'm not sure if I will see Christmas today. I'm just trying to be still, trying to comfort a friend who just lost his father." I realized that my voice was shaking. I was hurting also that Warren had to be going through all of this all alone. I knew how much guilt he would put on himself, and that was what scared me the most.

The gentleman said he would try and get me to be more relaxed. He played Whitney Houston's Christmas CD; it felt as though it was all I wanted to hear. I closed my eyes and listened to "Oh Holy Night" and had him repeat it three times until I got to my location.

When I got out of the car, I walked as quickly as I could to Warren's apartment. I had his spare keys in my wallet still, so it was easy to let myself in. The one thing I hated about Warren's apartment was that damned walkup; I despised it. I could only wish that someone would create some system so that I could access his unit more easily. Before I opened the door, I knocked. I heard no response, so I let myself in.

I felt as though I was at a reggae concert or walking into Bob Marley's house off Hope Road in Kingston, Jamaica. This wasn't the scent of weed; that was bush compared to this high-grade ganja scent that emanated from the apartment as soon as I opened the door.

Warren was laying across his bed on his back. He was wearing his white low-rise Prada briefs, and his head was hanging over the edge of the bed. In his hand, he held a lit joint.

I went over toward him and raised his head up. "Come sit next to me on the carpet."

He got up off the bed and sat next to me and rested his head on my shoulders. I put my hands around him, and I held onto my friend as tightly as I possibly could. He was shivering. I could feel his teardrops soaking my T-shirt.

"I know that it hurts, and there is nothing that I can say to comfort you right now. Just know that your God is alive, and he loves you. I am here for you. The pain is real, but we will get through this together."

We simply sat in silence, and we said nothing to each other. I could easily hear Warren's heartbeat. I had never seen him cry, other than when he was in the hospital after I had been shot. This time around, he didn't just cry; he wept, and he screamed. I held onto him tighter, as I knew that his pain was real. For a good twenty minutes, Warren just let go of his sorrow and pain.

His phone kept on ringing. He told me that he didn't want to talk. It kept on ringing, and I knew it had to be someone important. I decided to check to see who it was. It was his mother calling. I knew she just needed to know that he was okay, so I picked up the call.

"Good morning." I paused for a bit. "How are you holding up?"

"It is so good to hear your voice, Akime. Son, he fought a good fight, and he left us in dignity. I felt the pain of losing him all over my body. However, I know deep down that it's God's will. I will get over it; God will carry me though.

"How is my baby doing? I wish I were there with him, and I know he feels guilty for so much." I could hear the concern in her voice; it was the voice of a mother—a woman who is in pain but is staying strong not just for herself, but also for her family. She knew the strained relationship between Warren and his father because of his sexuality. The fact that Warren had never gotten an opportunity to say goodbye or make peace with his father would make the loss even harder for him.

I brought the phone over to Warren, and he just pushed it aside. I didn't want his mom to hear me talk to him, so I just held out the phone in my hand. He shook his head, and I realized that he just wasn't in the mood to talk.

"Mummy, he said he will call you later."

I knew she knew for a fact that I was lying, but her voice was more relaxed; she knew that Warren had someone at home with him and that he was safe.

"Okay. No problem, my son. Just tell him I love him and to let me know when he is coming home." As she hung up the phone, I looked at Warren.

Now I became emotional; I had never seen Warren ignore his mother before.

I went over next to him and yet again we sat in silence. This was a unique moment in my life because this was my first time ever comforting a friend who had lost a loved one. We lay next to each other on the carpet right by the bed until we both fell asleep.

I woke up around 3:00 p.m. to Warren sitting up in bed reading the Bible.

"Usually, I stay far from the Bible. This time around, though, I'm just curious as to what's going on here." I gave my best friend a nonjudgmental look.

"I'm searching for answers. I used to go to church with my mom every Sunday. I used to pray away this feeling, this urge and desire to be with men. I knew how much my father wanted me to take over the business. I knew he'd molded me to be just like him. I still don't feel as though I am fully a man. I'm battling with my father's expectations of me and feeling like I've disappointed him." Warren had his head down, and the tears were just flowing.

I went over to the bed and put my arms around him, knowing well that he needed to forgive himself for feeling the way he did about himself.

"Your sexuality doesn't define your masculinity; the last time I checked, you are a man. Your father loved you the best way he knew how. Your father struggled with the definition of masculinity and sexuality. Jamaica's colonial laws still hold that island paradise hostage. Your father felt he needed to uphold his cultural value system. And by doing so, he abandoned you. You did nothing to him; you're also not the cause of his death. You're hurting because you were looking for acceptance from him. With his death, the reality now lingers that there will never be hope or an opportunity to prove yourself to him. That harsh reality will hurt, but this too shall pass.

"Warren, look at all you've accomplished in the time since you left Jamaica. Look at the man you've evolved into. My friend, you have so much to be thankful for. I need you in this moment to treasure the memories you had with your father, knowing well that you had no control over his actions. We're going to go back to Jamaica and honor his memories. And like your father, you will stand strong." I was surprised that I was able to compose all of that shit, given that I also struggled with my own sense of masculinity and living up to my father's expectations of me.

"Akime, I so wish that Daddy had gotten to see me—to see the man I've grown into and not be so ashamed of me. I'm hurting because I know that I am a strong Black man. I will go home, and I will honor him. I will love him as I have always done." He slowly got up off the bed and headed toward the kitchen. I walked behind him, watching his every move.

"You know what? You won't be doing it alone. I'll be right next to you. This is my time to give back to you for all the love you gave me when Nathan passed away and during the time I spent in the hospital."

He turned around and gave me a huge hug.

"So, are we going to starve ourselves? I am not in any mood to cook. And I know damn well you're not going over any fire cooking any dinner today."

While I was talking his head was in the refrigerator looking for something.

As we pondered what to do, we heard the doorbell ring. We looked at each other.

"Were you expecting company to drop by? Maybe some unexpected trade who felt he had a right to just pop up out of nowhere, especially on Christmas Day?"

Warren gave me his *bytch-please* look. "As much as I would take some dick just about now to ease my pain, I am not in the mood for no random trade in my space." Warren walked over to the intercom and asked who it was.

"It's me, O'Neal. Merry Christmas, Warren. I knew that you wouldn't be cooking, and I knew Akime was here comforting you. So I decided to bring dinner to you."

Warren turned around and looked me dead in the eye, looking for an answer as to what he should do or say.

"I don't know why the fuck that *nigga* followed me over here for. After what he did last night, I am not even sure how to look at him again. Please don't ask me either, because you're going through too much. I won't let you focus on me and this trifling punk ass *bitch*."

My eyes flickered with anger; it was obvious that I would fuck O'Neal's ass up if he said the wrong thing to me right about now.

"So, should I let him in? This looks serious and I am not about to get into the middle of something or be part of a fight." Warren still gave me that look.

"Yes, let his ass in. I'm fucking hungry, and he knows how to throw down in the kitchen. He really didn't cook for me. He did this for you. So fuck it. Let's eat. It's fucking Christmas."

O'Neal came up with two huge bags, and he smelled fantastic. To be frank, it was moments like these that had allowed me to fall in love with him. He was just beyond considerate and thoughtful. O'Neal was a hard worker; he would go above and beyond for me. So many times while we were in London, he would surprise me at home with dinner, a hot bath, or just a nightcap in the den with wine and candles.

I knew I had fallen in love with him for all the right reasons, but I wasn't sure if I could move past what had happened last night. This relationship was different for me. I was actually in love with O'Neal. I just didn't want to get hurt again. There was a part of me that felt I was being hypocritical. I didn't mind him getting fucked. I just didn't feel that he should have allowed some other man to flood his ass other than me. That was my real fucking issue with the situation. This was all about my ego and my pride.

O'Neal didn't need much assistance. Even though he didn't know his way around Warren's kitchen he made use of himself. By the time Warren and I left to discuss his travel plans, O'Neal had already set the table. The table layout was beautiful, and all I could do was go over to him, give him one *big* kiss on the lips, and tell him that I loved him. I did love him. It was so sweet of him to think about Warren, so beautifully thoughtful.

We had fried chicken, done the way my grandmother would have done it back in Jamaica, along with rice and peas, curried goat, fried sliced snapper, and breadfruit salad done like potato salad with mixed vegetables. It wouldn't have been a meal without fried plantains, my favorite. When had O'Neal found the time to do sorrel and homemade carrot juice? It was mind-boggling. I was just thankful for his act of kindness, his willingness to just be there when you needed him the most.

I was happy to see Warren smile and get his mind off his father for a bit. We spoke about the party the night before and also where we saw ourselves for the new year. My life was about to change; it was God's will. They say things happen for a reason, and I knew for sure that there were no mistakes. I knew I had to find it within myself to forgive O'Neal and move past the hurt. I just wasn't sure how to start the conversation.

O'Neal and I both decided to spend the night with Warren, as we didn't want him to be alone. After dinner, we stayed up late watching reruns of *Will and Grace*, one of my all-time favorite TV shows. We all had a glass of wine. Although I loved the show, we all agreed that the lack of a consistent Black gay character was a sign that, once again, like it always is in entertainment, the Black gay narrative was being ignored.

Around midnight, Warren told us he just wanted to sleep. We asked him if he needed anything, and he reassured us that all was good with him. I was very proud of him. He seemed to be in a better mood compared to earlier. Also, he didn't have the desire to hook up with anyone. It was a sign that my friend was growing up.

O'Neal and I pulled out the sofa bed and made ourselves comfortable. Before closing my eyes, I held onto O'Neal tightly; thanked him for his lovely meal; and told him that, when we got up in the morning, I would like to have a conversation with him about the sexual adventure we'd had the previous night.

Chapter 8

I woke up the following day and turned the TV on, as always flipping to CNN. The story of the shoe bomb was all over the news. This time around, it was not Mr. Hot Ass Anderson Cooper. It was the holiday weekend, so the regular anchors were on break. This Black man had some sex appeal to him, though not like Anderson. He had a Southern accent, which allowed you to believe he was a gentleman.

"Officials charge Abdul Farouk Abdulmutallab with trying to blow up the Detroit-bound airliner on Christmas Day. The suspect was already on the government's watch list when he attempted the bombing; his father, a respected Nigerian banker, had told the US government that he was worried about his son's increased extremism."

O'Neal was still fast asleep; noise never tended to wake him up. I, on the other hand, was usually up at 5:00 a.m. and mentally ready for the day. Even on the weekends or when I was on break, I still got up early.

I lay in bed curled up in the fetal position facing O'Neal, watching him sleep. He looked peaceful. I would love a future with him, but I needed to ensure that the situation that had occurred the previous night wouldn't happen again. I needed to talk to him to get that reassurance.

I asked myself whether I had opened Pandora's box. This was our first time ever inviting someone in to either fuck with or watch us fuck. Don't get me wrong. I did enjoy the experience. I just didn't like him getting his ass flooded in my presence.

I got up to pee. In passing, I saw Warren sitting up in his bed reading the Bible. I decided not to disturb him, as it seemed as though he was looking for clarity.

I went back to the living room, sat next to O'Neal, and started searching for tickets to Jamaica. At this time of year, the tickets would not be cheap. I didn't want to wait until the weekend to travel. I very much wanted Warren to be home to spend some time with his mother. Thinking about cost led me to remember the airline points I had saved up on American Airlines. I could use them to purchase tickets.

I bookmarked the dates, hoping Warren would agree to travel within the next two days. I sent my boss a message and told him that my aunt in Jamaica had died and that I would be taking some time off. I gave the option that I could work remotely, just as though I was in New York, as that had been my original plans for the holidays.

I got up and decided to head to the kitchen and prepare breakfast. I wasn't trying to go all out this morning. But I felt like a traditional English breakfast. I was lucky because Warren loved beans, and he always had stacks of Grace baked beans and canned Vienna sausage from Jamaica in his pantry. In searching for ketchup, I found Ovaltine—one of my favorites from childhood. It didn't take me too long to scramble the eggs and toast the tomatoes. I was in a white T-shirt and my boxers.

I felt this very strong presence as though someone was in the room. I never turned around. Out of nowhere, I felt O'Neal's arms around me, and then his lips were kissing on my neck, and he was telling me good morning.

It felt good having O'Neal behind me; it also gave me some level of reassurance of his love.

"Good morning, sexy man. Are you ready to eat?"

He turned me around, and I could see his visible erection in his boxer briefs. He held onto my manhood and looked me in the eyes. "If we were home, I would have taken you in balls deep. But we have to respect Warren's home." He let go of me, walking away and telling me that he would go get Warren so that we could all have breakfast.

Warren had an eat-in kitchen. I got the table ready and waited for two of my favorite men to arrive.

Over breakfast, we talked about the trip, and Warren agreed he would allow me to take the lead on this one. It was the least I could do. Years prior, he had been there for me when Nathan had passed way.

"So Mister, we will be leaving two days after Boxing Day. I will reach out to my assistant and have her order two black suits from Zara for us. Is there anything you would like me to help you with? I know this is a very difficult time for you, and I'm going to try my best to be there for you as much as I possibly can. I have already reached out to the office, and I'll be taking the next two weeks off, doing limited work."

Warren held out his hands. The tears were flowing, and his lips were quivering.

I went over to him and hugged him, giving him reassurance that he would be okay—no matter how painful this experience was. I had never lost a parent before, so I was literally clueless as to how he was feeling just about now.

Warren got up and went to his room while O'Neal and I cleared the table and washed up the dishes.

While in the kitchen, I decided to have the conversation with O'Neal. I knew we had full transparency. It was also a given that O'Neal was fully aware that I'd spent some time with Warren and might have told him what was on my mind.

"I have decided to not even beat around the bush, so I won't go in a circle with what I am about to say. Last night, I really enjoyed fucking you and having our two hot Brazilian men join in. I was very shocked that you allowed him to come inside of you. I felt that he violated you. I honestly didn't mind watching him fuck you. I actually asked him to do it. I just felt that you would have told him to pull out."

He gave me this dumbstruck look and just stood still, holding the towel he'd been wiping the plates with.

"I am actually not sure what to say to you right about now. To be frank, I don't have much recollection of what happened last night, Akime." He never looked directly at me while he was talking, and it was a given that he was ashamed and embarrassed.

"Well, O'Neal, that is my point also. I know how much you drank. I have never seen you drink that much before. But I do know that, when you drink, you go all the way in. I guess the question in the back of my mind is, have you done this kind of thing in the past? Don't get me wrong. I am by no means judging you. I also have to think about myself. I love you even more for fucking with me raw knowing that I am positive and, yes, undetectable. However, if you were to get something and give it to me, it would further complicate my health; that is a risk I'm not about to take." I, unlike him, looked him dead in his eyes. I needed him to fully understand how serious I was about this.

"If we are talking about honesty, I think I should just give this to you. There was one time a few months back when I had gone out drinking after clubbing in Paris, and I brought home this Moroccan guy. Two days after, I saw a bit of dripping from my dick and found out that I had an STD. That was why, that weekend when I visited you in London, I decided not to have sex. I told you I only wanted to cuddle." This time he looked me in my eyes, and I knew for a fact that what he was saying was his truth.

The STD may have been a one-time thing. The fucking around, though, wasn't just a one-off. There were definitely others. I was in shock. The glass I held in my hand fell and broke. O'Neal quickly came toward me and pushed me away to ensure I wasn't hurt. He leaned in toward me and held onto my hands.

"Baby, I am sorry. I know that I fucked up big-time. I didn't mean to hurt you. I have some ways that I need to change. I also need to be more honest with you."

I squeezed his hands, thinking of what to say, but I was lost for words. He realized that I was speechless, so he came closer to me and just hugged me.

I whispered into his ear as I held onto him tightly. "I am no saint, but I always ensure that I'm safe with anyone I fuck with outside of you. I'm happy that we're having this conversation, because I have regrets every time I step outside. I can't justify the behavior. I just had assumed you were doing the same. I was just hoping you were playing it safe." There was a part of me that felt hurt. But I was in no place to judge; I was doing the same.

O'Neal got the broom and dustbin and started sweeping up. I was still bothered by the flooding of his ass; it may seem petty, but I wasn't sure if I could actually move past this hurt.

"I don't want to hurt you because I've grown to love you. Nonetheless, I realize I have some things that I need to work on. How about we give each other some space? You're about to head down to Jamaica in two days to be with your friend and his family. I don't want this isolated issue to break us up, Akime. I honestly shouldn't have allowed him to fuck me. We have never had a conversation about either of us watching the other getting fucked. I know it was in the moment of passion. I won't use my drunken state to justify my actions either. For what it is worth, I am truly and deeply sorry for what I allowed to happen."

I could see the sincerity in his eyes. There is just something sexy and attractive about a man when he cries. I went over to him, kissed him on the lips, and used the back of my right hand to wipe the tears from his eyes.

We both got dressed and headed home. I left Warren talking on the phone with his mom finally. On the way home in the cab, O'Neal and I sat in the back seat holding hands, silently looking out of our windows. Being honest with myself, I saw that I didn't want to break up with him; I just needed some space to think. His actions also brought back memories of Nathan and his lies and deception. I just didn't want to relive that experience again.

Chapter 9

The morning before I left for Jamaica, I was awoken by that dream—the dream with the guy in the mask, the very hot, muscular Black man who seemed to only want to watch me. His cock was huge, and I so wanted to suck him and have him fuck me. I yearned for him to just grab me by the neck and fill my ass with his dick, even if I wasn't able to handle all of him. I found myself twisting and turning in bed. I was tormented because of the dream—in which the man in the mask had walked off again, leaving me unsatisfied.

When I got up, I sat up in bed. I felt this weird feeling in my ass, a hungry feeling as though I needed to be touched right there. My ass was itching for dick. I needed him inside of me.

After our drive home from Warren's apartment, O'Neal and I had been very distant with each other. Something within me wanted to tell him I was sorry, I felt that I had been too hard on him. I also wanted to tell him that I forgave him.

The one thing I now knew for sure was that life is too short. True forgiveness came from saying thank you for the experience; it was literally my fault, though it was not a test.

As always, Power 105 FM was playing old-school R & B. It was raining outside, and the raindrops were hitting the window. It sounded cold with the wind blowing, but we were warm inside. O'Neal was wearing his white boxer briefs in bed. I was nervous; my heart was pounding. I desperately wanted to turn over in bed and sit on top of him. I was fearful of him rejecting me.

"Never Make a Promise" by Dru Hill was playing on the radio. I took off my boxers and slowly opened the nightstand drawer where the lube was kept and lubed my man hole. I lay on my back, massaging my anal opening. I was still covered, fingering myself and stroking my dick, hoping that the motions would awaken him.

O'Neal moved and turned on his back, but he never indicated that he was awake. Like a child lays still when he's in trouble, I just lay still in bed—not knowing how to move or what to do. One of the godmothers of soul was singing now. Listening to "I Apologize" by Anita Baker, I gained the courage I'd needed all this time. He was my man, and I was fucking sorry for how I'd treated him.

When I ran my fingers across his groin area, I realized he was already hard. I was still scared to touch him. But as I moved my hands up and down his shaft I heard him breathing heavy.

I went under the sheets and gently pulled out his john. I pulled back his foreskin with my lips. It had that musky smell from the slit of his dickhead. I licked the head with the tip of my tongue, as that piss taste was always a huge turn-on for me.

I pulled down his boxers and dropped them at his knees. I went in, all the way down on his shaft, balls deep. He moved his body and I felt his dick grow harder in my mouth.

He lifted up the sheets, looked down at me, and held onto my head with both of his hands. In a very soft voice, he whispered to me, "Suck on my dick, Daddy. Lick my balls too."

I looked him dead in his eyes. With his dick in my mouth I told him that I was sorry.

He raised himself up in the bed. I went toward him, still with his dick in my mouth and got to my knees with my back arched. O'Neal pulled the sheets from over my head, put his index finger in his mouth, spit on it, and entered my anal opening.

"Damn, Daddy, I see you're all ready for me. Not looking to get that ass licked on this morning I see."

I shook my head. Now I was sucking on his ball sack, using my right hand to hit my face with his fully erect dick.

O'Neal grabbed both my ass cheeks with his hands, jiggling them as though I was a footballer with a phat ass.

"I don't give a *fuckkkk* if your ass is lubed or not. I want to taste that shit." He came off the bed and positioned me to come to the edge of the bed on my back with my legs together and both hands holding onto them.

O'Neal let loose on my ass. He spat on my hole first. He spread my cheeks apart, using his wet, moist tongue to massage the opening of my hole. Without notice, he buried his head into my ass and tongue fucked the shit out of me.

"Just fuck me, O'Neal. Let me feel that dick deep inside of me." My body was relaxed, just hungry and relaxed, waiting for him.

"Yeah, you want this dick up in that ass, Daddy. Open your mouth, punk! And come suck on my dick," O'Neal demanded.

He fucked the spit out of my mouth. His dick head was hitting the back of my throat. I was gasping for air, and it was a huge fucking turn-on. His dick was now soaked with spit.

"Turn around. Lie on your back and put the pillow under your ass for support."

I did as instructed.

He placed the pillow right under my ass. I held onto both of my legs, pushing them as far apart as I could. As he stroked my dick, he spat in his hand and massaged his dickhead and gently put the head of his shaft into my hungry, waiting hole.

"How do you want me to fuck you, Daddy? By the way, you're forgiven. You are always forgiven, because I have always loved you." He came closer to me and bit my lips as he buried his dick deep inside of me.

My entire body shivered as I could feel his dick passing my second hole.

"Damn, nigga, you're deep as fuck, but it feels so fucking good."

It did not take him long to put me flat on my belly still with my back slightly arched.

O'Neal used both of his legs to spread my legs apart and held onto my neck with both of his hands as he slow fucked my boi pussy into man heaven.

As the church song says, "I surrender all to thee, I surrender all." I gave my man my ass, body, and soul, knowing fully well that I was loved, and he was allowed to fuck up at least once. He whispered into my ears and told me to sit on his dick.

I did as I was commanded. I actually squatted at an angle and raised my balls so that he could see the veins of his manhood as he went in and out of my hole.

My hole was wet and dripping, just the way he liked it. I could see his facial expressions in the reflection of the lights coming through the window. This time, I didn't go all the way down, I tilted my ass a bit, just riding his dickhead as I used my ass muscles to squeeze his dick head.

It turned me on even more as I would go ass deep, dropping my wet ass on him. My dick was fully brick hard. I held onto the headboard with my left hand, spat in my right hand, and jerked my dick.

It did not take long for me to feel my hot man juice firing up from my ball sack. I rode as though I was gliding on a slope.

I looked him dead in his eyes. "Open your mouth. Lift your head up closer."

He knew exactly what I was asking him to do. He moved closer to the headboard with his eyes closed and mouth open, waiting to be filled.

It was a slam dunk. I milked my load in his mouth. With my nut dripping from his lips, I held onto his face and kissed him as he held onto my ass and pumped his dick faster and harder into my hole until I felt his hot load deep inside my gut.

As I slowly got off his still erect, throbbing dick, his juices seeped out. And we both laughed at each other as we rushed to the bathroom to get cleaned up.

We got back into bed naked and curled up under the sheets. I went into my usual fetal position, and he lay behind me, both his hands wrapped around my chest. There was dead silence in the room. I could hear both of our hearts beating. It was that spiritual connection you have with someone after sex.

We often fool ourselves into believing that we can just keep fucking with someone on a regular basis and have no feelings at all. That, I must say, is impossible and madness.

The flight into Jamaica was smooth. On the plane, I held onto Warren's hands, giving him the reassurance that all would be good—no need to feel any certain way. We got stares, evil eyes, and all-too-familiar questioning looks. To be honest, I knew where we were heading, and I just didn't give one flying fuck. This was my friend. By the way, even if he was my man, I still would have comforted him like this. Prior to the plane leaving John F. Kennedy airport in New York City, I had a conversation with the flight attendants.

I had purchased first-class tickets; the red carpet was laid out for us. I was grateful for the attention and also for the support that was given to Warren.

I had a friend from high school, Orvile, who was a supervisor at Jamaica's immigration and customs. We had sex once, and he'd been begging me to fuck him again for the longest time. To try and expedite my arrival process, I promised him some dick. I knew he was going to be busy, with his wife just giving birth to their fourth child.

Orvile met us as we got off the plane. I handed him Warren's and my passports. He didn't give much eye contact; however, I saw his wandering eyes as they looked at my dick. He had that look that said he could drop on all fours and drain my dick like he was watering plants.

There would be no dick giving away on this trip. I would send him as many dick pictures as I could share in my phone. However, he wouldn't be draining my pipe while on this trip. After Orvile cleared us, we gave each other that hard-core Jamaican heterosexual handshake. I gave hm reassurance that we would be meeting. Warren said thank you and then walked away, expecting that I had some unfinished business with Orvile.

A car was waiting for us on the outside. As we exited the airport, that hot Jamaican air hit us like we were walking through a blazing fire engulfing a house. Warren's mother had arranged for a driver to come and get us.

On the way to the house, I decided to have a conversation with Warren, regarding his expectations of this trip.

"We are here to bury your father, my friend. I know that you and your family have some unresolved issues that need to be dealt with. This is, however, not the trip to do that. Your brother will be present, and you know, just like him, you were treated as an outcast. Be cordial and kind. It will hurt. Trust me, I know it will hurt like a motherfucker. However, you just have to let it go."

Warren held onto my hands. All he did to acknowledge what I had said was to shake his head.

"Remember, I am not family. Your dad and mom treated me as such even though I'm not blood. I'm here for you, my friend, and you are not alone. Don't forget that your two brothers from the outside will be present. The fight will come regarding who will take over your father's business. Your sister's husband may make some claim also, my friend. Look at me. You do not need this shit—not on this trip. I need you to be brave for him, for you; be the man you know you are. You know that your sexuality does not define you. My brother, my friend, just be yourself. Let your mother be proud of her firstborn." I knew it sounded like a lecture, but I had to give him one. I needed Warren to understand that he wasn't at war with anyone. His only job was to say goodbye to his father with grace and dignity.

Warren was crying. He had on shades, but the tears were flowing like a river. I knew deep down he was scared. He was the only legitimate boy for his father who no one had ever questioned. His two eldest brothers' mothers had been affairs. No one had ever done paternity tests. Warren was definitely no jacket. The expectation was that he was now going to own all the lands in Westmoreland, along with the cattle, the goats, and whatever business venture his father had owned.

"I'm scared as fuck. It feels like a dream, a nightmare actually. I just want it to be over with. I am feeling pain all over my body, but I can't pinpoint where exactly the pain is coming from."

I tried not to say much, as the driver was new to us. Gossip within this family started very easily.

"As someone who has been there before not too long ago, I can easily relate to you. I get it. It will hurt for an exceptionally long time too. Just let it out. Remember, crying is purging. It is natural and an extremely healthy process of grieving." I looked in the direction of the driver and back at Warren. He got it; we needed to end the conversation.

When we arrived at Warren's house, we were greeted by a young lady, who instructed an older gentleman to get our bags. I was hoping that Donavan would have been around to help with the family. When I greeted Warren's mother inside, she immediately told me that Donavan was in town getting food with the cook. It was known throughout the household that I had a keen interest in Donavan's education.

The house was packed with strangers. There were some familiar family members I had seen in New York. Most folks were, however, strangers to me. I didn't stay long enough to chitchat for a bit. I was having one major issue that needed to be addressed. I was dripping; some of O'Neal was still left inside of me. It felt good knowing that I was able to capture my man's juices and carry them all the way to Jamaica. But it was time to let it all out.

It was already discussed before I left that I would be sharing the pool house with Warren. I knew that I would be getting some fever for this. Mummy told me that, if anyone made a comment, I should let her know immediately. She reminded me before I arrived that I was just as much family as some of the "ungrateful" family members.

I went to the pool house and released myself. I choose not to mingle with the family. I knew my place. I wasn't blood. While I was close enough, I felt that it was safest to just keep my distance.

The hammock was still in its old spot. I took off my shoes, rolled up my pants, positioned myself, and put my straw hat over my face. It didn't take long for me to fall asleep. I'd spent several nights in this very spot thinking about my life, my purpose, my intentions, and my vision. I felt more at home at Warren's home than I did at my own mother's house. It wasn't that I was ashamed of my mother's house. It was the neighborhood and the fact that I just didn't feel safe there.

I woke up to the night sky, the flickering lights of Montego Bay and the city below. There was something different—a blanket over me. There was also a familiar face staring at me in the distance and a familiar body standing by a tree.

I wiped my eyes, as this felt like a dream. Since the last time I saw him, he had matured a lot. He'd grown facial hair, and he no longer looked like a teenager. He looked like a grown young man. His physique had also changed. His head was bald. I could see the white of his teeth. He had on a green polo shirt and khaki pants. Much time had passed, and Donavan had grown up.

I raised myself up a bit. When I had my feet on the ground, wiping my eyes, I was still fixated on the young man standing before me.

"You look so peaceful sleeping, just like the last time."

His voice had also changed; this had to be a dream.

"I see you remember."

I was literally lost for words. I just kept looking at him.

"I heard that you've been here for quite some time. I got you the cover, as I didn't want the cool air to wake you up." As he spoke, he came closer to me.

I couldn't help but keep my gaze on his crotch as he was showing so much. "Well thank you. It's very much appreciated and very thoughtful of you, Donavan."

As I stood up, he came closer to me. He held onto me, giving me a warm embrace and whispering in my ear, "Welcome home. Would you like something to eat or drink?"

I was thirsty and somewhat hungry, but I felt it best to join the family. I told him that I had to go up to the house.

"You don't have to worry about that. Everyone has left for the country, trying to find a suitable burying spot for Daddy. We are here alone. Food is in the kitchen, and I can go get you something. We have a new housekeeper Ann-Mare, and she made cherry juice with ginger; I know you would love it." He didn't even allow me to respond. He went running toward the kitchen in the big house.

I went to the pool house, peed, and washed my face.

By the time I got back, Donavan had already returned with a fully set tray. He only brought a Red Stripe beer for himself. He was sitting by the infinity pool. And yes, he brought out candles. What was this young man trying to do to me?

The last time he'd tried to make a move on me, I had been in such a fragile state. This time around, I had a man. I was now more alert as to his intentions and advances.

A gentleman should never turn down good treatment. And this time, I had every intention of taking advantage of Donavan's hospitality.

"I must say it is a pleasure seeing you, Donavan. You have grown so much. Thank you very much for the warm hospitality and the attention you have given me thus far." I had a huge smile on my face.

"That's not all I would like to offer you on this trip. I just hope you give me the opportunity to give you that island experience." He looked me dead in the eyes, and I knew for sure that he was dead serious.

I chose to not respond to his advances. "The fish is lovely. I haven't had boiled breadfruit in years. This must be country yam. The bananas are also incredibly soft. I need to get a hold of this chef." My head was in my plate as I spoke to him.

"So, have you decided what you're going to do after your finals?" Since my initial meeting with Donavan, I had offered financial assistance. I had also reassured him that, if he found a school in North America, I would assist as much as I could.

Donavan had a keen eye for numbers it seemed and had been studying accounting and economics. His ambition was to own his own consulting and accounting firm, helping minorities and the less fortunate start up their own business ventures. I had really taken a liking to him on my last trip.

"You have heard me say thanks so many times. And I will just say it again. My family has been very grateful for all the help you have given me. I actually paid the money to sit the exams early, and I got the results two days before Christmas. I was going to call you on Christmas Day to share the news, but you know how that day went down. I got four As and one B. My mom is sick, so I needed to take some time looking after her. With Daddy gone, I'm not sure if Mr. Warren will have work for me, seeing that he lives in New York and may have no interest in farm work." He spoke with a great deal of passion.

"You might be surprised what Warren might be willing to do. He hasn't said much to me about his future plans; however, I trust that he will make good use of his father's legacy." By this time, I had finished my meal and was looking at the night's lights.

"I will be taking you up on your offer in the coming months regarding schools in the United States. I'm going to try my luck and apply for a few scholarships. I would be most interested in accommodation."

I was impressed to learn that Donavan had put a plan in place.

While we were talking, Warren approached. Based on his mood, I knew it was time to cut my conversation with Donavan short. Warren seemed very emotionally charged. I rudely ended my talk with Donavan and headed in Warren's direction over by the rosebushes adjacent to the pool house.

"I am so not going to be doing this. I am going to *fuckkkk* a bytch up before I bury my father. Can you imagine the gall of these people? So, Daddy wrote a will. And guess fucking what? He left me the fuck in charge. I don't fucking want it, not one piece of this shit hellhole. You should have seen the look Patrick gave me when the will was read. He told me to my face that 'batty bois should drown in the swamp in the cow field.' My bytch ass sister feels that since her fucking husband is in banking, it would be best that I give him power of attorney until I figure out what to do." His face was all flustered, and he was stuttering, something I had never seen him do before.

"Mister, you will not be fucking up anyone while you are here. Calm down. Tell me what's going on." I realized that words wouldn't calm him down, so I just hugged him.

"I am not sure if I should have come. They don't see me, Akime. They only see my sexuality, and it hurts." He was crying hard; I could feel the pain as he shook with each sob.

"Look at me. I get it. You knew it wasn't going to be easy. It stings like a motherfucker. But you are going to get through this. So, they don't want to give you what's owed to you. I got this. I'm going to call Marlon; he's a lawyer friend of mine. I'm going to ask that you give me control for thirty days. I am a property manager. I will need to see the books and I will let you know if your family business is fucked or not and if you should sell."

All Warren could do was nod and tell me to do as I pleased.

"Right now, I just want to sleep. I trust you, Akime. I just can't bury him and do this with them at the same time."

I squeezed him tightly, giving him the reassurance that all would be well.

Chapter 10

My entire night was spent talking to Marlon about the card I thought Warren should play with his family. All I asked Warren to do was to call a family meeting around 11:00 a.m. the following day. I also asked Warren's mother if breakfast could be pushed back. It was crucial to have the whole family present at the emergency family meeting.

I got up early and met up with Marlon at his office. Marlon had had his assistant working on the draft letters all night. Marlon hired three armed security guards and had them meet us at his office. At first, I was nervous as fuck, as I felt that this was going overboard. I got the rationale, though, as someone may decide to make a move on Warren.

By the time I got to the house, everyone was anxiously waiting, wondering what was going on. I walked into the large eating area, with Marlon, Warren, and his mother by my side. All eyes were on us. We were now officially a target, especially me.

"Good morning, everyone. I apologize for the late start. For those who don't know me, my name is Akime. And as of this morning, I am now running the show for the next thirty days. I run a property management firm in London. As you were all made aware yesterday at the reading of the will, Warren will be managing his father's entire estate."

Warren's older brother started walking in my direction. To his surprise, the security guards showed their weapons, and he backed off.

"Me nah listen to no batty man; this ah fuckey." He was now trying to be the loudest.

"I guess we're not fully understanding what's going on here. So I'm going to lay it out for us all. I now run the show. These three security guards are here at my request. Warren and his mother will be taking care of the funeral arrangements moving forward." I looked over towards Warren's mother, looking for her motherly smile that would tell me she was pleased to finally be in charge of her husband's funeral.

"Ah who dah boi yah? Ah who you ah, fuck? You ah behave like say ah your father."

I looked at him, smiling. "It's odd that you of all people are talking about fathers. Yet this is my first time ever seeing you. If you insist on having this outburst, I will have you escorted off the property. You already heard what your cut will be; it's final. If your father felt that you were fit to manage, he would have left you in charge. You see, while most of you try to act more manly and have all kinds of names for Warren, the reality is that he has this shit, and he runs the show. If anyone objects, the door is behind you." I gave the immediate family members a copy of the terms and conditions of the thirty-day handover, along with the terms and condition of the security that was present in the room.

After the meeting ended, some family members came over and thanked me for taking over. To the group that came over, I said, "I really didn't want to take over. However, there are some who are present today who feel that, because Warren's mother was the helper when she was younger and dark-skinned that she and her son have no right to anything. Let us set the record clear. He is no bastard child. He is a legitimate child."

The internal fight within the family was a class and color struggle. Warren's aunts and uncles from his father's side of the family were literally white. In their minds, colonialism still existed, and the nigga boy wasn't getting shit.

As a poor country boy growing up in Jamaica, I knew my place in society. The only thing that would give me social mobility was my education. Even then, you could still be in some circles and be looked down on because of your dark skin. The house nigga mentality was very much alive in certain parts of the island.

I had Warren guide me to his father's home office to review paperwork. I insisted on having the door open, as I need our presence to be felt throughout the house.

The old man was ahead of his time. He had his reports in Excel, which made life easy for me. Things were not as bad as had been projected. He was losing on the goats due to stealing by locals. The cows were yielding in big numbers. The chickens supplied the local hotel industry in Negril's tourist sector.

I suggested to Warren that, if he wanted, he could form a partnership with his two brothers and sisters. He could split responsibilities with them. They all shared the same father, no matter who was from the first marriage and regardless of his bastard brothers' attitude. Half brothers or not, they were all family.

Warren agreed to think about my suggestion.

I also recommended that, while he may be a novice to this kind of work, I could have a property manager assist him. And if he wanted, he could hire one temporarily. Warren's father did an excellent job with the books, thus making it quite easy to make a transition to anyone.

I spent the next two days going over the financial records and the location of each farmland on the island. I had asked Donavan for help, as accounting was his line of expertise. He had a driver's license, so I hired him to take me around to the different farm sites, along with viewing the rental properties. Donavan was a huge help to me. I also got the opportunity to see rural Jamaica. I must say that, outside of the crime and the poverty that most Jamaicans had to struggle with, the inner parts of Jamaica were beautiful.

Warren got an update via text on every stop of my journey to the countryside. On the night before the funeral, I attended the Nine-Nights, which was a traditional Jamaican ritual. The entire community came out to say their goodbyes and share their memories of Daddy. I made a promise to Warren that I would have a final report to give to the immediate family after the funeral. I knew I wouldn't have any time on the day of the funeral to do anything. So the night before was all I had.

Finally, around 2:00 a.m., I added the last chart to the report. Warren never saw me at work or got an opportunity to see me working. The home office in the big house had a fully functional office. All I had to do was make several copies and have Donavan drop them off in Montego Bay to get them bound, early the following morning.

I saved the files to my flash drive, walked over to the bar, and asked Donavan if he wanted a drink.

"After these awfully long few days, I could take a stiff drink just about now. I'll have a glass of Appleton on the rocks please." He was lying on the sofa flickering through channels.

"I see you want a big boi drink tonight; I only hope that you can handle yourself and get up on time tomorrow morning for the big finale."

All he did was give me a big smile and nod.

I walked over toward him, handed him his glass, knocked the edge of his glass, and said, "Cheers." I decided to sit down next to him, hoping I would be able to see something on television that I would be interested in. About twenty minutes passed; there wasn't anything worth watching. I found myself drifting off to sleep.

I was woken up by Donavan's lips on mine. All I did was open my eyes. His lips were moist and wet. He was very gentle. Holding on to the back of my head, he massaged the inside of my mouth with his young tongue. I wanted to push him off me, but it felt so damn good; also this was all that I needed.

He was now sitting on my lap, just looking into my face and smiling. My eyes were wide open. I didn't know what to do next, as I knew I wasn't planning on or prepared to get fucked tonight.

Donavan leaned over toward me, put his hands on my crotch, and whispered into my ear that I should go to the bedroom. When I got to the bedroom, I found it lit with scented candles. I was blown out of my mind. I had no clue how or when he could have done this. I recalled him taking several bathroom breaks, so I could only imagine that was when he'd put this together.

He stood by the door, just watching the surprise on my face. He slowly walked toward me, kissed me on my forehead, and guided me toward the bed. For the first time in my life, I decided to just go with the flow. He walked back toward the door and closed it with the keys.

I was sitting on the bed. He gently pushed me to lay down. Slowly, he took off my shoes while looking into my eyes. I watched as he slowly took off my socks. The moment he started rubbing my feet, I knew his intentions. I told myself that he wouldn't, but he did. He started with my big toe and then moved on to the others. I had never had anyone give this much attention to my feet while massaging my calves.

As he freestyled, with my right foot in his mouth, he used both hands to cup my dick in my briefs. He used his muscular hands, spread my legs apart, and held them at an angle with his shoulders. Slowly elevating my butt cheeks, he took off my underwear. My dick was erect as a pole; all this young man had done was hold onto my shaft. He went for the kill; he buried his face right at my ass.

All I kept telling myself was, *Please, Jesus, let it only have that musky smell.*

The boi had skills beyond my imagination. He had both of my balls in his mouth, and he was gagging like a motherfucker.

My ass was next, Donavan licked from my balls to my ass crack. He used his tongue to make circular motions around my asshole. I literally jumped when he spat in my hole and then used his lips to create a suction at my hole. It felt tight. It hurt a bit, but the sensation of it was great. He grabbed onto both my cheeks, and he tongue fucked my hole until it was moist and open. He gently inserted his index finger into my ass in a downward angle. It was my G-Spot. My legs were shaking.

He slowly got up. He grabbed my dick, and without motion, he went balls deep. I just shook my head, as he was about to get to boy pussy heaven by fingering me and sucking my dick at the same time.

I knew deep within I wasn't ready for any dick. I wasn't about to paint a masterpiece on this young man's dick tonight. He stood up before me. All I saw was this huge, fucking straight pole staring me in my face. He must have pulled his dick out while sucking on mine. I needed no coaching on what to do. As I got closer, he literally slapped his heavy manhood against my face. I could feel its strength; it was solid as a rock.

I was intimidated by its length; it was beautiful. It was the first time I'd seen such a long uncut dick that was this straight. The head was not an odd color; it was clean. The veins were all over. There was one particular vein that was very pronounced and looked like it would hurt any ass. As I guided my mouth toward the tip of his dick, it started throbbing.

All I did was open my mouth and have him slowly guide his manhood to the back of my throat. Donavan grabbed the back of my head, and he forced my head all the way down. My eyes became watery, but I was loving the sensation at the back of my throat. As I was about to choke, he pulled out with lots of my saliva dripping from his pole.

I used both my hands to massage his dick as I went up and down with my mouth. I was now on my knees. I begged him to fuck my mouth. I was so in love with his dick, especially when it hit the back of my throat, which allowed me to gag. There was something about Donavan looking down on me; I saw the pleasure on his face as he fucked my mouth.

He motioned me to stand. As I stood firm, he whispered, "Come fuck my hole, Daddy."

I was taken aback. I remembered him telling me the last time that he would only flip with me. I was not about to turn him down.

Donavan, quickly got himself undressed and lay on the center of the bed, waiting for me to enter him. His ass was already lubricated. As he pushed the opening of his ass out, it got my dick throbbing even more.

I positioned Donavan's ass with the pillow below his ass. I put the condom on my dick, applying more lube. It took some effort to put my dickhead in, but eventually I was in. He gripped the head of my dick with the muscles around his opening, and he slowly guided me inside of him. His inside felt like heaven. It felt like wet velvet, moist and soft. As I went in further, I lay onto of him, kissing him softly as he wrapped his manly legs around me. Both of his hands held onto my butt cheeks, guiding me farther inside of him.

The crickets were making noises outside; it felt tranquil as I kissed his lips and glided in and out of his ass. I had him turn to his side, and I knelt between his legs, grabbing onto his neck. I eventually had him open. I took my dick out and just watched as his ass became open from my dick print inside of him.

I eventually had him at the edge of the bed on his back. I couldn't resist but spit in his open pink manhole. I instructed him to hold onto his legs. As he relaxed himself on his back, I went in slowly. As I entered his anal walls, I hold onto his dick, spit on it and guided it into my mouth as I fucked him. His facial expression was priceless.

I hadn't fucked like this in years. What made it so magical was the fact that he wasn't resisting. Donavan had surrendered his body to me. I was in full control. I could feel his muscles contracting; this was his way of telling me that he was close to erupting. I so needed his load down my throat. I edged his hole with my dick, as that was what got me to come quickly.

As I felt him tense up, I prepared myself to take in his babies. As he flooded my mouth with his milk, I made deeper strokes. I released my mouth from his dick and spat some of his cum into his mouth. I bit onto his lips as I released myself. It was one of the best sexual encounters I'd had in years.

I didn't feel like going to the bathroom. All I did was take the condom off. Then I guided Donavan farther onto the bed and held onto him in the fetal position. This was all that I needed; my mind was exhausted. Donavan eased his ass into my groin area, while holding on to my hands, which were wrapped around him. We fell asleep within minutes. To be frank, it was one of the most peaceful sleeps of my life.

Chapter 11

On the morning of the funeral, I woke up to that fucking dream again. I was twisting and turning. This time I was in the shower alone with him at the sauna. The sauna had a huge glass facing the open shower. I was alone in a corner taking a shower while he stood at a distance just watching me. I wasn't sure if the men who were coming in and out of the shower were aware of anything; however, they didn't stay around for long. They all came in and just left me all alone with this God of a man with his rock-hard dick in his hands jerking it. I stood under the shower. While the water drizzled down on me like raindrops, I played with my ass. All he did was continuously spit on his dickhead. This time, he erupted like a volcano all over his hands and his chest. He had positioned his dick toward his mouth. I could see the cum dripping off his lips.

I found myself getting up because my pillow was soaking wet. As I opened my eyes, I saw the artfully arranged tray next to me. It was piled with breakfast. Warren was in bed next to me, just looking rather intently at me. I was happy for the ackee and salt fish and fried breadfruit, not to mention the plantains with Jamaican hot chocolate. My tongue would be burnt from drinking the cocoa, but frankly, I didn't care. I got up and immediately started eating, even before I said anything to Warren. I was a bit nervous to ask where Donavan was.

"You sure were having a bad dream. You were out of it. You didn't say much. You just seemed to be fighting yourself.

"I know what you're thinking. And no, I didn't get you food. He got you food. I just asked him to get me some while he was at it. He must have fucked you good. Now you can't complain about O'Neal. So, is O'Neal now forgiven after this deep dicking you had last night?" He was having so much fun out of this.

All I could do was laugh to myself.

"Oddly enough, he didn't fuck me. I thought that was what he wanted. Warren, we made love. I fucked his ass while I sucked his dick. I couldn't resist it, but I swallowed all of him." All I did was laugh, just remembering what I had done hours before. I was naked under the sheets. Warren lifted the sheets away and, seeing my dick hard, squeezed it tightly.

"I don't want you fucking him again, you hear me." He held my dick as though he was talking to a mike.

"He finds you attractive. However, he has so much respect for you and your daddy; he said it would be too hard to fuck you—just out of respect."

He gave me that look, and then he jumped up out of bed. "So today is the big day. I'm scared. Don't forget that you're on the program, Akime."

I sensed a change in him, as though he had grown up. I'd been told that losing a loved one changes you. This was new for me actually.

I went directly to the shower after Warren left. I couldn't control myself. I just had to jerk off thinking about fucking Donavan. This time, I imagined him fucking me. As I jerked my dick, I used my left hands to finger my ass, as I so yearned for the sensation of Donavan fucking me. Carl Thomas's "Summer Rain" was playing in the background. It felt so tropical, I could imagine getting fucked outside in the rain. It didn't take me long to get that nut out, and it was heavenly.

The funeral service was going to be held in Montego Bay, and the burial would be in the family plot in Westmoreland. I had a car transport my mother to the funeral. I heard that my sister would be in attendance with my mom also. No matter how much we tried to build a relationship, it just never happened. It seemed she still struggled with my sexuality and the shame she felt it had brought the family. I'd often tried to build a relationship with her children. But I believe that she was afraid of my sins transferring over to them. It was a shame, how some people saw everyone's sins but their own.

Donavan had my rental car. He brought his mother, brother, and aunt with us. It seemed he had told them too much about me. They were all excited to see me. I had to do a double take when Donavan's aunt called me Mass Akime. I had to immediately stop her in her tracks. Akime was enough; I was not a part of the plantation life.

I greeted my mother, who was outside of the church, along with my bitter-ass sister. All I did was say hi to her. My mother gave me a look. I ignored it, as today just wasn't the day for me to give a lecture or be petty.

I made sure that my mother and sister got a seat. The funeral was one of the hottest tickets in town. Several dignitaries would be present, including both members of Jamaica's two political parties and members of parliament. The deputy prime minister was scheduled to give an address on behalf of the prime minister, who was away traveling.

Jamaica was exceedingly small. Often, people from all walks of life journeyed from afar just to attend funerals. My mother was known for doing that; I never got it. I wasn't sure if I would ever get it either. I saw a few familiar faces. Some approached me. Others I just did not want to have conversations with.

I had observed earlier on that the gossip mill seemed to be in full force, and it was inferred that I was Warren's partner. The irony of it all was that it seemed acceptable, and no one was bothered by it. It was the classism within the Jamaican culture that baffled me oh so often. If you had money, were educated, in the middle class, and had a trade or skill, you literally got a free pass. However, if you were gay and poor, that was when the real issue came up.

Too often, the poor gay guys were uneducated. They usually had no job skills or trade skills. Some actually had no desire to work, as they were so consumed by their gayness; they felt as though someone owed them something. The victim game was played every so often.

Another thing that the wider Jamaican community despised was the desire to act like women. Some gay men still held the view that, if you were gay and a bottom, inevitably, you were the woman and *must* assume the role of a woman.

There had been several incidents in which violence had erupted when men were seen in communities dressed like women—or, more accurately, like drags. Dressing in drag was a direct rebellious behavior that was detested by the society at large. It was a result of lack of education and an inability to fully understand sexuality, sexual orientation, and gender identity that left the poor gay Jamaican at a huge disadvantage.

There was a huge difference between dressing up as a woman because you were a bottom and doing drags. Doing drag was an art form and a craft. Not all drag queens were gay or acted feminine outside of drag. Straight women and men performed drag also.

There was also a criminal element within the Jamaican gay culture that involved men dressing up like women and weaponizing themselves to hurt straight men. There was great danger in doing this. And culturally, the gay community refused to accept or acknowledge this hidden reality.

As I walked into the church, I heard a remarkably familiar voice calling out to me. I told myself that it had to be someone else, as Delaney had never told me she would be in Jamaica. I was a bit nervous to turn around, as I knew I would become too emotional.

As I stood still, unsure if I should turn around, I felt a familiar touch. Her hands were so small, and she still had the same scent. I turned around, tearing up because, finally, I no longer felt all alone.

I squeezed her tightly, and the tears were just falling from my eyes. She lifted my head and held onto my face and wiped my eyes.

"I knew you would be surprised; but I had no clue you would be so emotional, baby boi. You know I got Warren. I heard about his father's death through a friend. I knew you were on big brother duties, so I made myself come to support you both."

I was so fucking lost for words. "To be honest, I'm not sure what to say. I'm so thankful that you showed up. I'm trying not to scream; however, I know it just wouldn't be appropriate. Thank you so much, baby girl. I know no matter what I can always count on you." I gave her another tight embrace and guided her to a seat.

"I came solo. The wife went to the south of France to visit her family. She said to give both you and Warren her condolences. She knew this was a time for us to just reconnect, and I so love her for always being so considerate. Now get me a program, and I will see you later."

I walked off, asking an usher to get the beautiful, insatiable woman in the black dress a program. I went off in search of Warren and his mother. I didn't give a fuck about any of the other family members.

Warren and his mother were in the back having a conversation with the pastor. Everything seemed to be going as planned. As I stood at a distance, I saw growth in my friend. He was finally growing up, and he looked handsome in his suit. His mother gestured for me to come over.

She squeezed my hands and gave me a motherly kiss on my cheek, saying simply, "Thank you."

I squeezed her hands harder.

We all went inside and sat at the front of the church. The family was in mourning, so there was no attitude or fighting today. Whoever had decorated the church had done an excellent job. It felt as though the decorator had gone around the island and picked all the exotic flowers and then arranged them in a fashion fit for a great man. It had a masculine feel, to be more precise.

An elder woman walked up from the back of the church, and she shouted out the Lord's psalms. Directly behind her were two young boys holding Bibles. The pastor stepped in, and all rose as he gave a benediction of life and death. It was powerful. It was as though he was talking directly to me. He spoke about our intentions in living our lives and the importance of recognizing that we are all created for a profound reason. Our only purpose was to spend our time trying to figure it out. Regarding our legacy, the pastor unequivocally stated that our legacy would only be defined by the lives that we had touched.

The church choir went up immediately after the pastor had spoken. They sang "Amazing Grace" with a twist, something more soulful and more full of life. Several members of the community went up, including the local members of parliament for both St. James and Westmoreland. I had no clue that Warren's father had been so much of a visionary. Nor had I realized how involved he was in education and community development.

With all the rift that was going on, it was agreed that the deputy prime minister would speak on behalf of the family. He would also talk about the life that Daddy had lived and the legacy he'd left behind. His tribute was powerful beyond words. I learned that he was Warren's godfather. The deputy prime minister did something that I found unconventional by addressing differences. Differences, in this context, referred to sexuality; he spoke to the role of the church and the wider community in being open to difference. This was outside of any box I had ever seen in Jamaica. It felt revolutionary, like a scolding of some sort.

When it was my time to go up, I asked Warren to accompany me. I needed him with me, not only to give me strength but also for me to be next to him, so that the community the deputy prime minister had spoken about could see what difference looked like. We walked up hand in hand. And yes, we heard the odd sounds. We saw the eyes and saw the lips move with whispers of gossip. I did not care. And frankly, Warren was wearing one of the bravest smiles that I had ever seen on him in my time knowing him.

"Today I stand here representing my best friend—the man who taught me what true friendship is. I am thankful to Mr. Brian Antony Rivers for his son.

"Most of you may not know that my mother and Warren's mother went to school together when they were young girls. Ironically, I never met Warren until he migrated to the United States. Over the years I met both his parents as they traveled to New York City to visit Warren. Mr. Rivers took a liking to me, and I called him Daddy simply because I did not have a relationship with my father. Today, I learned so much about Mr. Rivers—more than I knew when he was alive.

"What I know for sure is that his love is the greatest gift of all. It was his gift of love that he gave to Warren that built the relationship we have. Warren is like a brother to me; I would not have been here without him." My eyes started to tear up as I remembered that morning when Nathan shot me, and Warren saved my life. I took several deep breaths because the tears just kept on flowing, and I simply could not control them.

"Mr. Rivers took me in when most Jamaican families would have frowned on me. He loved me like his son. He, over the years, taught me how to be a responsible young man with a vision. On many of my visits to Jamaica, he would sit me down in the backyard just to talk about life and the importance of intention.

"I am proud to call Warren a friend and happy that he allowed me the opportunity to have spent that quality time with Mr. Rivers. To Mrs. Rivers, I cannot even fathom the pain you are feeling. However, rest assured that we all know that, as a wife, you were the pillar that supported Mr. Rivers, the rock. Behind every great man, there is a strong woman. My mother is here today. I know she will not get angry if I were to say that you have been just as much a mother to me as she is. Thank you for loving me and for opening your home to me.

"Mr. Rivers is in a good place. I am going to end with one of my favorite Bible verses. 'Let your light shine so bright before men, so that they may see your good works and glorify your father who is in heaven.'"

Warren and I stepped down from the podium together. After just a few moments, I stepped outside, as I was becoming too emotional. I never went back inside; I spent the rest of the time engaging Donavan in conversations about his future.

Chapter 12

The funeral reception felt like a star-studded affair. I had no clue that Mr. Rivers had such a lovely property in Westmoreland. It was not until this trip that I got to see what Westmoreland had to offer. Westmoreland was on the other end of the island, and we had no family in Westmoreland. The few things I knew about Westmoreland was the nude beach at Hedonism and the fact that both Richi Stevens, a singer, and the best weed out of Jamaica came out of Orange Hill in Negril.

First, it was an oceanfront property in Blue Fields, a good distance outside of the town of Savanna la Mar, which had me captivated. A huge tent was set up in an open section with the ocean as a backdrop. Mr. Rivers was buried at the family plot on a hill overlooking the property. Now if I were to tell my friends overseas that people in Jamaica lived like this, they simply would not believe me. This was old and new money mixed together. Mr. Rivers never lived lavishly. However, he surely did maintain that old-school colonial lifestyle. All this time, they'd had this property, and Warren had never brought me here. It was said that it was the summer home. Who lives in Jamaica—where it's hot year round—and has a summer home?

I made sure that Delaney had a seat. I finally introduced Delaney to Donavan. I introduced him as a friend of Warren's family so as not to embarrass him. I saw Warren walking around greeting guests, and I dragged him over to our table. We all knew he couldn't stay for long. We just wanted him to just take a break and be with some familiar faces.

"So, Mister, we see you have inherited a mansion and a beachfront cottage. You don't need to work again. Your daddy left you the coin purse. I had no clue Westmoreland was this beautiful." Delaney of all people, with as much money as her family had, really had to reprimand. I knew that she was just being playful.

"With what I heard your family has, my inheritance is more like cottage cheese."

We all laughed out loud.

"I'm happy that you're able to laugh, Warren, on this day of all days. I know you heard me say it earlier, but I will say it again. Thank you so much. And I love you unconditionally."

We hugged, and he ran off.

"You know the one thing I admire about you, Akime. It's your level of honesty, your ability to be vulnerable, and just the way you live in your truth."

I went over to her and hugged her.

"After what I went through with Nathan and God giving me an opportunity to live again, I simply have no other choice but to live in my truth."

"So, Donavan, what do you do for the family?"

I took the liberty of answering that question for him. "He is actually the bookkeeper for the family, and he will be Warren's right-hand man."

Donavan gave me an odd look. I was only trying to protect him and his past with the family. No one needed to know what he used to do for them.

"I see that you have a mouthpiece, Mr. Donavan." Delaney had to go in.

But Donavan was very polite. "I am grateful for Akime for believing in me and helping me get this job. Akime has helped me to complete school. He has also offered to assist me in getting into a school in the States."

I knew that was intentional.

"So, Mister, I see you're doing your part, not only mentoring but giving back financially."

All I could do was to give her a look that said clearly, *Shut dah fuck up*, just to end the conversation.

"How about we all go over to the food section? I'm starving, and the food is surely smelling good."

We all walked over in the direction of the food.

The setup was simply breathtaking. The sun was setting, the ocean was calm, and there was a stillness in the air. A traditional Jamaican mento band was playing. This was real country life, the life I read about in books. I promised myself to soak it up.

Most of my time was spent looking at the property and imagining its potential expansion. It appeared I was always in business mode. The family could keep the main house as their own. However, they had enough land to build small cottages. They could offer butler services. The beach was privately owned as well. This would be a great source of income without sacrificing the authenticity of the family home.

We all lined up to get served. I had to ask myself who dah fuck had picked out these waiters and servers. The women were young, they wore light makeup, and they were beautiful. The men were naturally toned, young, and just had that authentic Jamaican feel. I was really going to sell my idea to Warren.

We all got our plates full and headed back to the table. There were some elderly women who were sitting at the table. There was enough room for all, so we politely asked if we could join them. I'd never met these three women in my life. I asked them if they would like for me to get someone to get them some food, and they accepted the offer.

I called out to one of the servers, and within minutes, he brought over three plates on a tray. The woman with all silver hair was the most talkative. Her name was Shirley. One of the women seemed to have forgotten her age, as she dressed just as youthful as Delaney. Her name was Beverly. The other woman reminded you of the big-boned market women with their heads tied. Her name was Pauline.

Shirley had no hesitation in her conversation. She just dived in. "Mr. Akime you know say all ah wi did think say you was di lover. We were in the church when you walked in and someone pointed you out, saying that you were by the big house. We heard that ah you ah run the show too and you gave it to di family them."

"Hold up. How did you hear so much?"

The three women just look at each other laughing.

Pauline chimed in and gave her two cents. "Not fi nothing, I think di two ah you look handsome together. You two don't look like the chi chi man them. You both look like men. Back when I was younger, Beverly and I used to know of this guy in the community who was so. By the way, Beverly is my younger sister; she don't say much. Him use to tell us 'bout the parties that them used to keep in Morant Bay, St Thomas. Most of the guys had their women, and it was just something they did in passing. To be honest we use to believe that, once you so, you couldn't swim."

We all burst out in laughter.

"So what is your take on gays in Jamaica? Are you open-minded? Do you believe that they are a threat to society?" I was hoping Pauline would answer; she seemed more insightful.

However, Shirley took on the question. "Good question, mi boi," the eldest of the three shouted out. "I personally don't have an issue with two men doing that. My issue is when them trouble the little boi them and turn them so. It's not my place to judge. I leave them up to God. All sin is sin in my eye. What also bothers me is the one them who think say them a more woman than me. I believe them is a bad influence to the younger bios them." Her head was down in her plate; she refused to give me eye contact.

I felt obliged to give her a response. This was an opportunity to change the trajectory of her view of the world she lived in. "I will ask you ladies one simple question. Do I look gay? And if so, do I look like a child molester?" It was a straightforward question, and I was intrigued to see how they would respond to me.

They all responded in unison that I did not fit the typical gay look and that they did not believe that I would molest children.

"The reason I asked the question is simply that there is no specific 'look' to a gay man. It is not our lack of masculinity that defines us. It isn't that a boy has no interest in sports or even that he has a soft demeanor so he must be gay or that these things define all who are gay. To the contrary, if I were to show you some gay guys, I know you all would tell me that I was lying. To be frank, I think that too much emphasis is placed on sex."

We all laughed; however, it was the truth.

I saw everyone looking behind me. I asked myself, *Who could that be?* It was my mother and sister standing behind me. I turned around and greeted them both. My mother said that she wanted to talk to me. She asked if we could walk away a bit, closer to the rock garden by the ocean.

"I noticed that you didn't give us much attention today. It was as though we aren't family." It was my older sister. Our lack of a connection had been a fact for so long now that I wasn't even sure how I could rebuild that relationship.

"I got you both a ride to come and the best seats in the church. You didn't have to come to the reception. Nonetheless, the ride is covered." I just didn't know what more was expected of me.

"Akime, I have brought you up better than this. We are your family. And after that speech you gave, I am not sure if we are blood anymore."

I was stunned by their statements.

"Mama, did you even take much time to think about what you just said to me? Am I the only one with memory? Did you ask her to come with you? Why did you both agree to come? I keep my distance the same way I send money every month to pay your bills. By the way, Ms. Lady, do you even contribute to the household? No, you don't."

Upset crossed my mother's face; she looked furious.

"You're always throwing your money in our faces, and I so hate you for doing that." My sister sounded angry, but I didn't give a fuck.

"Hold up. Do you hate me as much as I hate you? Nah. Do you hate your father as much as I hate him? Are you fucking serious?

You used to watch your father molest me, and you said not one fucking word. When I told Mama, you told her that I was lying. Out of respect for Mama, I am going to be calm. Don't *fucking* call me out because your father fucked up your life and you're yet to say shit about it."

Mama was now crying. The right thing to do was to console her. But I couldn't find it within myself to do it. I was still angry with her for covering shit up.

"I cannot believe that we are still here. You kids are grown, and I brought it to God and let it go."

This was where I made my exit. This was the bullshit my mother said that was unbearable. "Mama, I am not about to do this with you or her. I am grown, and the past stings a lot at times, especially when those who should have protected you didn't protect you. While you were not there when he was touching me, I told you. I was your child, and it was your responsibility to believe me the first time I told you what was going on. You never did, so you have to take some ownership. The reality of it all is both of your children got raped under your watch, and you have yet to acknowledge it. Oh yes, you're in church every damn week. And what do you say to your God?" I started crying. I just could not control my emotions.

Delaney saw what was going on from a distance. She came right over to rescue me.

I honestly did not come to Jamaica for all of this. I walked away with Delaney without saying goodbye to either my mother or my sister. Delaney said nothing to them. She held onto my hands and instructed me to walk away.

"I know you love them, but sometimes you just have to let go. This is one of those things in your life you simply have no control over. And you just have to let it go, my friend."

I was so happy that Delaney had come. I needed that friendly face. I'd never shared much about my past with Delaney. She knew enough to know that it was time for me to walk away.

I didn't want the older women we'd met to see me like that, so we walked toward the gate. Donavan was running toward us with a concerned look on his face. I didn't want him to see me like this. He was all I wanted apparently. The moment he came over toward us, he held me tight and whispered in my ear that it would be okay. It had been an exceptionally long time since I'd felt that manly embrace; it felt so damn good.

We all walked in the direction of the car. Donavan noted that he would find a ride for his family, as he didn't want them to ride with us. I asked him to find Warren for me.

By the time Warren came, I had stopped crying, but he saw the look on my face. And he knew only my mother could have brought me there.

Just like Donavan, all Warren did was to hug me without saying anything. I knew no matter the time of day, I could always count on Warren to just be that supportive friend.

When Donavan arrived, I kissed Delaney goodbye and told her that we should link up before I headed back stateside. Warren said that he would be spending the night at the guesthouse. I knew there would not be enough space, so back to Montego Bay it was for me.

The night air was still. We drove all the way down without saying much to each other. I had no clue how Donavan found an old radio station that only played old songs, but he did. It was utterly relaxing; it helped to get my mind off things. I was reclined in the passenger seat, holding onto Donavan's hand in stillness, just thankful to have him around.

Chapter 13

After we got home, Donavan and I silently walked toward the pool house hand in hand. I was not in any mood to talk. I just wanted to be held. I didn't even feel like crying. All I wanted was to lie still and be with myself, giving myself the reassurance that all would be well. When I got inside, Donavan took off my jacket and my shoes and got me a cold Red Stripe beer. It was refreshing, and I felt the cool breeze from outside whispering through the curtains.

I heard Donavan in the bathroom. He was such a gentleman. Donavan filled the freestanding tub surrounded by stones. From the living room, I could smell the eucalyptus oil. It didn't take long for Donavan to come and get me. He literally took off my clothing and guided me into the bathroom.

I don't know how or where he found the time to do all he did. The floor was lit with candles, the windows were open, and the breeze coming inside was breathtaking. Donavan guided me, like a wounded warrior, into the tub. He just sat next to me in dead silence on the floor.

"Do you have any idea the life that I have lived and how damaged I am?"

He said nothing. I wasn't sure what to do, as the pain lingered all over my body; however, I could not pinpoint exactly where it was.

"I'm not sure if anyone can love me with all the hurt that I have been through, Donavan. I'm grateful for all the help you've given me; however, I don't want you to get too close to me. I frankly don't want to hurt you."

He slightly raised himself up off the ground and positioned himself to face me. "You do not make that call for me, Akime. We may have way more in common than you think. I may be younger; but I can easily relate to what I see you going through. To date, you are the first man who has given me as much attention as you have given me. The first time you turned down my sexual advances, I was embarrassed. I felt something was wrong with me. I know you are involved, and I'm not trying to break up that happy home. Just allow me in this moment to show you love and affection. You are deserving of it; sex is far from my mind. Furthermore, stop talking. That's the real issue it seems; you talk too much at times."

I did exactly as I was told. I literally shut the *fuck* up.

I had lain in the tub long enough to have fallen asleep. Donavan came in and woke me up, telling me I'd had enough soaking. As I stood up, I could see the outline of my water-soaked body. I couldn't even see my dick; it was all gone. I didn't remember the last time I'd seen it that small.

The view outside was breathtaking. The lights on the hills in Montego Bay were the perfect backdrop to fall asleep to. Donavan brought me into the bedroom and oiled my skin. My dick moved an inch. He stared me dead in my eyes and shook his head. I knew what that meant.

After he finished oiling my body, he put the covers over me and turned off the lights. He walked out, and I could hear the water in the shower beating on his back. It reminded me of Nathan, the first day I had gone over to his flat on campus. It brought tears to my eyes because I still loved him. I wanted to honor his memory. But it's difficult, knowing that he'd tried to kill me.

It didn't take Donavan too long to come and crawl into bed next to me. He moved me closer to him, and I laid my head on his shoulders. I could hear his heartbeat. This young man, right next to me, was mature. He far exceeded his age, I had to remind myself that O'Neal was in New York waiting for me. This was all a dream; all I could do was live in the moment.

I was woken up by my usual dream. My body was covered in sweat. I was scared because, this time, the man in the mask had come over, and he had fucked my mouth. He was overly aggressive; he was not gentle. He had on a cock ring, and the veins on his dick were thicker than a tree log. He forced every inch of his dick into my mouth. No matter how much he saw me choking on it, he never pulled it out. It appeared my choking gave him more of a kick. As he flooded my mouth with his nut, I could hardly swallow, I saw myself swallowing my own vomit. He spat in my face and just walked off into the darkness.

I got up gasping for air, I literally felt as though I was vomiting on myself. I was breathing very heavy; my heart was pounding like a horse on a racetrack. Donavan got up. He held onto me tightly. He rubbed the back of my head and asked me if I was okay.

"It was just a bad dream, Akime. You scared me just watching you. You seemed as though you were having a fight in your dream."

In that moment, I contemplated telling him about my dreams. "I've been having some horrible sexual dreams, where this man in a mask has been trying to fuck me at a bathhouse. The dream always ends with me fighting, trying to tear the mask off his face. I spoke to my therapist about it; however, I'm still trying to internalize the dream." I saw him looking at me very intently, wondering what the fuck I was telling him.

"I believe that often our dreams reflect something going on in our lives. If you look deeper, you may find out what it really means. Our dreams sometimes personify our fears and even our secrets." He held me tighter, kissed me on my forehead, and told me that it would be okay.

"Thank you for listening and not judging me."

He gave me a kiss and got up out of bed. He walked in the direction of the kitchen.

I walked toward the French windows facing the bed and drew the curtains. The naked light literally transformed the bedroom. I'd been making it a point of duty to read *The Daily Stoic: 366 Meditations*. It was more like a daily devotional. I got hooked on the book because it was only one page each day. The book challenged you to think beyond the message that it gave.

Today's meditation was called "Circle of Control." It reads:

> We control our reasoned choice and all acts that depend on that moral will. What's not under our control are the body and any of its parts, our possessions, parents, siblings, children, or country—anything with which we might associate.

> —Epictetus, Discourses, 1.22.10

When Donavan returned from the kitchen, he brought with him a glass of freshly squeezed orange juice and an array of fruits. He asked me what I was reading. I told him about my morning ritual of reading a page a day from my devotional—a collection of Stoic documents. I explained that I tried my best to read it religiously every day.

I read aloud the reading for the day, and we had a conversation about the things we had control over. Without saying much, Donavan noted that the verse was meant for me. He explained that, after yesterday's incident with my mother and my sister, I had to realize that I had no control over what they thought or said. I, however, did have control over my life, my thought process, and the people I chose to bring into my life.

I was in bed. I simply rolled over on top of him, looked him dead in his eyes, and kissed him.

"Thank you so much. If only you were a bit older, you would be the perfect man of my dreams."

He wrapped his arms around me, squeezing me tightly. "Age is just a number. I will definitely age with grace. I know that you are taken. However, I am open to being that guy on the side—just like the side chick."

We both laughed out loud.

My dick was now brick hard, and Donavan moved me closer to him and guided my dick into his mouth. The boy had some good gag reflex skills. He didn't waste much time in taking me all in.

Donavan instructed me to go to the edge of the bed, with him lying on his back. He had his legs open, just like a clip. His head was hanging off the edge of the bed. I opened both of my legs and dropped my rod in his mouth. I could not resist his man pole beating on my belly. I started jerking it at first. However, I just had to put it in my mouth. The taste was tantalizing. His pre-cum tasted like sweet sugar nectar. As I went balls deep, my eyes became teary, and that was the most enjoyable part of making out.

I went to the top of the bed and lay on my back. I held onto both legs while Donavan licked my balls up to my ass crack. I had shaved, and the hair was growing back. It made a tickling sensation with his face buried deep in my ass. Donavan inserted his index finger deep inside of my ass, slowly massaging my prostate as he sucked on my dick. I so wanted to nut; I couldn't do that to myself, as I felt relaxed enough to take dick. That was all I wanted from him, right in this moment.

Donavan went for the condom and lube. He did everything to lube me up like a well-greased car going for a ride. My dick was throbbing; the muscles were protruding. He poured lube on the top of my dickhead and rubbed gently.

I looked up at him. I was nervous at first. His dick was really long. I wasn't sure if I could handle all of him. The boy actually had some skills. I felt the head as he slowly pushed himself inside of me. My body was so relaxed I didn't feel much pain. I was literally using both of my legs to push him further inside of me. My facial expression said it all. My eyes were open wide, and I bit onto my lips. I used both of my hands to raise my hips higher to give him a better angle. He was pulsating inside of me as he made small circular strokes. I moved my head close enough to realize that he was only halfway in.

My legs were now fully wrap around him, my hands tightly around his neck. Donavan lifted me up and put me against the wall next to the French windows and he fucked the shit out of me. I realized that the tighter I wrapped my legs around him, the more in control I was. I didn't know how to let go, how to give this young boy control over my body. I owed it to myself to enjoy him and set myself free.

We ended up on the white rug facing the foot of the bed. It was here I went to work; I rode his dick like a stallion. I was now relaxed, and to my surprise, I took all of him inside of me. It had been a minute since I squatted on a dick in this position. Donavan reminded me so much of Nathan. I may have solved my misery with him. He was the younger version of Nathan, and God was allowing me to keep loving him.

It didn't take long for me to hear Donavan's heavy breathing; he was about to nut. I came off his dick, went on all fours and begged my young man to shoot his load all over my dripping wet ass crack. As he positioned himself, he used one hands to jerk his dick and the other to finger my hole. I caught myself jerking off and loving every moment of him. As he spewed his hot load on my hole, he rubbed his nut over my ass cheeks. I was so turned on by what he was doing, it didn't take me long to come. I surrendered myself on the floor while Donavan lay on top of me kissing my ears.

We lay in that position until late evening. My body was exhausted. I really needed the rest. I got up feeling a slight tingling feeling at my ass. It reminded me that I had gotten dick, some good dick at that. I know that I was in love with O'Neal; however, this felt different. Donavan, though younger, allowed me to feel safer and more secure.

I got my journal, sat in the corner, and wrote down my experience thus far, recording the details of the great sex I'd had earlier. I spent most of my time watching Donavan sleeping and wondering what I had done. It felt as though I had totally forgotten that I had a loving man who I'd left in New York City.

Donavan looked so peaceful sleeping. He had a heart made of gold, and I honestly would try my best to help him in whatever way possible. I knew he would be hungry when he woke up. There was always food in the big house, so I left to get us both a plate. By the time I got back, Donavan was in the kitchen washing up the dishes.

I placed the food on the island countertop immediately behind him. I went behind him and hugged him. He was taller than me, and my waist was by his leg. With his wet soapy hands, he held onto my hands and rubbed them, while playfully kissing me at an odd angle.

"What do you have planned for later tonight?" He was still holding onto my hands.

"I had made plans to meet up with Warren and his mother and discuss his plans for his inheritance. I hinted that you should stay on temporarily to help out also."

Donavan cut the water off and turned around. He held onto my face and plastered his lips against mine. All I heard was the wet of our lips and him going back and forth saying, "Thank you."

One thing I admired about Donavan was the fact that he had always been humble, and he was ever so grateful.

"There is a party going on tonight in St. Ann, and I would love if you could join me. It's going to be outside of your comfort zone, but I think you should experience this side of Jamaica. It's more like an underground gay party. It is totally safe; lots of guys from Kingston will be there. It's by invite only. No cameras are allowed. And discretion is highly advised."

I'd heard about these parties before, but I'd never been invited to attend one. There wasn't much of a need to go.

"If it's not too much, would it be okay if I were to invite Warren? Like myself, he has been far removed from the Jamaican culture. With all that he's been going through, this may be what he needs in his life."

Warren had so much going on. I figured taking him out to just let loose might be the right thing for him.

Warren had decided to not stay back in Westmoreland and brought his mother back home. He was up for the excitement and noted he'd been wondering when he would get some time to hang with his best friend.

Later that evening, we all got dressed and headed into a remote country area in St. Ann. While slavery had ended years ago, remnants of the plantation period still lingered on the island.

Arriving at the entrance, we found a pathway lined with several decorative garden lights. Cars were parked to the far end of a nursery. The music wasn't overly loud, yet one wondered where the neighbors were. We all walked up, and Donavan was greeted by a very tall individual. I was unable to identify a gender. And in conforming to the LGBTQ slogan, gender conformity was not all that important.

By the looks of things, this was going to be a fierce party. We didn't get the memo. The gods were out in their colors. Heels of all shapes and sizes were visible. The hair and makeup were on fleek. The atmosphere was very colorful. I didn't mean to laugh. However, there were a group of lesbians dressed as warriors. Warren and I were laughing about our childhood television series *Xena: Warrior Princess*, as some of the women seemed as though they had come for war. I had never seen anything like this before in my life.

What stood out the most for me were the men and women dressed in all white with headbands. I had to ask myself why a group of revivalists were present at a gay party of all places. As we walked further down, we saw a huge firepit. Let's just say that I felt I was entering the Twilight Zone. Warren and I were just looking at each other and laughing.

Years ago, I read about a religious sect in Jamaica and how the spirit would transform the men. They were called Poco people. They took some elements from African religion, along with voodoo. The only time I'd ever experienced anything like this was as a teenager. I'd attended a Nine-Night function, and the band leader had been transformed. It was said that he was transformed by the spirit. In the transformation form, he no longer encompassed a gender. The local rum, JB, was used to summon the spirits of the dead.

The drumming was spiritual. The beat and rhythm forced your body to move. It made you feel as though you had the spirit within you. Donavan had left us for a bit. While observing the gathering, I saw someone come behind Warren and me. We were startled, as we knew for a fact that no one here knew us. To our surprise, it was Donavan, dressed in his white robe and headband of bright blue.

"What dah fuck? Are you serious? I had no clue that you were …" I didn't even know how to end my sentence, as this had come from out of nowhere. How did I never see this coming?

"Donavan, what dah fuck is this? Are you telling me all this time when you were working for us, you were involved in this?" Warren was filled with rage and anger.

"Mr. Warren, I supplied both your parents with whatever supplies that they needed. I depended on them as much as they depended on me and the spirits that I protected them from. Your older brother has been trying to kill you for years. My mother has been your guardian angel since you were born. Due to her illness, she is no longer able to do the rituals, so I took over from her."

We both looked at him in shock, completely lost for words.

"I'm not sure what to believe. You're like a mystery man. Hold up, are you an Obeah man or a Reader man, Donavan?" I was praying under my breath that he was neither, as I just couldn't do this. I couldn't see myself helping him. To be honest, I wouldn't be judging; I just couldn't see myself doing it.

"Hey, I have to go. I'm in charge of the service tonight. We welcome the LGBTQ to our services, as we strongly believe in inclusion. It isn't our place to judge God's children. The spirit can be immensely powerful. When transformed by the spirit, we see no gender identity. The transgender community in Jamaica struggles, as there are no social services within the varied communities that offer support. I wasn't sure how to tell you guys. However, I hope you both will see a different side of Jamaica."

I honestly didn't know what to say. He seemed genuine; the cause seemed noble and humble enough. I nudged Warren a bit, looked him in his eyes, and just hugged him.

We followed very slowly behind Donavan, not having a clue what to expect. The people looked country; there was just something about the mannerisms that reminded me of deep rural Jamaica. It dawned on me that I was coming off as elitist and overly privileged.

I hadn't been brought up with a golden spoon. But because of my education, my job, and my socioeconomic status, I was in a position to do things differently. I had never once forgotten my humble upbringing; this was just all new to me.

We all stood in a circle, surrounding the open bonfire. Donavan stood before a table with several bottles before him. There were three drummers close by, along with several men and women all dressed in long white dresses. Two men came out dressed in white wrapped underwear. They looked like ancient wraps, something slaves would wear.

The drums were loud, and the singing was in unison. Warren and I, however, could not make out the language they were singing in. It seemed like a ritual of some sort. Donavan started reading from a book going around the circle. He had a rum bottle in his hands and, on occasions, he would take a sip and spit it out in the crowd.

Both men were dancing close to the fire near the other dancers. After twenty minutes, I wondered what would be next. The men were both drinking; they were obviously drunk now. They both went atop of the table that Donavan was standing before. All three men started kissing, passionately at that. I held onto Warren's hands, as I was in a great deal of shock.

Donavan stood aside with a fire stick and the bottle of rum in his hands. He literally blew fireballs at the men as they got naked. I would have assumed the patrons would be in shock. Rather, they all chanted for the men to get naked. What happened after blew our minds.

The more attractive of the two guys was transgender. He had no breasts; however, the male parts weren't visible. They started making out, and the action was hot. Donavan went over and covered them both with some special oil. There were two short people burning herbs in a can. I had never read or seen anything like this in my life. It felt like something from a history book or a Steven Spielberg movie.

Now the weirdest shit happened. The masked man from my dream was here in the flesh. I had shivers all over my body. I'd never had a conversation with Warren about my dream, so I didn't even know how to explain it to him. The man scared the fuck out of me. I stood there, watching him nervously, telling myself that this shit was all a dream. By this time, the two guys were by the firepit fucking, covered in a white sheet.

The music was blasting, and the drums were pounding. I saw the masked man walking in my direction. I so wanted to walk away, but bytch ass Warren held onto me so tightly I couldn't even run.

"Yo, he is coming for me. If he stops, I am sure as fuck going to give him some ass."

All I could do was laugh, hoping and wishing that he was correct.

"Bytch, if he comes for you and you want to go, I will not hold your fucking ass back." He held onto my hands tighter, and we both look at each other, laughing.

As the masked man came toward us, he held out his hands. Based on his gestures, Warren knew that it was me. Warren pushed me toward him, and I obliged. As he grabbed my hands, he blew something into my face. I found myself falling to the ground. I have no recollection of what happened after.

I got up the next morning in bed next to Warren.

"Good morning."

I turned around to look at Warren. My head hurt and I had so many questions to ask him. My first question was, "What happened?"

"Don't fucking good morning me. You and that nigga stole the show last night. That masked dude must have known you. He brought you right over to Donavan. He stripped you naked, and two girls painted your body in red, green, and yellow. Both you and Donavan were in the spirit form. You were speaking in a different language. Let's just say, you may never forget or remember last night. I know for sure that Donavan is your soul mate, Akime. You guys made love in the open as if no one was there. Yo you deep no bloodclath; all of his shit went up in you. You were gliding on his dick."

I didn't know what to say. I knew my ass felt nice—not hurting or burning—just fucking nice.

I got up out of bed without saying anything to Warren. I went in the direction of the outside shower. I stood under the shower, just allowing the water to cascade down my back. I had this new joy about me. I just could not explain it. I felt renewed. I felt as though someone had given me life. There were so many unanswered questions. I frankly didn't want an answer to any of them.

All I wanted to do from this moment was to just live. I wasn't ready to leave Jamaica, but I knew I had to go. I was going back home feeling transformed. I wasn't in love with Donavan. But I had to acknowledge that he had given me a different experience. I hadn't come for love, but I had gotten something deeper.

I'd never had interest or desire in younger men. But I would spend the remaining two days with Donavan, soaking up as much of him as I possibly could. I left the shower and spent the rest of my day in the hammock looking out at the Caribbean Sea. I only wished this were the backdrop to my new office.

Chapter 14

Warren spent the next six months in Jamaica, sorting out things with his father's lands and holdings. Donavan continued to work with Warren as his right-hand man. O'Neal moved into my London flat with me after getting a gig in a West End show. Life with him wasn't perfect, but I loved him, and he loved me. I didn't communicate much with Donavan, as I didn't want to complicate my life.

My brother's girlfriend got pregnant. I told them they could stay with us. She was French white and did not want to share for too long. My dad forced my brother to do the manly thing and marry the girl. I was the best man at the wedding. They moved out at the end of the summer before I went on vacation.

O'Neal was in high demand for his show and wasn't able to travel to New York with me. Donavan got accepted to Columbia University in New York City that summer. I had offered him the house in Brooklyn as a place to stay. I'd made some changes and rented out the basement unit as a one-bedroom apartment. I felt that having someone staying at the house would be the best thing to do. I'd been looking into finally purchasing a property in Westchester County, outside of the city.

To be frank, since I'd left Jamaica after Warren's dad's funeral, things just hadn't been the same. I found out that, while I was in Jamaica, O'Neal had attended two sex parties in Midtown Manhattan. I forgave him. In Easter when he had already moved in with me, he had gone to Rome with a few of his friends for the long holiday weekend. I didn't want to go; I had some work I needed to catch up on. He returned with an STD and literally blamed me for giving it to him and having to get treated. I forgave him for that too. O'Neal would come in late almost every night, using rehearsal as an excuse. I found out he was lying; he was fucking this young dancer. I forgave him for that too.

I was no innocent bystander; I had done my own shit too. I had a fetish for African men, and I have stayed over late at the office.

The communication gradually lessened. We communicated mainly via text messages, which would lead to endless arguments. We both lived separate lives it seemed; though the love was still there. There were nights when I would get home early and cook for him. We had our occasional date nights. Sex was sporadic and often not planned, more by accident.

One morning I was in the shower jerking off before getting ready for work. He had left but returned for something. He heard me in the bathroom and came in fully clothed. We made love standing in the shower. He still gave me good dick. I still enjoyed fucking him. There just was something missing, and neither of us was man enough to use our words and say what we desired of each other or what was missing.

Closer to the start of the summer, I came home earlier than expected and caught O'Neal fucking this young, slim, well-toned white dude in his early twenties in our bed. I had not had sex in weeks. It was such a turn-on that I ended up joining in without getting upset or angry with him. We never had a conversation about what he had done after the guy left.

By midsummer, we decided it was best that we seek professional help, seeing that the love between us was still strong. We found a West Indian gay therapist, as we wanted to engage someone in conversation who was about the life. We had three one-hour sessions and felt that the time was well spent. We agreed to work on things. We agreed to talk more and to no longer hide things from each other. I very much wanted us to work. I wanted to live happily ever after with this man. It was extremely easy for me to forgive him and start all over.

Classes started in late August, so to help Donavan get situated at school, I had to visit New York by the second week in August. The weekend before I traveled, O'Neal and I went to the south of France to visit his best friend Roger. Roger lived with his partner and their two daughters. It was a great weekend. His partner noted that he was going to plan something special for Roger.

The day of Roger's birthday, his partner approached me over breakfast. He noted that Roger wanted to have two African guys come over and we would all fuck them. The birthday request was that both O'Neal and I join in. At first, I figured that O'Neal wouldn't be down. Ironically, everyone was waiting for me to give the go. It was for Roger, so what the heck? I agreed to join in the festivities.

The birthday night came. We all fucked the two African guys. As couples we didn't even touch each other. We were only focused on the two guys taking dick.

The following night, after dinner, O'Neal and I took the train and headed directly to Paris. On the way into Paris, we spoke about the relationship, what we would work on individually, and what we would work on as a couple. I was confident that things would work out and that no one could ever come between our love.

I did not pull any strings for Donavan to get his scholarship. The only thing I offered him was accommodation for his four years in school. My only expectation of him was that he take care of the house, which I knew he would be able to do. The tenants in the basement were a family friend with a small boy. I never had any issues with them. They paid the rent on time. And if there were an issue, they would resolve it and give me the bill after. The backyard was mine, and I had asked Donavan if he could maintain the lawn and the garden. He had laughed at me when I made the request. It was a given that he would have company over. I just asked that he respect my space and refrain from having parties.

The arrangement I made with Donavan worked out in my favor, as I didn't want to leave the house all shut up without someone living in it. By this time, Warren had swapped his desk for high-top water boots with the lush greenery of Jamaica as his office backdrop. I didn't have Warren around to house-sit. Donavan was the only person I felt safe enough living in the house. I thought about subletting, but where would I go when I visited New York? Warren had leased his apartment. I had already told him that he could stay at the house whenever he made a trip to NYC. He still had a copy of the house keys and would always hold on to them.

I had asked my job for an extension so that I could meet up with Donavan and get him acquainted with New York City. I knew that it was going to be a bit much for him living in a foreign country. I promised him I would help him navigate the train system. Warren was no longer around, so Donavan would have to figure it out all by himself. Within no time, the winter would be here. I was confident that Donavan would figure it out all on his own.

I arrived in New York two days before Donavan's arrival. I gave Donavan the bedroom closest to mine. I had bought him a desk so that he could use it for school. My office space was now rented in the basement. So, there wasn't much that could be done regarding that space. I also went to Pottery Barn and got new sheets and towels for Donavan. There was an extra bedroom adjacent to the one he would be in. There was a pantry in the kitchen, and I ensured it was packed with enough essentials to last him for three months.

The morning Donavan arrived in New York, he landed at 6:45 a.m. at JFK International Airport. It was the end of summer, the week before Labor Day and also just a few days leading into West Indian Day Parade. The march would pass the house, so I never had the need to go to the parkway. This would be an interesting introduction to all things gay and colorful in the Caribbean community.

He spent some time getting through customs and followed my instructions and found his way to the car. I had given him a smartphone when I was on my last trip to Jamaica. He called me when he got outside, and his chocolate complexion seemed to shimmer in the morning sunlight. There was something different about him. I held my composure, as I had made a promise not to have sex with him again. I was too emotionally involved with O'Neal; the idea was to stick to the plan.

When Donavan arrived at the car, I helped him put his luggage in the trunk.

"So, you finally have arrived in the *Big Apple*, and I am so excited you're here. How was the flight?" I hugged him and rushed him into the car.

He gave me a huge smile and held onto me tightly, whispering in my ear. "Thank you so much for coming to get me and for helping me."

I could hear him choke up, and I gave him a reassuring look to let him know that all would be good.

"So how was the flight? And did they give you a hard time at customs?"

He seemed exhausted and overwhelmed, and he looked like he just wanted to take it all in.

"Hey, you look beat and drained. Would you like something to eat?"

He shook his head, and as we drove off, all he could do was look out at everything passing in the window. I figured he was just asking himself if this was all real and if he was really here.

"I didn't eat much on the plane. Mr. Warren drove me to the airport, and he had the chef make me an egg sandwich. I had never flown on a plane before, and no matter how hard I tried to sleep, I just could not. The flight attendant girl was very polite and helpful, and she assisted me in filling out the customs and immigration form. I had a seat to myself, and I told her about school and how excited I was to see New York." He paused for a bit and looked at me.

I used my right hand to rub his leg and told him that it felt scary, but it would be okay.

"The city is huge, and there is so much happening all at once. All I can say is trust your gut instinct, and don't be ashamed to ask questions. I've taken off work to show you around. I'm giving you a crash course, and hopefully you will get the hang of things while I'm gone. I'm also fucking proud of you."

While I spoke to him, he looked out the window as though he was drifting, and he just nodded. He was captivated by the city and all the tall buildings.

For the next couple of days, I brought Donavan over to Columbia campus in Manhattan. I got him a metro card for the month, along with a subway map. I told him it was okay to get lost, as that was the only way to find his way.

While Harlem had lost most of its Black occupants, Harlem was going through a different renaissance now. The white folks had moved in, and the brownstones were no longer cheap. Harlem was, however, one of the best places to get authentic Southern food.

I didn't care for the Bronx much; however, I did venture over to Gun Hill Road. Eventually, I would be making regular visits if I decided to buy my dream home in Westchester County. Donavan was all smiles, noting that some sections of the Bronx looked like Jamaica—they felt and looked like Jamaica. I jokingly told him that, if he had lost any friends he hadn't seen in a long time, this was the place to find them—right on White Plains Road.

The Sunday before the West Indian Day Parade, I brought Donavan down to Church Avenue side by the Q Train across from the famed Bobby's Department Store. There was a West Indian food market across from the train station that sold fresh produce. I wanted to give Donavan the opportunity to see as much of the neighborhood as possible so that he would feel at home.

We went out to dinner twice; all the other meals we shared, I cooked for Donavan. In the process of cooking so much, I realized how much I had missed cooking. I decided I would make a conscious effort to start cooking more when I returned to London.

Despite the time difference, I spent most of my nights up late talking to O'Neal. It seriously felt like old times all over again. O'Neal was such a romantic. I was eager to get back home and literally spend the rest of my life with him. I was even contemplating proposing to him. I was passed thirty, and settling down was just the right thing to do. I couldn't see myself loving anyone else but him.

The night before I was ready to return to London, I got a rather strange text message from O'Neal. It read, "We need to have a serious conversation when you return. I have come to a decision, and I feel its best that I share it with you face-to-face."

This came out of nowhere, and I simply was taken off guard. I didn't know what to do or say. I didn't respond. I knew I had only a few hours before I would get on the plane. I trusted that all was well and that he was going to be giving me a huge surprise.

That night, when I was leaving, I took a cab, even though Donavan was insistent that he accompany me to the airport. It was a kind gesture; however, I needed some space to think. I was heading back with a new perspective about myself. I was ready for love and all that came with loving someone. I believed that I had fully gotten over Nathan. The love that O'Neal had for me was real and genuine. He was the first man I'd met after Nathan; he had brought me to the next level of loving.

I boarded British Airways Airbus A380 double-decker from JFK with a direct flight to London Heathrow. I never accepted less than first class if it was available. As I got settled on the plane, something strange came over me. I wasn't sure what it was. I just knew that it felt as though something was missing. I put on my headset and selected the *Waiting to Exhale* soundtrack featuring Whitney Houston. By no conscious intention, I selected, "Why Does It Hurt So Bad." Oddly enough, that was exactly how I was feeling.

I jetted across the Atlantic reading *A New Earth: Awakening to Your Life's Purpose* by Eckhart Tolle. After Nathan died and recently with the death of Warren's father, I'd been taking a different look at life. I wanted to give back. I wanted to live a life with meaning and purpose. I wasn't sure what was going on. I just knew that these songs by Whitney Houston were having me feeling a certain way. I was having mixed feelings about that text that O'Neal sent me.

I told myself I just had to be open to the possibilities that presented themselves. I felt as though he was about to break up with me. I did not see the rationale for it, though. Things were going great—well, so I had believed.

The flight attendant in first class was incredibly attentive. She was a beautiful young lady from South Africa. I wasn't sure if she saw the worry on my face, but she was very attentive to my needs.

I arrived in London at 6:27 a.m. It didn't take me too long to go through customs. I got a cab and headed directly toward my flat. London rush hour traffic was bad; but I didn't feel like taking the tube with my luggage.

When I got home, I dropped my bags in the living room corner and went directly to the market. O'Neal usually got home after 6:00 p.m. I wanted to cook him a fish dinner with pumpkin rice and plantains. If I marinated the fish early, I would have an opportunity to take a nap before I started cooking.

It didn't take me long to go to the food market by Brixton. This was the closest place I could go to get a Caribbean market that could rival those in New York. I was familiar with the market, but it was no comparison to Jamaica's Coronation Market.

When I got back home, I seasoned the fish and chopped up the pumpkin for the rice. I didn't feel overly exhausted, but it was becoming somewhat challenging to sleep. The good old Pornhub would do its job. I went to the site and selected Remy Mars, one of my favorite porn actors. I didn't need lube. I was naked in bed. I spat on my dick and went to work.

I hadn't had sex while in New York; I very much needed this release. I found myself grabbing the lubricant in the top nightstand drawer. I tipped a bit of lube onto my index finger and rubbed it around my butthole. The sensation was amazing. I could not resist myself; I had to put two fingers in. I closed my eyes, imagining O'Neal pounding the shit out of me, literally. I felt my ass muscles contract. The muscles in my dick became more erect, and I exploded in my face. I intentionally opened my mouth to taste my warm nectar of man juice.

I slept like a baby in the night. I got up around after 4:00 p.m. and immediately went to the kitchen to cook. The television was playing reruns of *American Idol*. I was in such a good mood; I even had a glass of wine I was sipping as I prepared the food.

After five, I headed to the bathroom to take a shower and to do my ritual. I needed dick tonight. I needed him inside of me balls deep. I would not settle for any accidents tonight either. At the rate I was drinking, I knew I would have him fuck me with my head out the windows looking out.

O'Neal walked in around 6:20 p.m. I took his bags from him and plastered a kiss on him. I asked him to wash his hands, as dinner was ready. His embrace wasn't as warm as I had anticipated. I told myself that he'd just had a long day at work. We both sat eating, and I soon realized I was the only one talking.

"So how is the food?" I had to say something, I just could not handle both of us sitting in silence.

"The food is good as always, Akime." That was all he said. O'Neal was a man of many words, and that was all he had to say; something had to be up.

"How's work?" I no longer knew what to say. I honestly felt like crying.

"Akime, I don't want to continue the small talk. While you were away, I had some time to sit and reflect. I don't think that you're the right man for me."

There was a fucking long pause. I didn't say anything. My eyes didn't even blink. I just kept looking at him.

"I love you, but I'm no longer in love with you. I just can't see myself being with you any longer. I think it's best that we just be friends. It's best that we just end the relationship." He was eating while talking. I found that to be so disrespectful and rude.

"What happened while I was away?" That was the only question I could have asked; I just did not see this coming at all.

"Nothing happened, Akime. I just took some time and self-reflected on all that has happened in the past. And I just see that my basket is full, and I don't think I can do this any longer."

I sat looking at him, and the tears just started flowing. My body felt numb, my hands were shaking, and I didn't have any words to speak. I wished the ground could take me in just about now. This was not what I'd come back for. I had come home changed. I had come home looking to love him even more than I already did.

"So, what happens next? Is this a breakup or are you asking for a break?" I was confused as fuck. When I say this shit came out of nowhere, I mean nowhere.

"No, Akime, this is a breakup. I no longer want to be in a relationship with you. I honestly believed that I could do this with you, but I can't."

I was now filled with rage and anger; he couldn't even give me a solid excuse for the breakup after all of his fuckups. "So, you have a basket. What dah fuck is in that basket? I have a fucking basket of my own. Yet here I am with your sorry ass after all the shit you've done." I was filled with anger.

"Akime, I don't want to argue. I still love you and all. I just can't see myself being with you. I just don't think you're the right man for me."

His words stung like a bee. My body felt as though someone was stabbing me in my heart. I had not returned home for this.

O'Neal held out his hands to mine. He scooped both of his hands around my right hand and kissed it. My eyes were wet. I was an emotional wreck. I was sitting there looking at the man with whom I was in love only to hear him tell me I wasn't the man for him. He came over toward me and, standing behind me, kissed me atop my head. I used both of my hands to hold onto his arms. It felt like a dream, a bad dream at that. Something was missing. I felt empty and lonely all at once.

"I'm not trying to hurt you, Akime. I know what you went through with Nathan. I just got to a point where I have to do the right thing for me. I'm not going anywhere for now. We can build on the friendship. To be honest, I just need some space, some time to figure things out for myself. I moved to London for a better life. Look at me. A struggling artist, trying to make ends meet. I'm living with you in an apartment that I hardly contribute to. You pay for literally all our trips. This isn't about you, Akime. It's about me and doing what's right for me."

I started crying because I heard him. Only, it just wasn't adding up.

"If we decided that we are building a life together, that means that we are a team. As a team, we should be doing this together. I get your point; but I'm here for you. I just can't believe that this is happening, O'Neal. How will this work? Are you moving out? If not, what's the transition point? How do we make this work?" I finally got the strength to stand up and hug him. I just couldn't stop crying.

"Come and sit with me. So much has happened, Akime. I need to be at peace with myself. I have never loved another man as much as I love you. I just know that, right now in this moment, you're just not the man for me. I'm hurting too; this wasn't an easy decision for me."

We both went over to the sofa.

I found myself laying in his lap, looking for comfort and peace. Ironically, it was from the man who broke my heart. I had never felt this pain piercing in my heart. The last time I had felt this level of pain was on the morning Nathan had shot me. Not even after Nathan died had I felt this way. As I lay across the sofa, I closed my eyes questioning God. *Why?* I asked. I desperately needed answers to my question. I had known something was up on my way home; I'd felt it.

My breathing became heavy; this was just too much. I closed my eyes and told myself that this was all a dream. I turned to my side, said the Lord's Prayer in my head, and drifted off to sleep. I just needed to clear my mind. I figured in the morning, I would wake up, and it would be just a dream.

Chapter 15

I woke up the following morning to my new reality. O'Neal was no longer next to me. I found myself still lying on the sofa all alone. I rubbed my eyes, telling myself that this had to have been a dream. I looked in the direction of the dining room; the table was not cleared. The only thing I felt like doing was crying. I didn't want to go back there again. I needed answers.

I needed to have a conversation with myself. It was important to seek clarity and find my center. I went to the room; I had assumed that O'Neal would be in bed. No, he wasn't. I had to hold myself, simply because it was a Sunday morning. O'Neal did nothing on a Sunday but just lay in bed. My daily devotional was on the nightstand. I took it up. I wasn't sure what I was looking for. I just turned the pages and opened to "The Path to Serenity." It wasn't the day's reading; however, the universe has its way of guiding us in the right direction. It read:

This morning, remind yourself of what is in your control and what's not in your control. Remind yourself to focus on the former. And not the latter.

God has a way of bringing things to light. I was hurting. I felt pain all over my body but couldn't pinpoint where exactly it was. I needed an escape from all of this. I wasn't about to run away either.

I made myself some coffee with French vanilla. I picked up the phone and called Warren; he didn't pick up. I called Delaney; she didn't pick up either. I found myself calling my house phone in New York, just to hear a familiar voice on the other end of the line.

I was silent for a bit; I just didn't know what to say. Donavan just kept on saying, "Hello. Hello. Hello?" He would know the call was from London, as it would have shown up on the caller ID.

"Akime, are you okay? Say something to me please." I could hear the concern in his voice; it was genuine and real.

For a good five minutes, I said nothing—just sat there breathing heavily. Eventually I broke down. I couldn't stop crying. I needed the release; I had to let it all out. I felt safe with Donavan. I knew he wouldn't judge me.

Eventually, I was able to use my words. "He broke up with me last night. It came out of nowhere. I told you I came home to make that change—to do right by him. I never expected this to happen, not in my wildest dreams." I went over the details of the prior night.

"To be honest, Akime, not to sound insensitive or anything, but you deserve way better than what you were getting. I remember our conversations in Jamaica on your last trip; you weren't happy. I know you love him; he was also the first man after Nathan to have shown and given you love. Look at it like this: you needed some time alone. It's time for Akime to be alone and spend some time with himself."

I sat down on the edge of my bed, realizing that this young man was mature way beyond his years. He was right. He was dead fucking spot on. I had to be honest with myself for a bit. I was scared as fuck.

"Who am I talking to?" I laughed out aloud. "I just left you yesterday, and here you are giving me advice on life and how to live. You are indeed right, Donavan. It will hurt; the hurt will go away. I do love him; I was willing to put my all in it. I realize that I have no control over his decision. No one has ever broken up with me before. Well, my husband killed himself and left me all alone. I'm going to take a walk in the park. I'll call you back later."

I hung up the phone, got dressed, and headed out to the park.

For the next seven months, I tried to cohabitate with O'Neal. It wasn't always easy, especially when he came home late nights and took a shower. Even though we had an extra room, we chose to sleep next to each other. There were nights when I desperately wanted to fuck but had to resist and keep myself from touching him. I caught him on a few occasions jerking off next to me in bed.

There were a few occasions where we had small arguments here and there. They weren't anything major; it was just rehashing the past and who had hurt who more. I made a decision—one I wasn't sure I could keep. I decided to give up sex and random trades and focus my energy on myself. I realized that, in order to be my better self, I had to spend more time with me. Sex was fun, enjoyable, and enlightening. I spent too much time focusing on getting a nut and not enough on me.

For the next couple months, I found myself traveling to different countries in search of a new me. I realized that I had relocated to Europe without exploring the mainland. Africa was so close, yet I never took the opportunity to explore. I was far from rich; however, I was comfortable enough to do certain things.

Two Years Later

I spoke to Donavan literally every day. I couldn't have asked for a better friend. He shared with me his adventures in New York. I scolded him a few times. School was going great; he even made the dean's list.

Late one night while we were talking on the phone, Donavan said there was something different about me. I told him I felt different also. I had become more centered and still. I now had more clarity about life, my purpose for living. I had made up my mind that I would start my own business. I had given so much to my company. I would be able to replicate what I do for them on my own.

Christmas would no longer be the same if I stayed in London. I opted not to do New York either, as it would have reminded me of what had occurred two years earlier. I yearned to be home, the land of my birth. I desired Jamaica of all places. I didn't want to go alone, so I invited Donavan as a friend to tag along with me. I offered to purchase his ticket and give him spending money.

Donavan and I arrived in Jamaica the day before Christmas Eve. Warren was excited to see me; when he arrived at the airport, it was all hugs and smiles. He didn't give a flying fuck what anyone thought or felt. He just knew that I was in Jamaica with him yet again. Donavan had landed earlier and decided he would wait on me. I didn't think Warren liked Donavan. I thought he believed Donavan was a gold digger or something of that sort.

We all met up and packed ourselves into Warren's van. Warren had purchased an apartment in Kingston, as he had several business meetings there. Within the short time since I'd left Jamaica, Warren had made some changes to the property in Blue Fields in Westmoreland. He'd finally taken my advice and told me he would be creating a bed-and-breakfast on the property.

We arrived at Warren's new home in Westmoreland after 11:00 p.m. Warren didn't like to cook, but he made white rice and stewed peas with spinners. Sweet ripe plantains were on the side, along with avocado. I was, from a distance, just observing Warren. He'd matured so much. Warren indicated that we could choose any room we desired. Donavan and I selected the rooms farthest from each other.

"Hold up. So what the fuck is up with you two? You don't need to pretend with me, missy." He was busy sharing out the meal.

"I keep telling you that we're not together; we're just friends. I'm on a break from all that. I haven't had sex in over a year now. Ever since O'Neal broke up with me, I've been focused on me."

He looked at me side-eyed. "Bytch. Please, get the fuck out of here and stop lying. Did you buy a dildo or a flesh light or something, Akime? You're talking to your best friend."

I knew it would be exceedingly difficult for him, of all people, to believe me. "I'm doing this for me. I'm spending more time with myself. I won't lie, I miss sex a lot; I so want to fuck too. I just don't want to be with anyone like that now." I had to change the topic, so I went over to help him and started taking the food outside.

Warren had created an outside lounge area in the backyard. The ocean wasn't too far away; it was the perfect lookout point. Donavan was already outside looking out at the ocean. I went over to him, just to see how he was doing.

"Is everything okay with you?" He didn't look himself. He seemed worried or bothered about something.

"It's just odd. I honestly don't feel a part of all this. Two years ago, I was working for Mr. Warren. Four Christmases ago this time, I was working for his father before he died. I just don't know how to function." I could see the hurt and confusion in his face. Donavan had never fully accepted his father as his dad.

"Let's put it like this—you've evolved. You're now in a privileged group, and you're just going to have to own it. I get it. It's a new feeling; it seems surreal, as you can remember the life you once lived as though it was yesterday. I felt the same way when I returned the first time. I'm here for you; just enjoy the moment and space that you're in. Most importantly, tell yourself that you deserve every bit of it."

I held onto his hands and added gently, "At some point, you're going to have to stop saying Mr. Warren. Don't forget; he's also your half brother." I gave him a hug and went back inside for the lemonade with ginger.

"I'm confused," Warren said. "You said you guys are just friends, yet you were just outside hugging him."

I was trying to determine whether it was jealousy or bitterness I detected in his tone.

I told Warren about the struggles Donavan was going through and how reassuring I was to him as a friend. I also reminded Warren that Donavan was his biological brother, and he couldn't keep ignoring that reality.

"Akime, he was my family's gardener. He used to work for me right after Daddy died. He was the yard boy, for heaven's sake. Now you're on vacation with him, and he's my houseguest. He's not in my class, and it's going to be a challenge to accept him in." Warren said this with so much attitude.

In that moment, I wanted to hate him, simply because I was another version of Donavan; so that meant he had not accepted me fully. "I will not do this with you, Warren. I grew up just as poor as Donavan. I know how he feels. I've been there before. You grew up with money, privileged and a part of the Jamaican elite, yet your sexuality brought shame on your family, and you became an outcast. So, no you don't have a right to not accept him, simply because it's not your call to make." I was so fucking upset with him and wished that I could smack the fuck out of his face.

"I am so sorry, Akime; it wasn't my place to say that. I'm just looking out for you as a friend. I don't want you to get hurt. Donavan is a great guy. I just have my reservations." He seemed sincere, and I accepted the apology.

"You have nothing to worry about. We're just friends. We had sex in the past, and that's over and done with. I really do enjoy his company and the conversations that we have. Don't forget that you're no longer close to me, and you no longer have as much free time on your hands." I could see the hurt in his eyes when I made the last statement.

He came over to me and hugged me very tightly.

We walked over to the outside table. Warren did something that I really liked; he went over to Donavan and hugged him. I was so pleased that he wanted to at least try and be cordial.

The conversation revolved around the New Year's Eve party we'd been invited to in Kingston. Warren apparently had been dating a minister who was in the current Jamaican government administration. The gentleman was single with no children; he did, however, have a woman for show. She was aware of his situation, as she too was a part of the life.

Warren also gave us an update on what he had done since I'd last seen him. Apart from the bed-and-breakfast, Warren had decided to end the goat business. He decided to keep the cows, pigs, and chickens. Regarding farming, the banana industry was striving, so that was a definite stay. Apparently, hot peppers were a lucrative business. Overall, Warren felt more comfortable keeping the ground produce farms, as he felt it was important to support the local agricultural markets.

We literally fell asleep outside, just listening to the waves coming ashore. Donavan said he woke me up after my snoring was getting out of hand. He lifted me up and took me to bed and covered me up.

I woke up the next morning to the smell of fried plantains, fried dumplings, ackee, and salt fish, along with the sweet smell of cocoa with nutmeg. I changed into something more comfortable and went outside.

I could not have asked for more. I found Donavan and Warren cooking in the kitchen. I stood at a distance, observing them, just hoping that, as times went by, they would get along.

The view outside was spectacular and more breathtaking in the daylight. Warren had gone all-out with the flowers and the layout. This was a full experience. He came out and, seeing me, gave me a cup of hot cocoa and pointed to the hammock.

"That right over there was created just for you. You will always have a place in my home."

I was emotional, just acknowledging the kind of friendship I had developed with Warren over the years.

To the far left of the backyard experience, Warren had constructed an infinity pool. This would be a great incentive to the bed-and-breakfast crowd.

Warren's mother had opted to travel to the Cayman Islands to spend Christmas. She felt that it would be too much to spend Christmas in the house without her husband again. She wanted to be around her friends and not be in Jamaica. The relationship between Warren and his siblings hadn't improved; however, he had gotten them all involved in the business.

Donavan and I spent the day exploring the property while Warren went out to tend to business. There was a river a distance from the property, so we decided to venture out and find its origin.

What we found was magical. It was an actual untouched waterfall, covered by lush greenery. There weren't any houses in proximity. We both sat on a rock just taking it all in.

We heard a splashing and got up, startled. To our surprise, we discovered the splashers were two extremely attractive young men playing. It was so much fun just watching them play in the water. Donavan, the friendly person he was, went over to them and asked if we could join. Who could resist Donavan in any case? Hold up. I forgot to mention that both guys were nude. The younger of the two laughed and said we could join in only if we got naked.

I could not have asked for a better day spent with two strangers. The younger one's name was Roger and the older one Mark. They asked if we were together, and we both playfully said yes, we were. They were both under twenty-five years old. They told us how they'd met in high school late one evening after football practice. It was a story made for movies. I was intrigued by the tale and the story of young Black gay love.

I took the liberty of inviting them to Christmas dinner at Warren's. It was refreshing to see these two guys together. Their outlook on life was inspiring and revolutionary. When we got back to the house, Warren was there, and I told him about our discovery. At first, he was upset; however, he too was intrigued to meet the young couple to stay mad for long. I made it clear between him and Donavan that none of us would be fucking any of the guys after dinner tomorrow. We all laughed out in unison, as the idea was right at the top of our heads.

The following day, we all got up early and had something light for breakfast. Warren had the weirdest tree for a Christmas tree. I guess he was thinking outside of the box. I helped him to decorate, while Donavan was in the kitchen cooking. I had invited the guys to come over around midday. They were on time, another positive for them.

They both came dressed in white, I don't recall the all-white memo, but they looked cute. The moment they got settled, they asked what they could do to assist us. It made life so much easier.

We learned about their simple upbringing and how committed they were to each other. They lived in the same community, not far from Warren in the hills. Both of their parents were dead, and they had little or no family support. They shared a house together with the eldest paternal grandfather.

They noted that the community members all believed they were related. The issue was, at times, too often, they would forget that, even though they were in an actual relationship, cuddling just wasn't allowed. Both had the desire to get a higher education, but the funds weren't there. When we asked about their grades in high school, we learned they'd both finished at the top of their classes.

Mark worked as a manager at a popular hotel in Whitehouse. Roger was a teller at a bank in Savanna-la-Mar, the town of Westmoreland. I would very much have loved to help, as this was what true survival commitment was.

Over dinner later in the evening, Warren said he had a surprise; he decided to be bold by offering to pay Roger's college tuition. I could not have been prouder of him. These guys were strangers. He didn't know them; he hadn't even wanted them at dinner. I was just proud of him.

"This morning I had a conversation with Akime. After some reflection, I realized just how privileged I am. My dad always told me that to whom much is given much is expected. I have a responsibility to give back to the gay community. I believe that education is the only way out."

I held onto his hands and wiped tears from my eyes.

"Sir, I am not even sure how to say thank you." Roger was wiping tears from his eyes while his partner held onto him. "I have always believed in God and trusted that, one day, he would give me a way out. I will not disappoint you, sir. And anything you ever need help with, please let me know." Roger was emotional; his lips were shaking as he spoke.

"Roger, you don't owe me anything. My only expectation is that you be focused and give school your best shot possible. I never got a chance to be myself when I was younger. I was shipped off because my family was ashamed of me. You both have given me hope that love is alive. It's not always the beating and killing that go on in Jamaica."

We all raised our glasses to Warren.

As the evening evolved, we spoke about politics and sports in Jamaica. It was an eye-opening conversation. So much hypocrisy pervaded the island when it came to homosexuality. Mark was heavily involved in sports and gave us a list of very prominent Jamaican athletes who were gay and in the closet. Roger had a strong distaste for the local LGBTQ organization, as he strongly felt that it wasn't representing the majority gay population. Too much attention was given to the negatives. Roger believed that, too often, young men just needed support and guidance. The conversation revolved too much around HIV prevention, advocating for homeless gays, and those tagged as "Gully Queens." It attracted international attention and fueled financial support to the local gay rights movement. This was at a cost to tourism and Jamaica as a brand.

Around midnight, we sat by the pool and reminisced about old country time in Jamaica. Our two guests and Donavan were young, so they didn't have much to say. Warren and I spoke about the fun times we'd had in primary school and high school. We spoke about Miss Lou, Oliver Samuels, Titus, and the list of musical legends.

The topic of Buju Banton came up, and it was very heated. Banton's "Boom Bye Bye" is still seen as the hate anthem to gay killings in Jamaica. I had a different take on that. Everyone was taken aback when I told them I enjoyed fucking to "Boom Bye Bye," simply because Buju was only imitating art. The song was more of a social commentary, and it was an escape from accepting that the gay killings too often were gay-on-gay crime.

We spoke until early morning, taking in the sunrise. I didn't recall having had that much conversation in a very long time. Warren dropped off our guests. Donavan and I went to our separate rooms and slept throughout most of Boxing Day.

For the remainder of the trip until New Year's Eve, Donavan and I just relaxed by the pool. We spent a couple of nights in Negril and Montego Bay.

I did go to St. Ann to look for my mother. My brother and his wife flew in to surprise my mother. My brother and I had become somewhat distant, as he had accused me of abandoning the family. He felt that the way I'd spoken to my mother at Warren's father's funeral was unacceptable. I was honestly at a point where I no longer gave a flying fuck. I had to do what was right for me now. Whatever was in my basket belonged to me and me alone.

Spending time with Donavan's family was interesting. His mom, who was very open, was of the view that we were in a relationship. Donavan's younger brothers were just as hot as he was. To be poor wasn't a crime. I really enjoyed my full day with Donavan's family. We all valued different things in life. The greatest gift of all was love. No amount of money could buy you love. While Donavan's life would be forever transformed, he still remembered his humble upbringings. Just watching him attend to his mother and seeing the affection they had for each other made me respect and admire him more.

New Year's Eve morning, we all journeyed to Kingston. I decided to drive, as I wanted to give Warren a bit of a break. It must have felt freeing for him not to be driving today. Before arriving in Kingston, we got stopped by the police three times. I was polite on all three stops, though it did seem as though I was being hit on, on all three occasions.

My only observation was that I had no clue Jamaica had so many gay officers in the police force. They must be free balling in the black-and-red striped pants, as I all I could see was dickhead hanging down. I so wanted to be patted down.

The last guy who stopped us knew what was up. He literally asked where the party was tonight while holding onto his gun. Well, you could easily see his dick because it was so close to his hand.

Warren was such a tease, he invited the officer to the party and requested that he come in uniform. I was Mr. Quiet, as always; I got the fucking number without being a slut. See, it pays to just sit and be still. There was a thicker one who stood at a distance and had a phat motherfucking ass. Those were literal cakes and beat to the Gods; he had dick too. I took his number, and I asked the young cute officer to bring his friend along if he didn't mind our kind of party.

We were expected to spend the night and the weekend with the minister at his home in the hills of St. Andrew. When we arrived at the minister's home, we were greeted by a doorman—let's say a houseboy, as he was no more than twenty. I gave Warren a look meant to say, *What the fuck is up?* The young man was extremely helpful, polite, and too damn young to be doing this shit. It was none of my business, so I was going to just take my bags and shut dah fuck up.

After getting settled, we all went downstairs. My mouth fell open wide; I couldn't even call his name, and I still won't. Let's call him M moving forward. M held an important position in the Jamaican government. He looked like royalty and, damn, his pepper grey beard and bald head were such fucking turn-ons. He looked way better in person. He smelled like old money; his voice moved you. I could imagine him fucking Warren; just having him whisper in my ears would let me have several orgasms.

M greeted us and escorted us all outside. It felt very formal and businesslike, somewhat old-school. I felt as though I was in some English country club. We were having tea in the Jamaican heat. Now that was just a bit too much and overdoing this privileged shit. You know what? I was all for the pageantry and fuckery. I ate biscuits and sipped tea with my little finger hanging in the air like everyone. Donavan kept hitting me, telling me to cut out the attitude.

M was the conversationalist, as I would have expected him to be. He spoke about the party and his plans with Warren for the New Year. He seemed genuine, just a real old soul. That smile could get your ass wet and dick dripping any day. If I had to kick Warren under the table, using my lips to mouth, "Bytch, he is fine as fuckkkkk" and "old boy got *dick*."

All Warren could do was laugh.

M noted that he was elated to meet me, as he'd heard so much about me. He extended an invitation for Donavan and me to go to St. Thomas with them for a few days and celebrate the start of the new year.

Donavan seemed very intrigued by him, and M was giving him a bit of attention. Donavan was still my guest, and I wouldn't want that line to be crossed. M stated that Donavan and I made a very cute couple.

"I always like to see young love. Now this is my kind of love. Growing up as a young boy in Jamaica, this was totally unheard of. Warren has brought so much joy into my life. I finally feel I have a chance to live."

There was something about what he said that made me question the kind of love I was seeking.

M was somewhat taken aback when Donavan and I both noted we were just friends. It seemed as though everyone saw things that we were not seeing. I had become more fond of Donavan; I felt safe and comfortable around him. As a friend, I knew that I could say anything to him. It felt like a partnership too. I frankly could think of no reason we couldn't be in a relationship.

After tea, M left, saying he had a last-minute errand to run. Donavan, Warren, and I drove to Sovereign Center to get food from Island Grill. It wasn't just the food that brought back memories; it was the location. I remembered the days when Delaney and I would meet up and have lunch together. I ordered my usual, jerk chicken breast, callaloo rice, and fried plantains. This was somewhat new for Warren. Donavan stated that he'd had only BBQ chicken and festival from them.

After we were served, we sat in the eating section by the elevator. Something came over me, an emotion I hadn't felt in an exceptionally long time. I was overjoyed with love and happiness. I just started looking into space, reminiscing about my kind of love, the kind I'd had with Nathan. I was still torn by my love for Nathan—still trying to find a balance between that love and the hurt he'd caused me, along with the love I had gotten from him. The scar from the bullet was very visible. There were days when it hurt, but I tried to just deal with it.

The good thing about having friends like Warren and now Donavan was that I didn't have to explain anything to them. They both knew where my mind was, and they said nothing. After having my moment, I came back to reality and drilled the hell out of Warren about M. I'd heard stories about gay politicians. But to see one as prominent as M just blew my mind.

Warren seemingly was taking his time with M and not rushing anything. There was a difference in how Warren spoke about M, compared to the way he'd always talked about the others he'd been with. Apart from just the obvious maturity, it was a given that M would not settle for bullshit. M came off as a father figure; he may have provided all the things that Warren yearned for in a father. I was simply happy and overjoyed that my friend had finally found someone to love him.

We didn't spend too much time out, as I needed to get some rest before the party tonight. When we were walking out, Donavan came over to me and asked if there was anything he could do to comfort me. While it was a sincere gesture, I wasn't sure if anyone could interfere with my love for Nathan. I thanked Donavan and reassured him that I was okay.

When we got back to the house, I went to my sleeping quarters. Donavan went by the pool, while Warren glued himself to the television. I got up around 7:00 p.m. in time for dinner. I guess because it was the final night of the year, M decided he didn't want to go out for dinner. As I said earlier, I wouldn't even complain; I am gluttonous. We had the luxury of serving ourselves dinner in M's huge dining room.

We had guests for dinner; M's mistress and her lover were present. I had to laugh to myself, as this cover-up was a plot for a movie script. Hey, it wasn't any of my business. I was introduced to the mistress and her lady as Ms. Angela and her best friend Natasha. They were both lipstick butch, so pulling off the best girlfriend thing was easy.

Angela and Natasha were both genuinely nice, pleasant women. They too needed an escape, and like anyone, they were doing what they had to do in order to survive. While they were all privileged and elitist, they had a social status they had to maintain. I applauded them for going this far to pull off this cover-up just for love. Some would see it as cowardly; but in truth, it was brave of them to be doing what they were doing.

We all had a great conversation getting to know each other. It was interesting learning so much about the Jamaica that most people didn't get to see or hear about. Life in Kingston, Jamaica, was totally different from life in Montego Bay and St. Ann. It was like living in a different world on the same island. The mannerisms were different, the expectations were different, and just the way people looked at each other was different.

Who knew that our dinner conversation would end up being a prelude to the New Year's Eve party? The party wasn't far from M's house, so after dinner, we all rushed to get dressed, hoping that we could get to the party by 10:30 p.m. at the latest. I had brought three outfits with me, just in case.

Thank heavens it wasn't a mask party; I so wanted to see faces. It wasn't anything over the top. All the men wore jeans. Both women were in heels, faces made up, sisters showing, and they were beat for the gods.

When we arrived at the party, we found the music in full swing. Though it was an open bar, we were greeted with wine at the entrance. This place could rival any New Year's Eve party in the Hamptons. Whoever was the host had gone above and beyond. It felt like a winter wonderland on a tropical island. That was the only part I didn't get—the winter theme. Who would want snow on an island? I guess to each his own.

The lighting on the inside wasn't all that bright. At least seventy or more people were present. It was an inside/outdoor affair. Soca music was playing by the time we arrived. Soca wasn't so much my thing; however, Donavan was all for it. He wasted no time in grabbing me by the waist and dancing with me.

M and Warren were profiling it seemed. So, I had one criticism thus far. They were both stuck-up and too caught up in what people think of them. Warren was only reserved because of M. I knew my best friend; he wanted to dance. M had expectations of him that he had to live up to. I wouldn't fight him for it either.

The party apparently was by invite only, so the guests were those who were in the know. Picture taking was a no-no. It wasn't a secret society. It was just one of those places where everyone literally knew everyone. Most individuals who attended knew the social code. No one would be putting anyone—or any of the details of the party for that matter—in the headlines of tomorrow's news. It was a safe space for Jamaica's privileged gay elite.

When the music changed to hip-hop, I knew it was my cue to head to the bar and get something to drink. Donavan ordered rum and Coke for both of us. We found a spot in the backyard where we could observe the crowd. For Donavan, this was all new, as coming from the countryside of Jamaica, he'd never had access to this kind of party. The parties Donavan had attended would be looked down on by this group.

There were some familiar faces, and I did engage them in conversation. I introduced Donavan as my friend—which opened several doors for Donavan, who was insistent that his door would be shut tonight. Having Donavan around was so much fun. Tonight felt different. I felt safe. My mind was at ease, to be honest. It had been some time now since O'Neal had broken up with me. I had grown closer to Donavan; I knew for sure that I wasn't looking for a relationship. I needed time to be by myself—to figure me out. Donavan wasn't just an escape; he gave me all I desired without the sex. I wasn't even missing sex, to be frank.

As midnight drew near, like in any Cinderella story, we all got our glasses ready to toast the new year in. I had no clue who was hosting this damn party, but whoever he was, he had to have some serious money. There were fireworks, motherfucking fireworks, at the party. The night sky was open, and you could see stars. The fireworks made it even more romantic.

With Celine Dione from way back in the day playing, what better mood to set? This was way better than Times Square, with all the cold and the crowds. Most of those in attendance, coupled up or not, held onto someone. Only a few individuals stood alone. Bob Marley's "This is Love" was playing, and I could feel the genuine love of everyone.

The DJ was hyping up the crowd, and we were into it. At midnight, we all counted down with our glasses in hand. We had a moment of silence as someone offered to pray for the new year. Donavan held onto my face and kissed me. It came out of nowhere. I, however, did not push him back. I released myself to him, surrendered myself. I felt as though I was all alone, and he had come to rescue me. How many times had Donavan done this? Too often.

Donavan looked me dead in my eyes, while biting onto my bottom lips. He seemed emotional; it was the first time I had seen him this vulnerable. He held onto my hands and stood at a distance, looking me in my face.

"Akime, I could not have asked for more. You have given me so much attention and help to give me a better life. I never imagined we would grow this close to each other. I just knew this was meant to be. The moment I met you, I knew I had to have you. You're all the man I ever needed, and this is my kind of love. This isn't a proposal or anything. I just need you to know that I am in love with you. I would like to spend the rest of my life with you too. I know now isn't the right time, but I am willing to wait."

My eyes were wet, simply because this was what I needed to hear. All I could do was hug him.

"You're right; this is my kind of love too. I'm just scared—scared of loving all over again. The hurt still lingers, and it hurts skin deep. I so want to be with you. But I'm not sure how or where to start. I know that I'm ready for love. I only ask for some time and space. Let's build on the friendship. And when it's right, we'll both know it. Then we'll make it happen."

I held onto Donavan tightly for the rest of the night, just dancing to the beat of R & B and reggae music. I knew deep down that I was ready for love and all that came with it. It was the start of a new year; a new beginning. I had decided to do things differently; I had chosen to live by my own rules.

I needed his friendship most of all. I needed his trust, time, and affection. In that moment, I promised myself to let my guard down and to be open to the possibility of trust, love, and vulnerability. I knew deep down I had a lot of work to do on myself. I needed to forgive myself for believing that I was undeserving of love and happiness. I had to mend the relationship with my family. I knew it wouldn't be easy, but I had to do it for myself.

Donavan and I spent the night together in each other's arms. It was the safest I had felt in an awfully long time. The universe has a funny way of guiding us in the right direction, exactly at the right time. It was never easy seeing our way through the lights. I now know for sure that there were no mistakes; mistakes were literally the universe's way of guiding us in the right direction. The universe had guided me to Donavan, and he would be my man.

Chapter 16

For the next year, Donavan and I courted from a distance. I realized that I had to get both Nathan and O'Neal fully out of my system. I went back to therapy, just to try to deal with some of my demons. It had taken O'Neal some time to move out of the apartment. There were occasions when we had sex, and it made it feel like we were going back there. Each time we tried, he kept fucking up. And I was just over forgiving him, over and over again.

When O'Neal moved out, it brought me into a phase of depression that I had never seen before. Donavan was so far away, and I felt all alone. I needed someone there with me to hold me, to make me feel safe and whole again. In the end, I realized that I needed to spend more time with myself—to just be by myself. I had to learn how to love again; more importantly, I had to know how to love my self first. I had to keep whatever was in my basket for me and me alone.

I came up with a one-year plan to leave London and head back to live in New York, where I would start up my own property management firm. I had the skillset, along with the money, to do it on my own. My eyes were set on my dream home in Westchester County. It was an old white house, a fixer-upper. The property was surround by the woods, and there was a pond in the back.

On one of my visits to New York, Donavan and I had spent the weekend there. The owners said that the house had been in their family for over a hundred years. They were looking for the ideal buyer, someone who would not destroy the home. The old couple's children didn't want the house. Several individuals had made offers; however, they noted there was something about me they liked and admired.

At first, I felt that my sexuality would be an issue. The old man, Tom, had a private conversation with me late one evening. He expressed how much times have changed and progressed. He told me that it was former slaves who had helped his great-great-grandfather build the house. He mentioned that the house was always staffed with Black people. He felt that, for him, it would be an honor to sell the house to a Black man. Tom shared with me one of his biggest kept secrets—that he'd had a male lover when he was younger. However, his lover had died, and he'd never looked at another man again.

I was beyond grateful for the offer to purchase the house at way below market value. Donavan and I bought the house, cash up-front, as I didn't want to take out another mortgage. The house was near the Metro North train station. That meant it would be an easy commute to Manhattan and Brooklyn. I would eventually purchase a car.

Donavan was with me all throughout the process. Surprisingly enough, we still did not have sex with each other. For the most part, I had a sexless relationship with Donavan. I wanted the relationship on different terms, not one based on sex. I realized that sex was the cause of so much of my troubles. I had used sex, not only as a drug, but as the one tool to get love and comfort. Don't get me wrong; I did get an occasional ass on my travels, and I did open it up. I just lessened the act as much as possible.

My intention was to not sell the house in Brooklyn. I transformed the house into a livable two-family house. I decided to leave the basement unit vacant so I could use it when I was in the city. There was something about the city that I enjoyed very much. I couldn't see myself moving out completely.

I moved back to New York the day Maya Angelou died. She was one literary luminary who stood for so much. I had always had a profound love for Oprah; it was Oprah who had introduced Maya to me. I wasn't ready to let her go. She had so much to offer the world. *Till I Rise* has resonated within so many of us. *I Know Why the Caged Bird Sings*, though it tells the story of Maya's life, in its own way, spoke to me and the abuse I faced as a male child.

I had all of Maya's books. I'd even had the opportunity to have her sign two of her books for me.

I moved back to the Brooklyn house as a transition before moving into the house in Westchester. Donavan came home in the evening to find me crying. He held onto me very tightly, trying to figure out how to comfort me.

I remembered an episode with Oprah where she interviewed Maya in her bed. She spoke about the one lesson she would never forget: "When someone shows you who they are the first time believe them." Maya had given the world so much. I just wasn't ready to say goodbye to her.

That night Donavan cooked us both dinner, and we ate in the backyard. The summer had literally just started; the weather was temperate. Donavan got us a blanket and we spent the night outside just holding onto each other.

There was a new side of me that was starting to be more assertive and vulnerable. I had enough confidence within myself. But I just didn't know how to believe I could do it all alone. As young as Donavan was, I found a great deal of comfort in talking to him. By this time, I was over both Nathan and O'Neal.

Strangely enough, O'Neal had become more like a stalker, as he now wanted to get back with me. I just couldn't see myself going back after all that he had done—not to mention the way he'd broken up with me. Donavan had to intervene at one point, just so he could stop the phone calls.

By the middle of the summer, Donavan and I had become full-fledged lovers. We had spent plenty of time talking and getting to know each other for over two years. We'd both dated other people and obviously had sex with other people because of our distance. This was my kind of love—a love where I felt whole, alive, wanted, and desired; and most importantly, this was love with a man I could also call a friend. This was exactly where I needed to be in my life. I had to have gone through the roads I had traveled just to learn some of life's most precious lessons.

I was in love finally. I felt it in my bones. When I got up in the morning, I turned to face Donavan, reminding him on each blessed day that I loved him.

I had rented office space in Midtown Manhattan. I needed to get out of the house. I had hired a personal assistant just to help me with my day-to-day schedule. The office in the new house was adjacent to the kitchen overlooking the garden. I could not wait to move in and just take it all in. For the first few weeks leading up to the move to Westchester, Donavan would come by the office on occasion and take me to dinner on his way to school. This time around, it was different. My mind was at ease; I had greater clarity. To be frank, we had less sex. However, when we did have sex, we made love to each other passionately. Who knew that flip fucking could have been this intense?

We moved the day the beloved comedienne Joan Rivers passed away. I was hurt that the bytch died, as who would give me my laughs on *Fashion Police*. The Golden Globes and the Oscars were nothing without Joan. The world mourned her death, and Ray Jay Brandy's kid brother looked as though he missed the old bytch's pussy too. Joan, at eighty-one, looked way better than her daughter. I had met her at Lincoln Center for Fashion Week, and I just fell in love with her.

We had rented a truck to move some of our belongings from Brooklyn. All we talked about was Joan. Donavan had befriended a young man from his school named Terence. Terence was from North Carolina and moved to New York to pursue his degree. Just like Warren and me, Donavan and Terence met late one night, fucked, and became best friends after.

Terence had the hots for me. I wouldn't however cross that line. I had thought about Donavan and me fucking him, but I didn't want to go there with his best friend. I knew for a fact Donavan could not fuck Warren, even if he was master of any motherfucking house. Terence was a diva and a fun travel companion to ride with.

When we arrived at the house, there were workers already there. They were a godsend, as I wasn't in the mood to pack the truck and unpack it again. Three guys came over and unpacked the truck and brought the things inside. Donavan was such the handy man; he had been coming by the house secretly and cleaning it up. Each passing day, I just kept falling in love with him. There was literally nothing for me to do but organize my office space.

Terence was excited, as he literally had nothing to do. I decided I would cook some chicken foot soup. Terence was beyond comical about the idea of eating chicken foot. Donavan, however, gave him a tutorial on how we do it in Jamaica. Since I'd met Terrence, he had been on and off about wanting to go to Jamaica. The media had distorted his mind; he had become frightened of the idea of going. I wasn't even sure what words I could say to him to tell him that Jamaica was a safe place for him to visit. The few Jamaicans he knew outside of Donavan made it seem as though the island was a war zone for gay men.

Later that evening, we all had large bowls of chicken foot soup in the living room while watching basketball. To be honest, it was Donavan and Terence who were watching, as the only ball game I knew was the one with a stiff dick attached to it. Donavan was annoying me; he kept getting up for no apparent reason. Donavan at one point did go back for a few seconds. He backed out, licking his finger like a kid. I caught him on a few occasions licking his fingers and even the inside of the bowl.

I knew I had a long day ahead of me, so I kissed him goodnight. Terence decided to spend the next two days with us, just to help around the house. As I walked up the stairs, I smelled an odd scent; at one point, I was convinced that something was burning. At the top of the steps leading into our bedroom were white flower petals on the floor. On both sides of the wall hung votive candles, lighting the room.

My heart was full, and my eyes lit up as I held my hands to my mouth, just smiling. When had he found the time to do all this? Where had he gotten all these flowers from? I literally felt as though I was in *Coming to America* with Eddie Murphy. When I got to the top, by the entrance to the bathroom, I found live orchid plants all over. It did not take long for the tears to flow. This was all I'd ever wanted; I had dreamt of having someone give this much to me. The splash of raindrops falling and birds chirping sounded in the background.

No one needed to tell me to get in. I wasted no time in taking off my clothing. There was a huge walk-in shower at the entrance to the bathroom door, and there were at least twenty candles in there. The tub was right by a huge bay window; a lantern and candles rested on the windowsill. The scent of eucalyptus and spearmint filled the bathroom. The water was as hot as the hot springs at Bath in St. Thomas, Jamaica. I laughed at myself for believing that I was stepping into hot lava. By the time I fully emerged my body, I felt a heavy weight lifting off of me.

So, I figured that the night had to end with a bang and an explosion. I quickly got out of the tub and got myself ready for the happy-ever-after that my young man would be giving to me. I deliberately asked to have the toilet separate, as I hated when Donavan watched me clean myself. I tell you, taking dick isn't easy, especially when you want him to hit that second hole and not come out muddy. It took several times for me to go before the water was clear. Finally, it was clear as crystal, and it was time for me to enjoy my bath.

When I got out of the toilet section, Donavan was sitting on the floor waiting patiently for me. I walked slowly over to him with my heart beating fast and my legs shaking. It was love, pure, unconditional love. He helped me to step into the tub, and as I lay down, he plastered a kiss on my lips. We both laughed as my dickhead kept protruding from the top of the soapsuds.

We spoke at length about the house and the new move. I told Donavan that I knew I had moved him away from the city, away from his friends; and if he wanted, it was okay to stay at the house in Brooklyn. He wasn't having any of it. Donavan reassured me that he was right where he should be. My eyes were shut, just thinking about how much love this man had given me. Out of nowhere, I felt something soft falling atop my face. It was a shower of red flower petals. As I opened my eyes, I saw the black velvet box with the diamonds just shimmering staring at me.

Like a nervous fool, I found myself going under the water. This was too much, too unreal, too played out and with so much detail.

As I got back up, "I Am Ready for Love" started playing in the background. I cried, only because I had buried the words of that song when I first visited Nathan's grave in Jamaica. I was emotional because I was more than ready for love. I loved Donavan with all of my heart and my soul. I was happy I'd laid off sex. I had no regrets about having taken it slow with him. I knew getting to be his friend and earning his trust was more than I could have ever done in my life before I'd made the decision to focus on me.

Donavan placed the ring on my finger, and I kissed him passionately. I held onto his face with the soapsuds on my hands, making him a beard. I told him yes; he didn't even have to ask me to marry him. It was a *fucking* yes. I could not have asked for a more supportive, understanding, caring, and loving person in my life. All that he brought to me was my kind of love—the kind I'd been yearning for over the years.

As I stood up, soapsuds dripped off my body. I motioned Donavan to get into the tub with me. He got naked, and we both stood fully erect facing each other. Today, I needed to feel him inside of me. I wanted to have him hit my second hole and make sweet love to me. I needed to be one with him tonight.

I went down and worshiped my now husband-to-be's pole. Tonight, he owned me, and I had to go that extra mile. I don't know how I did it, but I did. I took all his manhood inside of my mouth and held it there for a good minute. He pulled out with my saliva dripping from the shaft of his dick, and he gently slapped my face with it. He spat on his dick and faced fucked my mouth. As I was about to gag, he quickly pulled out.

I sat on the inside edge of the tub, while Donavan stood at the top of the tub and, in circular motion, peed on me. I had no clue where that came from, or why he felt I would be interested in being pissed on. I didn't give a fuck tonight; he was my husband to be, and nothing was off limits tonight. As he shook his dick, like country boys did on papaya trees in Jamaica, I grabbed onto his dickhead, using my open lips to play with the slit of his dickhead, still filled with piss.

It was my time to get serviced. I positioned myself toward the bay window as my man ate my ass and sucked on my dick. I had both of my legs open wide as I placed my right hand between my legs and buried his head into my ass. I had never felt myself getting so wet since Nathan. Donavan spat on his dick and made circular motions with his dickhead. As he played with my manhole, he was jerking my dick.

My ass was aching to feel him inside me. I realized he was just teasing me. With his dickhead positioned at my anal opening he spat again on his dickhead. This time, he went in. I slightly arched my back just to give him enough angle to enter me. I grabbed onto his neck, flinching as I felt his dickhead slowly entering me. Donavan was no easy ride. And I had to close my eyes and take myself to that other place. It wasn't so much about the pain; it was knowing that I was able to connect with my man and pleasure him.

I found myself sitting on the edge of the tub, with him between my legs, all wrapped around him, using my legs to control his thrust. More than ten inches of dick isn't easy to handle, not even for a pro. I knew how to make him nut quick though. I grabbed onto his ears, playing with them and massaging them. Donavan grabbed onto my neck with his right hand while using his left hand to jerk my dick. I felt my dick throbbing, and I refused to nut before him tonight.

As his rhythm intensified, I held onto him closer, kissing him passionately. I could feel his heartbeat. I could hear him breathing faster. He was now only halfway in, but I needed more of him inside of me. I allowed my body to relax as he held onto my ass cheeks, just bouncing me up and down his dick. It took me by surprise, it was like a burst of fire as he unloaded himself inside of me.

As I held onto him tighter, I could now feel his warm man juice seeping through my inner walls. He positioned me back to the window. He motioned me to push out. I smiled, as I knew what he wanted me to do. I used all my muscles to squeeze his juices out of my now bruised manhole. As I pushed out his babies, I spat on my dick and jerk myself to completion as Donavan ate his cum out of my hole.

We both took a shower, speechless. We said not one word to each other. We dried off our bodies, blew out the candles, and went straight to bed. In bed, I curled up in my usual fetal position. I jokingly told him that I would oversee the wedding; he only needed to show up. Donavan held onto me tightly. For the first time in an exceedingly long time, I felt safe in the arms of another man. I closed my eyes, thanking God for his unconditional love. I drifted to sleep, knowing that, in the morning, it would be a new day, the beginning of a new journey with Donavan.

Chapter 17

For the next couple of months, all my time was spent thinking about the wedding. I was overly excited. The first person I talked to about the engagement was Warren. Warren still wasn't convinced that Donavan was the right one for me. Nonetheless, he sounded incredibly happy and excited for me. O'Neal and I had developed a decent enough relationship. I could not see myself ever having sex with him again, but I did get to a place of forgiveness. I felt safe enough calling him a friend, and I also shared the good news with him.

The winter before I got married, I spent the new year with Warren and the minister in Italy. Nicole came with her partner; Delaney never missed a good outing, and she turned up with her wife. I had invited O'Neal, who was seeing this older guy from Israel. It was not going to work out, as O'Neal liked dick too much to fully commit to a total bottom—even when the coins were rolling in his direction. Donavan warned me against inviting O'Neal, as he felt I should leave my past behind me. Warren also invited some of his friends. It turned out to be a couples' retreat.

The trip was one of the best I had ever had in my adult life. It wasn't about sex; it was more about spending alone time with my husband-to-be. I finally was in a space with people who were in love with each other. They too understood what it meant and took to maintain a relationship. News flash— never take advice from a single friend; there is a reason why they're single.

We stayed up until late into the night, just talking about politics and the changing world. I tried staying away from politics, as I only wished that Obama could have run a third time or that Michelle was interested in running. I had my reservations with Hillary; but I was sure Donald Trump wasn't even capable of getting elected. Oddly enough, the minister was rooting for the Donald, and it changed my views about him.

We had rented a villa on Airbnb off a small fishing village on the coast of Italy. It was the cutest remote village I had ever seen. We hired a personal chef who had the time to cook. You know you have money when you can take a trip with your friends and have your own personal chef. It wasn't really money; we pooled our resources together. Roberto spoke few English words; however, he could cook his ass off. The man had a sweet tooth and made us some of the best cocktails I had ever tasted in my life.

Most of our days were spent by the ocean just talking. Late evening, we stayed outside watching the sunset and the stars. We were all at peace—until two nights before we should have left. There was a heated debate about my wedding. Donavan made it noticeably clear that his job is only to show up for the wedding. O'Neal apparently was drunk and started making fun of Donavan. At first, we all laughed too and called him the jealous ex. It turned nasty when O'Neal started using profanity, calling Donavan all kinds of names. I saw a side of O'Neal I had never seen before.

O'Neal apparently could not take any of his own medicine and felt offended when Donavan told him he was a fool to have broken up with me. Donavan also broke the long-held secret that O'Neal and the Trini guy who lived in Brooklyn across from my house used to fuck whenever he visited New York. On top of that, O'Neal also revealed that he had a threesome with Donavan and the Trini guy once.

I sat in amazement, not sure who to be angrier with, Donavan or O'Neal. O'Neal got so angry he got up and punched Donavan in the face. A fistfight broke out, and Donavan broke O'Neal's nose. The neighbors called the police, and we were asked to leave the following day. Not only was I hurt, I also felt ashamed and humiliated. That night, I slept alone, questioning what I was really getting myself into.

The following day, we all took a train and rented a hotel in Rome. I asked Donavan for time and space, as I needed it. The thought of Donavan fucking O'Neal knowing that I was still trying to pursue a relationship with him was hurtful. It was also an act of betrayal, as he'd kept the secret for an awfully long time.

It was in Rome that I found peace, just sitting down in the ruins overlooking the Colosseum. I met an old couple who had been married for over seventy years. Their English was not the best, but I had to ask them the real secret of their love. They both said patience, compromise, communication, and unconditional love. The husband laughed and told me that this new method of communication via text and email wasn't real communication. A phone call, hearing the person's voice, was always best. He stressed the importance of using my words with my partner. Ask and it shall be given to you.

I had to let one of them go; O'Neal should have known better. Not only was O'Neal older, but I also trusted him. Well, I felt that I could have trusted him enough to not fuck up on this level. He also knew my history with Donavan. I won't give or find excuses for Donavan's behavior; however, he was young and trying to find himself. He also did betray my trust, and it would take some time to forgive him. My love for him was still strong; it seemed forgiving him should be easier than forgiving O'Neal. However, something within me made it so much harder.

We flew back to New York not speaking to each other. I just needed some time away from him. I needed space to be by myself. I hadn't felt this much hurt in a long time. I wasn't sure if I was more upset about the fucking part or the betrayal. Or was it the case that both were equally great? At the JFK airport, Donavan took all my bags without saying a word to me. I knew he was hurting also, however; I just didn't know how to start the conversation.

I had requested a Black Star driver, who picked us up in a black SUV. It would have been a challenge trying to get a yellow cab to take us all the way to Westchester County. On the way heading home, he palmed my left hand. I looked him dead in his eyes, and the tears just kept flowing. The fucked-up part about love was that sometimes the people who hurt us the most tend to be the same people we go to for support. It's like getting stabbed with a dagger, pulling it out, and using the same dagger to cook with. The memory lingers longer, and the hurt becomes numb.

I had no one else to turn to. Warren was no longer around. Delaney wasn't anywhere around either. All I had was Donavan. The few friends I had were more social acquaintances than friends.

I fell asleep without even recognizing that we had stopped. By the time I realized that we had stopped, Donavan had already unpacked the car. I thanked the driver for taking us safely home, and I walked inside the house.

"How much longer will it take for you to talk to me? How many times am I going to apologize to you?" Donavan's voice was loud and filled with rage and anger.

"For as long as it fucking takes. All of a sudden, you can speak and is shouting? You better lower your goddamn voice up in this house. You fucked up! I don't give a damn how long it takes for me to talk to you. Just let me be." I went directly to the kitchen to make a cup of coffee.

"Akime, back then, I was young and stupid. I just didn't want to say anything that would hurt your feelings. It wasn't planned or anything. It just happened. Can you just believe me please?" He sat at the island, watching me as I waited for the water in the kettle to come to a boil.

"Donavan, I don't want to do this. I don't want to have this conversation right now. Not only did you betray me, you also embarrassed me in front of company just because of your motherfucking ego." I reached to the top of the cupboard for the tea bag.

There he was, standing behind me and holding onto my hands as I grabbed the tea bag. As I turned around, he held onto my waist and kissed me passionately. I needed it. I didn't resist him. I so wanted to hit him, to scream at him, to fight him. There were so many negative things I wanted to do; however, I didn't have the strength to do or say them.

I realized in that moment that I needed to let it go. I needed to forgive him, as what had happened was long gone and in the past. I had to forgive him because I had done some fucked up shit also. I just needed some time—time to heal. I needed time to let go of the hurt of what he had done to me.

That night, we slept in separate rooms. As much as I needed him next to me, I had to let him realize there were consequences for his actions. I also felt like a hypocrite, as I too knew what I had done when I was younger and in love with Nathan. I kept reminding myself that Donavan and I had had sex more than once while I was in a relationship with O'Neal. I wondered if this shit was just karma, as no motherfucking bad deed went unpunished.

I was completely in love with Donavan; I adored the ground he walked on. He was the man I wanted to spend the rest of my life with. An act of betrayal for me was often one that wasn't forgivable. This time around, I needed to forgive him. I had grown so much; I realized it was important for me to just let it go and move on. I just needed time to be with myself.

I woke up the next morning to my favorite breakfast—ackee and salt fish, fried plantains, and fried roasted breadfruit, along with fried dumplings. Wait a minute! Donavan found hot chocolate, the Jamaican one with the oil on the top. I could do this every day with him. I knew his game plan—treat me with my favorite comfort food. I definitely was going to eat the food, and I would thank him too. However, it wouldn't be this easy.

Donavan opened the French doors in the bedroom that overlooked our huge deck with only a view of the forest adjacent to the house. He lay on the carpet by the bed watching me eat. There was a part of me that wanted to punish him. I was still angry with him. I thanked him for taking the time to prepare one of my favorite meals. It had really made my morning.

I decided to take a shower downstairs. I didn't want to be in a tub. I yearned for hot water cascading down my body like a waterfall.

We had renovated the bathroom and installed a surround system compatible with our iPads. Back in the days when I had just moved to New York City, I had fallen in love to the soundtrack of *Brown Sugar*. The moment I walked into the shower, I selected the soundtrack.

The shower could literally hold up to six people. There were three showerheads in total. Hanging from the top of the shower was a huge showerhead that delivered its spray like rain, and that one was my favorite. We also had one with a hose—just in case we did have six people in the shower all at once. I didn't want a curtain, so Donavan and I had glass installed around the shower.

I stepped in with both hands against the wall just meditating in silence. I now had learned the importance of keeping still. The water felt great; it fell atop of my head like raindrops. The music brought me back to my youthful days and how much fun I used to have. Was it wrong of me to deny Donavan the fun he so freely wanted? Why couldn't he have just left it in the past, given that he had chosen to hold it back from me so as not to hurt me?

Oddly enough, this very moment brought me back to my better days with Nathan and how deeply we had been in love. Even though I hated seeing Nicole, I use to love getting fucked at their house, knowing she was taking care of my man while I serviced him. That night when she caught us fucking in the laundry room was devastating. However, it was one of the best sexual experiences I have had to date. There had been times Donavan had been fucking me, and I had taken myself right there.

Out of nowhere, I felt hands on my shoulders. I felt the tip of his dickhead beating on my ass. I didn't move. He wrapped his arms around me. I felt light. I could no longer hold my body weight. Donavan realized I was about to fall, and he held onto me. We never spoke a word to each other; he respected my silence. We stood for some time, with the water beating on our bodies, listening to the vocals and lyrics of Jill Scott.

I was hard as a rock; however, my mind was far from anything sexual. At one point, Donavan held onto me, jerking my dick. It felt good; however, I was not looking for that kind of release. I knew how much he wanted to have sex; I wasn't about to get vulnerable enough to let him fuck me, though. I was not in the mood for sex period.

My dick was hard. He was rubbing on it. I told him point-blank it was not going to happen. I never wanted to disappoint him. And most importantly, I was not about to start something I knew darn well I couldn't finish. A hard dick didn't mean shit, and it was obvious that I still had a deep sexual attraction toward him, even when I was angry with him.

Donavan asked if he could jerk off next to me. At first, I was inclined to say no, but I decided to allow him to please himself. As he jerked his long dick, I soaped my fingers and fingered him. I grabbed onto his butt cheeks as I finger-fucked him hard. I literally wanted to hurt him, I wanted so badly to punish him. I was hard as a rock, but I refused to participate in this ritual.

After Donavan released himself, he washed himself off while I stayed still with the water beating against my back. I found myself crying, as I did love Donavan. This situation might get out of control if I allowed it to.

Boi knows I had not been a saint all my life. I too had made some fucked-up decisions when I was younger, and I would have wanted to be forgiven by my partner. I made up my mind that I had to let it go. The situation wasn't current. I did feel ashamed about the way the information had come out. If this man was about to be my husband and in order for me to love him unconditionally, I had to move past the hurt.

When I got out of the shower, I could hear Donavan in the backyard chopping wood. It was somewhat off for this time of year. I stood by the kitchen side window watching him. He was hurting too. I could see the pain, anger, and frustration in his face.

I no longer wanted to hurt him. Goddamn, I had a wedding to plan, and I couldn't do it without him. I went to the room and got dressed in my outdoor clothing. I had on boots, as I had every intention of helping him cut some wood.

When I walked outside, Donavan gave me the side-eye. I stood by the porch door just watching him, holding a cup of hot tea in my hands. He was literally ignoring me. I slowly walked over in his direction. I stood before him, far away from the blade of his ax. He laid the ax down, just staring at me, wanting to say something. I went over and put my right index finger on his lips. He playfully licked it with a smirk on his face.

"I was upset. I am still somewhat disappointed. I guess it was the public embarrassment and humiliation that I had to deal with that got me so upset. I also feel that it's an act of betrayal that you messed around with O'Neal of all people, knowing that, at that time, I was still trying to be with him. We had already built a friendship; you should have warned me about what was going on. I trusted you. I confided in you. And as a friend, it was your responsibility to protect me at all costs. I would never have betrayed your trust like that, Donavan. You proposed to me. You professed your love to me. I'm scared that there are other things going on that you may be hiding from me." I spoke with a great deal of passion and clarity. My eyes were wet. I was more emotional about the unknown than the betrayal I was dealing with.

Donavan held onto me and hugged me tightly. I held on tightly to him too. "Akime, I am so sorry for betraying you. It was my ego and pride in Italy that got the best of me. To be honest, I didn't want to tell you about O'Neal and his infidelities, as I didn't want to hurt you. Also, I should not have fucked him. It was a stupid and immature decision, and I have lived with that regret for an awfully long time. I didn't do it with the intention of hurting you."

I looked him in his eyes, and I wiped the tears. I knew deep down that he had regrets. It was no longer my intention to let him feel guilty for his actions. It was my deception and my infidelity with Nathan that had gotten me shot. Two wrongs didn't make a right.

"I have no choice but to forgive you, Donavan. I am too much in love with you. I cannot hurt you or myself. The wedding is in five months. We need to be more open and honest with each other.

I have done some shit in the past that I've regretted. I would like to move past this hurt."

Donavan held onto my hands and led me into the open grass area. "You have taught me so much. All that I am is because of you. You never once took advantage of me, Akime. From the get-go, you only wanted the best for me. And I am always thankful for that. This too shall pass; I am learning so much from this experience. This is my kind of love—the love where I feel forgiven; I feel vulnerable; and I cannot only stand in my truth but also embrace my shame and my past."

The evening sun was about to go down, and we both just sat on the grass holding onto each other. I honestly couldn't have asked for more. I was exactly right where I needed to be in my life. Few men my age got to experience this kind of love. Donavan was incredibly supportive and understanding, and he made me feel so alive. We just sat in total silence, enjoying the sun and the cool air.

Spring came around quickly; it seemed to take us both by surprise. Donavan had landed a job as a consultant at a firm in Midtown Manhattan. My work was kicking off, though not at the rate I would have liked it to be. I spent most of my mornings going to Home Depot to purchase garden supplies and plants. I was in love with rosebushes, lilies, and hydrangeas. My intention was to have the garden in full bloom by our wedding day.

The conversation between Donavan and me had improved greatly. We hung out in the city a few nights a week. We both agreed to take a break from sex until the honeymoon. At first, I felt I could not withhold sex from Donavan. I also didn't want to risk him going outside looking for ass. Two months in, we decided to just jerk off with each other—at least just to get that nut out on a regular basis. It helped the sexual frustration we were both facing. The break didn't last that long.

I took a break and traveled to the Bahamas just to be alone. I needed some time to myself to find my core and my bearings before the wedding. I knew I loved him; I just needed time away from him. I asked that we not even communicate with each other for the few days I was away. Donavan didn't like the idea; however, he was respectful of my wishes.

The five days and four nights I spent at the Hilton Bahamas were magical. I pampered myself. I had breakfast by the pool almost every morning. I met a guest from Switzerland who invited me to hang out with his best friend and his wife and a few friends on his yacht. My evenings were spent on their yacht, watching the sunset and having conversations about life.

It's freeing to have conversations with strangers without feeling uncomfortable about your sexuality. Dan, the guy from Switzerland, told us that he was on a break after losing his partner of more than ten years to cancer. Just watching Dan live and hearing his experience of death and how much more he valued life brought me back to Nathan and how he'd left us.

I eventually revealed why I was on a break, and I invited Dan to the wedding—well if he could make it. I used the opportunity while on the yacht in the open ocean to dive and explore the underwater world. The waters off the Bahamas are crystal clear. The sea life could rival that of the man-made Atlantis.

Dan's friend had a personal chef, and I so enjoyed fine dining. The owners were an old couple from South Africa who had survived apartheid, sold their far lands, and relocated to the Caribbean island of St. Kitts. I was intrigued by the couple, and each evening, I asked questions about their take on apartheid and racism. While it was a very heavy topic of conversation to delve into while on vacation, I was curious.

On the contrary, the couple did not come off as racist. They spoke about the struggles of inheriting lands versus surviving and giving the lands away to the Blacks. I guess that I was lucky to have met a white couple who gave back to South Africa. Like Oprah Winfrey, they too had built a trade school for boys. The argument that they presented was that they alone could not win the race war. There were too many whites who were hell-bent on maintaining the status quo. They explained the popular views of the whites when Nelson Mandela came into power, saying it was similar to the way white America treated Barack Obama, the first Black president in the United States of America.

As an immigrant, I had a somewhat objective view; I had come from the outside with a system designed and built to hold Blacks backwards. I gave my take on institutional racism and how much the "system" may not change, adding that I believed education was one of the easy ways out, other than land and homeownership. As difficult a conversation as it was to have, I also had to point out that there are still Blacks in America who believed that someone owed them something. There were a few who were waiting on that acre of land and a mule.

The real hurdles were the social system, along with religious and cultural values. There was a cycle of young women getting pregnant at an early age and young men getting arrested and sent to prison at an early age and the breakdown of the family structure. There needed to be better examples from within the Black community. However, too often there existed a mentality of not openly sharing or the ability to give back. The trauma within the Black community stemmed back far and was greater than the economic disadvantages suffered; it was rooted in the trauma of slavery, Jim Crow, segregation, and this post-racial society that we live in—a society that refuses to speak truth about the real evils of America.

The following day, I bid my new friends goodbye and got myself ready for my flight back to NYC. My heart was pounding. I was excited to see Donavan. I felt like giving him some ass the moment I landed. I had a wild fantasy of sucking his dick in the backyard and having his nut in the back of my throat. I knew he would still be hard, and I would ride his shaft until I released myself and get off before he got a second nut. He would crucify me if I were to ever pull a stunt like that. His dick was way too long for me to just slide off; he would have filled the opening of my ass even before the head was out.

I had a layover in Miami before taking a direct flight from there to JFK. I spent the time waiting on my flight catching up on some US news. The Donald seemed to be navigating the news wave. Hillary was confident as ever, yet she still lacked that personality so many of us were looking for. There was a voice within me that said Donald would win the election. And it wouldn't be because he was the best candidate; it would be because, for too long, whites in Middle America had been neglected. No matter how you looked at it, it was racist in nature; however, many poor whites had felt disenfranchised with this current administration. They also hated the idea of being governed by a Black man. To be less politically correct, the negro factor from slavery was still very real in America.

I slept for the duration of my flight to New York City. Donavan was outside in his favorite black-and-white sweat pants, with the shaft of his manhood just protruding from them. As I approached the car, I got hard just watching him leaning up against the passenger side of the van. As I went up to kiss him, I held onto his dick, and he was sure at attention. I had missed him dearly. In that moment, I realized that the space and time away from him was extremely healthy.

We spoke the entire length of the ride home. It felt as though I had been away from him for a month. There was so much excitement between the two of us. Donavan apologized for his behavior while on our trip. His apology was sincere and from the heart. No matter what, I had to forgive him because I loved him. We all make mistakes. The fact that I had done my own shit kept me from having any upper hand or call to punish Donavan for too long.

The moment I walked into the kitchen, I knew the night would be a long one. The smell of ackee and fried plantains and white rice spilled throughout the house. This was what get me all the time, and he know it so darn well. His mom had sent him breadfruit, and there it was all fried up. There was a huge avocado out and I knew for a fact that he'd gone to that old Jamaican woman off 225th Street and White Plains Road in the Bronx.

We had dinner in the man cave in the basement watching past seasons of *Empire*. Even though I had seen most of *Empire*, Donavan was playing catch-up. We had a heated debate about how homosexuality was being portrayed on television now and how inclusive it had become. I pointed out that there was still a struggle to normalize feminine traces within Black gay men. All I believed was that the definition of masculinity was subjective. However, if most of the characters portrayed on television showcased the feminine side of men, then the younger generation would grow up believing that to be gay was to be weak, feminine, and flamboyant. This wasn't an accurate representation of what it meant to be Black and gay.

Donavan hinted enough times that he wanted sex. Oddly enough, though I wanted some myself, I was not in the mood to get up and get prepared. I sure as hell was not about to make a mess after not having sex with him for such a long time. He wouldn't have cared. I did, though. And I wanted to make it a treat for him. I felt the need to let him go deep and let me be vulnerable.

We ended up falling asleep in the basement. I woke up the next morning to Donavan's eyes watching me. I felt loved, safe, and secure and, most of all, fulfilled. If only someone could have told me when I was younger that this was how love felt, I would have focused more on work and just waited. I had no regrets, however, for the life I had lived. Mistakes are just the universe's way of guiding us in the right direction.

My intention was to get up and make Donavan breakfast. It appeared he had other plans on his mind. As I tried to get up out of bed, he held onto my legs and pulled my boxer briefs down. My dick was already at attention, with my morning hood jumping eagerly for his hungry mouth. He went for my ass first; thank God, it was clean. Donavan spread my ass cheeks apart and spat directly at my manhole. He went face down as though he was diving in an ocean. I had not felt that much intensity at my ass in weeks. It had me weak for a moment; my moaning sounds were intense.

He grabbed me by the legs and raised me up a bit, wrapping his tongue around my dickhead. He slowly took it all in, including my fucking balls. While my legs were raised, I went head down and showed him that I had gag reflex. I held onto both of his feet and I took all that manhood in my mouth without gasping for air. It was an intense moment for both of us. My aim was not only to have him nut; I also very much wanted to swallow all his babies. The intention was to get him to nut, so he didn't ask me for ass. Honestly, I didn't want to get fucked or fuck.

I guess he was more excited than I had anticipated; my trick work. Unexpectedly, after I'd wetted my index finger with my lips and played with his manhole, Donavan unleashed his load in my mouth. I could hardly gasp for air. Luckily, I had good gag reflex and just swallowed it all down. There was some satisfaction from the intensity of his dick throbbing in my mouth as he released himself. I took in every bit of cum, and I grabbed the shaft of his dick and milked him like a cow. I had to ensure that he was fully satisfied and drained.

As Donavan lay lifeless on his back, I squatted over his face, putting my ass at just the right angle so that the top of his tongue was on my hole. I spat on my dick, while using circular motions to rub my dickhead, shooting my load all over his chest. I guess I was in the mood for nut this morning. I found myself arching my back, licking up the rest of Donavan's nut and my own cum. Eventually, after getting in my full cup of protein for the day, I lay next to my man, just listening to his heartbeat.

It didn't take him long to fall asleep. That gave me the opportunity to head to the kitchen and look after breakfast. I turned on CNN, which had Donald Trump all over the screen. As much as it scared me, I felt like the Democratic Party was about to lose this election. Hillary had all of the qualifications; however, the likeability factor wasn't there. The email situation wasn't just a distraction; the calculated way she handled it was also very problematic. Personally, I wished a woman could finally win a US presidential election. I had one serious fucking issue with CNN; they were covering this election more like news entertainment than the actual serious news it was. It seemed like a fucking joke every time I heard Donald Trump's voice.

We were a month away from the big day. The trust factor between Donavan and I had been slowly rebuilding. There was no doubt in my mind that he loved me. Nor did I doubt the fact that he was the right one for me. Not only did he say that he loved me; I also saw it in his actions. Donavan had made the travel arrangements for our respective families. I was excited about his level of responsibility and commitment. Since I had more free time, more of the planning was left up to me. Planning the wedding did bring back some fond memories of Nathan and me. Age, maturity, and experience had taught me, however, that it was more than just the ceremony; it was a fellowship with those we loved.

I was out in the garden tending to my flowers when I got a phone call. It was from a delivery company. The young man said he was at the front door and just checking to see if I was home. To my surprise, he had a bouquet of spring flowers and a card attached to a small Tiffany box. I signed for the package with a huge smile, like a teenage girl in love with the star football player.

The box contained a Paloma Picasso knot bead. I held myself, laughing out aloud to myself. About two weeks ago, I had gone to Tiffany to clean our bracelets. I had been captivated by the bracelet, but I'd told Donavan that the price wasn't right. It was what I had desired. If my man felt I deserved it, who was I to turn it away? The note just said, "Love you, sexy man. Dinner at the mall by Columbus Circle."

I saw my neighbor, the closest one to the house, doing her usual power walk. She waved at me. You know you're in a white neighborhood when you cannot see the house closest to you.

I spent the remainder of the day in the garden ensuring that the flower bed was ready for the big day. I did get some help, as there was no way possible I could have done all the work by myself. On the way home from the Metro North train station, where I dropped Donavan off, I stopped by Home Depot. I picked up two young day laborers, who, I might add, did not speak much English. They were both highly creative and used Google translation on their phones to communicate with me.

I left both young men in the garden to finish up while I went inside and got dressed. Columbus Circle was one of my favorite spots in the city to hang out. I knew the restaurants by the shopping mall were rather expensive. The neighborhood catered to a certain demographic; that was what had drawn me to the location years ago.

After getting dressed, I went outside and showed the men where to wash up and paid them. I even offered them a ride to the train station.

While on the Metro North heading into the city, I just sat there thinking about married life with Donavan. I must say, Donavan had made many changes in the past few months. I now looked at relationships differently. When I was younger, I had been so caught up with sex; the consistency of sex was what I'd yearned for. I had a new love for Adele, so I closed my eyes and drifted away listening to her latest hits.

By the time the train arrived at Grand Central, I had drifted into a deep sleep. A very beautiful blonde young woman nudged me to get up. As I stood up, I realized she was all smiles. Her eyes were on my crotch, and I looked down at myself to see that the boy was in a semi position. All I could do was return the smile and tell her, "Thank you." It was evening rush hour, and the terminal was busy with passengers. I decided to walk to Bryant Park and take the D train to 59th Street Columbus Circle.

There was something about the day that felt weird. I was overly excited to meet up with Donavan too. He hadn't said much, so I didn't know what to expect. I had gotten myself prepared just in case we decided to take a late-evening walk in Central Park.

On the way to the train station, I gave a homeless young man twenty dollars, as he seemed as though he needed it. As I approached 5th Avenue, I assisted an elderly man to cross the street. I was having an out-of-body experience. The universe was guiding me; it was trying to tell me something. The universe, at times, has a way of guiding you in the right direction.

When I arrived at Columbus Circle, I received a text from Donavan, saying that he was running about ten minutes late. I told him that I would stay outside of the Coach store across from the taxi stand. While waiting, I was going through Facebook. I ran across a rather odd post from Jason.

"Mi can't believe say them kill Denver Potter."

To be honest, at first, I was upset. I asked myself why people were so fucked up and loved playing jokes. I scrolled down farther. And there was another one.

"Them kill Denver to Bloodclath."

My hands started to shake; this shit could not be real. I sent Jason a direct message, as he was very close to Denver. Jason's response was not only a confirmation, it was also cold and chilling.

"Yes, them kill him. Di duty nasty battyman them stab him up, rob him, and left him to die."

My entire body was shaking. I didn't see crime of passion. I just saw the goodness of another human being and someone taking advantage of that kindness. I knew Denver. I used to communicate with him back in the days when high-five was around; it was the old version of Facebook. Denver was a class act, someone who embodied free spirit. He lived an authentic life; he was never ashamed of who he was. He was a fashion trendsetter. Humble was what came to mind first. Sometimes we die the way we live—just being kind to others who take our sense of vulnerability for weakness.

I got two random calls from two friends in Jamaica I hadn't spoken to in years. I knew Denver. We weren't tight friends, but most times when I returned to Jamaica, I would be in his company. Denver was a friend of Donavan's. I didn't know how to share the news with him when he arrived. I played out so many scenes in my head. I would rather he heard it from me directly than see it on social media.

Donavan looked so attractive in his work clothing. I had always admired how he was able to make that Jack Spade tote bag look so masculine. We hugged each other and walked through the revolving door of the shopping mall. As we got to the top of the third floor, I hugged him and held onto him tightly.

I tiptoed as he was so much taller than I am and whispered in his air. "Denver is dead. He was found dead in his house early this morning."

We stood in total silence. As I looked up into his face, I could see the tears flowing. He held onto me tighter as he choked up; he asked me if I was sure. I affirmed to him that it was true and that all would be okay. I knew all too well what it was like to lose a friend. I told Donavan that, if he didn't want to go to dinner anymore, we could just go home and take a cab home, rather than riding on the Metro North.

Donavan decided that dinner was still on because it was my special day. I held onto his face and gave him a wet kiss. Over dinner, Donavan wasn't his talkative self, which was expected. I tried my best to make small talk with him, just to pass time. We had gone to Porter House, a bar and grill by Columbus Circle. The food wasn't cheap. We were the only set of Black folks inside the restaurant, other than the waitstaff and the host, who were constantly coming over to ask if we were okay. The food and the service, might I add, were excellent.

Out of nowhere, Donavan stretched his hands across the table. I held onto them, and out of nowhere, the tears just started flowing. He wasn't crying; his eyes were just filled with water, and it was coming down with a heavy flow.

"I have never called Warren brother—for the simple fact that I don't see him as a brother. I am not entitled to anything that Daddy left. I was his bastard son who was his family's yard boy. That was the most he offered, simply because he was ashamed of whom I am. In his eyes, he was helping and protecting me. There was a point when I was hurt, as I felt I was cursed. I am thankful for the experience because I would not have met you and fallen in love. So, if anything, Daddy gave you to me. I never felt comfortable having this conversation with you, as I know that Warren is your best friend."

I sat across from him, watching him and the pain he was in. I knew this was a moment for me to be silent and just listen. Sometimes, supporting someone means to just be still and say nothing.

"I know I don't always say much about my past, and I am thankful that you came into my life. I appreciate you for all you have done for me also. It wasn't until Daddy was sick that I knew he was my father and that Warren was my brother." His hands were shaking, so I knew he was coming from a deep place.

"Back then, I was more grateful for you and the help that you were offering myself and Warren." He wiped his eyes and looked me dead in the eyes.

Warren refused to accept Donavan as his brother and noted that his father died with the truth. We all knew a simple DNA test would solve all that. I was between a rock and a hard place. I just hoped that, soon enough, they would both come to terms with the fact that they were blood relatives.

"Denver was my first lover, my first at so many things in this lifestyle. I met him at a teen fashion show in Ocho Rios back when I was in high school. He wasn't just hot; he was like a fashion god. His dreadlocks made him look so masculine. When he walked out in his shorts with no shirt on, my dick got so hard. I was embarrassed just standing there looking at him."

I wasn't sure if I should smile or just give him an odd look. In my head, I was asking myself why he was telling me this. I didn't want to look insensitive and rude. All I did was hold onto his hands tighter and listen to his story.

"I spent several weekends at his home. No one knew what was going on. I was just seen as the country boy Denver was helping. I will say this, he had a heart of gold; he helped so many lost young gay boys. He gave so many of us a safe space, especially the many who had no home. He was young. He was one of the few who helped without taking advantage of us. So many young men are abused in Jamaica, and he was a godsend to so many. When I met you, that was when I lost feelings for him. I knew where I stood with Denver; it was just sex. The fact that you turned me down so many times was such a huge turn-on. Akime, you taught me how to value myself and my self-worth. I am going to miss him; it hurts because it is his kindness and compassion—his always wanting to help others—that has killed him."

I was shocked at his candidness in sharing such a personal story with me. Donavan had grown so much since the time when I met him. He not only was my rock star, he was also the light that shone so bright within me. I told Donavan that my hurt had more to do with coming to terms with trusting people. I remembered helping many friends while living at the house in Brooklyn.

After dinner, we walked hand in hand to Times Square, just watching the tourists and their fascination with the city. It was the first time in a long time we'd just spent some time together in the city without a plan. Times Square had changed a lot. A huge H&M store seemed to be the highlight of Times Square. We took a stroll over by Bryant Park. I ran across to the Starbucks and got us each a tall cinnamon dulce soy steamer. We both just sat in silence, enjoying each other's company.

Often, mourning the death of someone we know forces us to question life. I knew I had many questions in my head about my existence and my contribution to society. It was sometimes sad to be a young Black man, brimming with potential and love to give, in a world that was far too often lacking in acceptance and offering up hurt. At times, in these moments, I got upset with God, and I was forced to question my faith. I had, however, learned this much; nothing in life happens out of context.

Although Denver's life was cut short, he had given back a great deal to the Jamaican LGBTQ community. He'd taught so many young people how to live in their authentic skin. I'd learned, most of all, how to stand in my truth and to own my sexuality; and I'd also come to fully understand that I was not defined by who I slept with.

That night when we got home, Donavan and I both took long showers in separate bathrooms. As the water cascaded down my body, I realized that I had to move past my hurt with Donavan. I had to find it within myself to just let it go. No one in this life was perfect. I have already made a commitment to marry him and spend the rest of my life with him. I could no longer hold him up or have ill feelings toward him. I had to move past the hurt and give myself freely to him. Tomorrow was no guarantee. And, in that moment, I made a pledge to myself to live as though each day was my last. I knew I had a reason for living, and my goal in life was to find my purpose and my calling. Fully understanding that was all I could do.

By the time I had gotten myself ready for bed, Donavan was already in bed watching TV. I had put on the white Calvin Klein jockstrap underwear that he liked to see me in. He knew what was about to go down; all I saw was the white of his teeth. Just the excitement on his face made me visibly hard. I could no longer control myself, and tucking my dick was no longer an option. I just pulled it out and had my manhood firmly nested on the side of my leg.

He didn't have to ask me to worship his manhood. I squatted on his face, and I went head down. I realize that I was getting better at this. I had had all of him inside of my mouth, and the pleasing moan he made let me know that he was satisfied with how I was handling myself. My gag reflex was extraordinarily exceptional today, and I aimed to please. Donavan had put the TV on mute, and all I heard was his moaning. Without notice, I felt a familiar taste in my mouth, and I knew I had completed my task. I took it all in and licked my lips. I went over to him and kissed him passionately, knowing fully well that he was satisfied for the night.

I wrapped my arms around him, trying my best to make him feel as secure as possible. It did not take long for Donavan to fall asleep. I looked at him dead in the eye with the reflection of the moon coming through our bedroom window. I asked myself if I was ready to do this for the rest of my life.

What I knew for sure was it felt good. I honestly could not see myself being with anyone else other than Donavan. He literally completed me. And not only did he make me see the best within myself, he also pushed me a lot. I no longer questioned love. I realized that I alone could define my love, and this was "my kind of love."

Chapter 19

The pastor went into my study with O'Neal, and they were locked up in there for well over thirty minutes. Donavan was sitting next to me, trying his best to comfort me. He was apologetic and told me that, if I wanted, we could just go to the courthouse and get married there on Monday. I was hurt. However, I was not getting married for the symbolism of the wedding. I was doing it because it was the right thing to do. There was too much at stake to not get married.

The pastor asked if he could have a conversation with all three of us. I was unsure as to what that would do. However, I realized that the aim at this moment was to convince the pastor that the union was legit, and there was no objection to our union. O'Neal could not make eye contact with either Donavan or me. I had already told Donavan to remain calm and to just allow me to do all the talking.

O'Neal started off talking, and as apologetic as he was, I really didn't want to hear the fuckery from him. I just wanted him to do the right thing and tell the pastor that he was over me, and it was okay to continue with the ceremony. Based on the conversation, the pastor gave us the go-ahead. It was agreed that O'Neal would be escorted off the property. I had someone reach out to Warren and told him that the ceremony would be going on. The guests had had to wait for just under two hours. By this time, the sun had already set; it was still painting the clouds amber, which set a romantic tone.

Donavan and I exchanged our vows before God and the world. It wasn't what I had planned. The reality was, it was finally over.

We went off to the study and signed off on the marriage certificate. We were both excited and totally happy that we'd finally tied the knot. I held onto Donavan the entire time, as I needed to feel secure in myself.

As we watched our guests eat, waiting for our arrival, I asked Donavan to give me a moment to myself. I went up to the second floor to get a better view of the garden and reception area. I often told myself and close acquaintances that I was skeptical of people and I simply did *not* trust people. I was wrong. The real issue was I didn't trust myself. As odd as it may sound, it was the truth.

I feared letting myself down in some of the decisions that I had to make. I feared not pleasing people. Culturally, we Jamaicans come from a pleasing tradition, stemming from slavery. I didn't trust myself enough to say no, even to those I loved and admired. Too often I didn't trust myself in the way I spent money and, over the years, how I'd chosen my partners.

My biggest fear was trusting myself that I would be able to make the right decision. That applied even right now, in this moment, to trusting myself that I'd made the right decision with Donavan. My issue with O'Neal was I knew the hurt he had caused me; I knew that he'd betrayed my trust. Yet, I struggled to trust myself that, after all the hurt he'd caused me, I would be okay.

Looking back at my relationship with O'Neal, I saw there were signs—obvious signs at that. What came to mind was a parable I'd learned as a child—God throws a stone, and you throw a brick. My issue was knowing how to trust the pebble that God often threw at me. It is only when we become still and centered that we ever hear that soft whisper from God. It was what I called my inner GPS. Trust me, it is always right when you're in tune with who you are as a person.

The ceremony continued, not in the twilight I had dreamt of. The most important thing was it had happened. I'd finally married Donavan. O'Neal and his guest were escorted off the property. I joined my husband for our first dance. We'd decided to go old school and had created a compilation of Whitney songs—"My Love Is Your

Love," "I Learned from the Best," "I Have Nothing," and "Run to You." That, however, was not the highlight of our dance.

After our dance ended, we invited our guest to join us on stage. My mother's face was lit, just watching all the same-sex couples having fun. The strangest thing happened. My brother decided he wanted to have a dance with me, just out of love and support. His woman was all smiles just watching us. To be honest, this was one of the happiest days of my life. It wasn't just that I had married my best friend, my partner, my confidant. It was that I was able to show my friends and family what "my kind of love" looks like.

As the night progressed, Donavan and I had the opportunity to greet our guests and give each of them a personal thank-you. Around 1:00 a.m., I was ready to take my shirt off. Most of the guests had already left, and mainly close friends were staying around just for the free liquor. I held Donavan's hands and brought him over to the rosebushes and sat on a bench.

"Thank you so much for making this day one of my best days to date. I felt like we'd never get here today after what O'Neal did earlier." I laid my head in his laps, all teary-eyed, as, deep down, I knew I had found love.

"After our trip to Italy, I honestly believed you were going to end the relationship. I didn't know how to give you space. I knew I had deceived you, yet I felt like less than a man because I'd kept the secret from you for such a long time."

Donavan positioned me to turn on my back and look him dead in the eyes. He saw the tears in my eyes. I tried my best to hold them back, but I couldn't. I was in a vulnerable position. I felt safe also. Donavan's eyes became watery, and as he wiped my wet eyes, his teardrops fell into my mouth. I laughed out loud, telling him his teardrops tasted dry as fuck. He held his head down and kissed me passionately on my lips.

"I know for sure that the road ahead won't be an easy one. You are going to fuck up. I am going to fuck up *big-time*. I will get jealous and obsessive and act crazy. You will fuck an ass and get hooked; you will at times fall out of love with me. We're going to argue and fight. In the end, I only ask for honesty. The marriage is just the legal process. Don't be going out saying my husband this or my husband that. Call me by my motherfucking name and my own fucking last name, as it's all I have that's worth something of value in my life."

As I spoke to him, Donavan held onto my hands, playing with my fingers. I didn't often get a chance to see him this vulnerable. "I know for a fact that the road ahead won't always be an easy one. One thing I can say to you is I am fully committed to you and looking forward to spending the rest of my life with you. I know you get worried about my age. I know your views on Millennials and how much you believe that Gen Xers are more focused on relationships. I have so much to learn, and you have taught me so much already. There's one thing that gives me peace. And that's the fact that I get to sleep with you every night no matter what."

We just held onto each other in silence for a few minutes before heading to the bar area.

The bar had an interesting mix of people. Our close friends all stayed behind it seemed. Warren held it down for us and kept the party going. I knew he and Donavan had things to work on. He knew that I was happy, and he wanted me to be happy too. Warren's desire was to get married; however his politician lover wouldn't do that. He had given Warren a rather expensive promise ring, but that wasn't enough.

There were just fourteen of us total, and I felt it best to go inside, knowing fully well no one had intentions of leaving. Everyone apparently wanted to know when we would be leaving for the honeymoon. The big surprise was we had no intention of taking one—not any time soon. Donavan and I had traveled so many times together, so we'd both decided to take our honeymoon trip in December. It was my way of showing him my kind of love—on that island of our birth.

Our conversations were dominated by politics, an unfortunate subject, as most, if not all of us, had reservations topped by anxiety about Donald Trump winning the election. As much as Hillary's emails were not serious for me, the Benghazi issue was a political witch hunt, and her limited ability to connect and seem human was a huge factor. I was a Democrat to my core. However, the Democratic Party had seemingly become out of touch with Middle America.

The orange-headed man, as he was most popularly called, had grown on people with his unconventional approach. His Twitter usage had boosted his popularity, and he had connected with Middle America. He had used the word *jobs* so many times he was literally associated with the word. The cross section of America that was white, uneducated, poor, and racist was able to relate. Warren was adamant that, no matter how we looked at the political race, the Donald would be our forty-fifth president.

The conversation moved over to the untimely passing of music legend Prince. We all started singing "Purple Rain," as that was the first song that usually came to mind. Who could seriously have a conversation about Prince and not mention the fact that he was short as fuck and had a banging-ass body? Hold dah fuck up. Did I forget to mention that little man was fifty-eight years old? They say age is just a number, but this number was turned up. I told myself that I wanted desperately to look that fucking good when I got older.

The few women in the group noted that they didn't give a shit if he was bisexual as long as he ate pussy like it was his last meal. If I were to take heed of my elders, they often said short men came packing with big dicks. If that were the case, Mr. Purple Rain had it all set both back and front.

It was always sad when someone as talented as Prince passed away. The too-soon sentiment was somewhat cliché, as no one knows their end time. It left us having an honest conversation about death and what preparations we had made for our loved ones. An untimely death for those who were unprepared could cost loved ones an economic burden. Death was always an uncomfortable conversation. The idea of dying and leaving this world was scary and depressing. But it was inevitable; it was the one thing we were all guaranteed.

What I have learned to date regarding death is that acknowledging its reality must lead to an understanding of the importance of time. After Nathan's death, I've looked at losing a loved one differently.

Even though I tried to not remind myself about getting shot, the scar was too visible to forget. I had had my own personal scare with death. So I tried to live each passing day as my best—as though it were my last.

Delaney was like a spiritual guru, who looked at life differently than the ordinary man. We were the same age, yet she looked the same as she had when I'd first met her. Every time something popped up in my life, she asked me if I had control over the situation. If I didn't, she would advise me to move past it and focus on what I had control over.

I knew the night was winding down, and it took Delaney to put things into perspective for us. She opened her phone and pulled up a quote from Seneca. We listened as she read it out loud:

Life Is Long—If You Know How to Use It

It's not all that we have too short to live, but that we squander a great deal of it. Life is long enough, and it's given in sufficient measure to do many great things if we spend it well. But when it's poured down the drain of luxury and neglect, when it's employed to no good end, we're finally driven to see that it has passed by before we even recognized it passing. And so it is—we don't receive a short life, we make it so. (Seneca, *"On the Beauty of Life"*, 1.3-4a)

Chapter 20

Our summer and fall were spent completing renovations on the house, along with hosting friends. Donavan got a promotion at work and had a flexible work schedule. My new business was taking its own course; it was a new learning curve for me. We got robbed by a contractor, so we decided to do some of the renovations on our own. I must say, in the beginning, Donavan was against the idea. We spent many late nights working into the early morning. We had two basic rules—we would not touch any electrical wiring and no water pipes.

The teamwork brought us closer together as partners. There were nights when we did not sleep in our bed; we were too exhausted. We unofficially had two separate bedrooms. We decided to create a man cave in our basement. It was a spa-like experience with our own vision. What we decided was, in the event either one of us wanted some alone time, we could visit the man cave.

We had yet to spend quality time there, as a friend of ours from Paris had encouraged us to list the space on Airbnb. With the fact that I worked from home, renting the space out gave me a sense of purpose. I enjoyed hosting guests and interacting with them. We never got much of an opportunity to use the man cave ourselves though.

I did, however, steal away to Donavan's bedroom some late nights just to cuddle next to him. When we did have sex, it was spontaneous and anywhere we ended the sex was usually the room we spent the night in.

Now that the work was finally finished, it was time to get ready for our long-awaited honeymoon. We'd decided to wait until my business was fully on the ground and running before we took the trip. A year had already passed; we were adamant that Jamaica was the getaway destination. A few weeks earlier, I'd been watching CNN, and one of the anchors had talked about spending time at Strawberry Hills in Jamaica. The picture was breathtaking, so we'd made some changes and decided to book our reservations at Strawberry Hills Spa. It had been years since Donavan and I had spent Christmas in Jamaica. While the trip was meant to spend quality time with each other, we decided to incorporate our families.

How could we plan a trip and not have Delaney with us? Warren, though he lived on the island, was obviously invited. I hadn't spent time with my godkids lately, so I also invited Nicole and her husband to come along with the kids. I also invited four of my closest friends who lived in Harlem to spend Christmas with us.

And I totally forgot that O'Neal was invited. Quick story—he did get some help, and I forgave him and attempted to rebuild our friendship. We were now back on good speaking terms. Before heading to Jamaica, I called to confirm the booking and O'Neal confirmed that he would be at the hotel.

Because I had an unexpected interview to be a consultant at a small management firm in Midtown Manhattan, I had to push my trip a day behind. I would still have the flexibility to run my own business. I preferred doing consulting jobs, as it would be a great opportunity to get back into the job market and collect a pay stub. If I got the job, I would have to start by the end of January. The firm had reached out to me directly, so I had been somewhat excited when I'd received the phone call.

Donavan and I got the first flight out of JFK to Montego Bay, Jamaica. We were seated in first class with all the tourists heading to Jamaica for the Christmas holiday. I hated the fact that we felt like token Blacks in first class. I kept thinking that, if I could change seats and move to the back, I would have. We decided to make it happen.

Donavan and I opted to give our seats to an elderly Black couple. They were beyond thankful, as they have never flown first class. I must point out that we were not the only people of color in front; the others spoke, acted, and seemingly felt that they were white. Some were Jamaican born and had migrated and now felt that their shit could make a pie. This was just the sad reality of dealing with some Black folks from the island who felt as though they had arrived.

As sleepy as I was, I couldn't resist watching *Almost Christmas* with Monique, Kimberly Elise, Danny Glover, Gabrielle Union, and Nicole Ari Parker, just to name a few. It was all laughs from the moment I pressed the play button. Donavan, on the other hand, was fast asleep, his head resting on my shoulder.

Shortly before the plane descended, I took some time to look out through the window, asking the universe for guidance. I had so much to be thankful for. My aim was to spend some quality time with my family and show them what it meant to have *my kind of love*.

Donavan had made the arrangements for the pickup from the airport. Oddly enough, neither of us had touched another man since we'd gotten marry (well, I knew for a fact, I hadn't; I can only speak for myself). Our driver was young and tall, about five foot eleven; sported a low Caesar cut; and had an even-toned chocolate complexion. I wondered if he worked out, as he was fully toned. His smile and teeth were as perfect as the day God made the heavens and earth. He was also very polite, professional, and manly. I couldn't resist looking at his behind. Let me not even make mention of the trunk of dick print he had neatly resting on the side of his legs.

When we arrived at the Hilton Rose Hall Resort and Spa, we were greeted by a butler service. The agreement was to meet up with everyone at sunset for dinner on the beach. Donavan, with his clever self, had taken the driver's number and placed it on the bed with a note. "After I am done with you, we can have him for a nightcap."

I loved him dearly. He knew me that well, and that was why I'd fallen in love with him.

We both undressed and took a hot shower. There were two overhead rain showers in the bathroom. We had a view of the ocean, which made the experience even more magical. It felt as though we hadn't spent this much quality time together in a long time. I needed this time with him. I found myself growing and maturing beyond measure. In the past, there was no way possible to be naked and this close to a man and not desire sex from him. I had evolved to a point where I now desired a more spiritual intimate connection between myself and Donavan. The sex would just be the topping on the cake. What I did know for sure was that I loved him unconditionally.

We spent the remainder of the evening on our balcony with his arms wrapped around me, just looking out at the calm Caribbean Sea. The view peaceful—a scene of complete tranquility. My alarm went off, reminding me that it was time to get dressed for dinner. Donavan held onto my arms as I eased myself away from him. I knew he didn't want to go to dinner; and, more importantly, he hated the idea that O'Neal was here.

We both dressed and headed down to the lobby area, all smiles on our faces. Delaney and her partner were both dressed in yellow and white. Warren had informed me that he would be late. Our guests from Harlem seemed to be soaking up the sun and loving it. As I approached the dining area, a short, muscular young man came toward me.

"Hi, Akime. My name is Shevon. You don't know me, but I'm O'Neal's lover. I know the history, and I just want to reassure you that he will be on his best behavior. He is too ashamed and embarrassed to speak with you directly. I know you've both tried to rebuild the relationship long distance, and he is grateful for the invitation. However, I reassured him that all would be well and that he had nothing to worry about. What he did at the wedding has torn him apart, and he just wants you to know that he is sorry."

While the young man seemed sincere, I was not about to play some bullshit welcome party to the man who not only had tried to destroy my life but had also fucked up my special day. I was very polite to the young man. I was having second guesses about having invited O'Neal though.

"Thank you so much for gathering the courage to come over to me. I have forgiven O'Neal a long time ago. Will I forget what he did? No. I do not think so. Do I want to consume myself with negative thoughts or hating him? *No!* All I ask is that he keep his distance and stays on his best behavior. He isn't welcome to my family Christmas dinner. The other outings he already paid for, so I can't stop him from attending."

"Thank you for your honesty and your truth. I reassure you that he will be on his best behavior."

Donavan came over to me. I introduced him to the young man, and then we both walked away.

We arrived on the island three days before Christmas Day. I had asked Warren if it was okay to use his mom's backyard in Montego Bay to have my family dinner. All I had to do was show up and host the dinner. My father and his wife, along with my distant sister from Paris, would also be in attendance. I knew for sure that my mom hadn't been too pleased when I'd told her that Daddy would be coming. I had some family members I hadn't seen in years, and it was an opportunity to have everyone together.

Since Donavan and I were married, his family was also invited. We did have some issues with some members of our family, especially those who made negative comments about us on social media. Those individuals were not invited; however, they had the option to send their children. Those who openly called us "batty boy" could not sit at our tables. Those who we felt could not control their behaviors were asked to not attend.

Our aim was to create a safe space for all. I wanted our families to see what an alternative union looked like. More importantly, I wanted my mother to understand what *my kind of love* looked like. Donavan's mother had such a warm heart. Every time I saw her, she would tell me how grateful she was to have me come into her son's life. The dinner was not a sign of my money or my influence; nor was I hosting it to flaunt my success and throw it in my family's face. My purpose was to have our families, especially those who could not attend the wedding, come together as one family unit.

Warren drove into Montego Bay on Christmas Eve and spent the day with us at Doctor's Cave Beach. Two cruise ships had docked, and the beach was overcrowded. Delaney had opted to go to Dunn's River Falls with her partner and I'd begged her to let O'Neal tag along with her. My friends from Harlem had opted to go to the Falls also.

Warren didn't seem himself, though it was obvious that he had gained some weight. This was my first time I'd seen him since the wedding. It wasn't that Warren was out of shape. In the gay world, an extra ten pounds is much to do about something. I knew he worked long hours and traveled around the island a lot, so exercising and eating right may not be the easiest of things to do.

Donavan and Warren did exchange some levels of pleasantries with each other. The relationship wasn't perfect, but it had improved dramatically. It did not take long for Donavan to give Warren and me some space to talk. I watched Donavan as he walked away. The young girls were all over him. The young, toned, well-built white guys all wanted to play volleyball with him. He knew I trusted him enough. Furthermore, it was Jamaica. What the fuck was he going to do down here?

Warren and I walked over to the section of the boardwalk that protruded into the ocean. Warren wasn't giving me eye contact, so I knew something was off. The one thing I constantly had to remind myself of in Jamaica was my inability to show affection to those of the same gender in public.

"What's going on with you, Warren? Do you miss New York yet?" I had to find a way to lighten up the conversation.

"I have my moments of just not wanting to live on the island. However, I'm living my best life ever. Island life is sweet. Yes, crime is escalating daily, but I'm not personally impacted by it. Jamaica has now become the scamming capital of the world, and Nigeria has lost its crown. Being a farmer isn't easy. I'm still learning. I had some issues owning my social class and the fact that I am, indeed, a Jamaican privileged elitist. I miss your company. I know we talk every darn day, but just having you close to me is enough to make me want to move back to NYC."

I wanted very much to hug him. I missed him dearly.

"The move was the right thing. Look at how life has turned out for you. You found love. You're rich, young, and fucking one of the most powerful politicians on the island. You get to wake up to paradise every fucking day my friend. Who could ask for more?"

He gave me an odd depressing look, as though he was about to cry. "It sounds as though I have it all. I don't. Half of Kingston is fucking my man under the covers of the dark. After Denver's murder, I have become scared as fuck. I've been hiding something from you too. I've decided to settle for an open relationship—well, let's say, some components of an open relationship with an understanding of honesty." The look in his eyes told me there was more to this new story and revelation.

"The first question is, are you happy with the decision? Is this something you want to continue to do in the long run? If you're settling just to say that you're in a relationship to make him happy, please don't do it." I could see the pain and hurt in his eyes.

"I love him; but he fucks every young boy in Kingston and Ochi. He lies so fucking much; it just hurts too much. He treats me well though, so I told him that it's best that we just have an open relationship. After I got back from the wedding, I went by his house, and there were five guys in the pool house fucking. Yeah, he wasn't there, but I was still fucking upset."

I so wanted to hug my friend. Regrettably, I knew I couldn't do it in this setting. Well, it wasn't exactly that we couldn't. It was the attention and questions I wasn't up for.

"At the end of the day, you just have to do what's right for you. What Donavan and I have is somewhat open. Trust me, my friend, it's better doing that than cheating. If you get everything as the husband, let it the fuck go. Have a set of rules that you know is practical. As long as it works for you, let it go." I took a seat just looking out at the deep blue sea.

"I was simply scared and didn't want to feel judged or even jealous. I love him. It's sad that we won't get married. I have fucked out on him before; it felt great. I just hated the idea of an open relationship. You know what? I so needed this conversation, my brother."

Warren's mother decided to tackle Donavan and Warren about their relationship. Warren admitted he was jealous of Donavan, as hard as it was for him to say. Warren was emotional and started crying. He asked his mother why she hadn't said something all these years. The only response she gave was, "I too was hurt, as I was forced to have the son of the woman my husband cheated with work in my yard." She noted that so much time had passed, it was important that everyone move past the hurt. Both men agreed to work on their relationship, and Warren finally called Donavan brother.

Donavan, Warren and I spent the remainder of the evening by his mother's pool house, watching the sunset. After the conversation Warren and Donavan had had, they both agreed they would work on the relationship. Warren's mother said she had known all along, and she too was struggling; that was why she'd paid special attention to Donavan. Donavan was adamant that he did not want any of the inheritance, but Warren insisted on a mutual partnership.

I was filled with joy, just knowing that the two men in my life weren't just on speaking terms but were also working on becoming better brothers. To be honest, there wasn't anything I could ask for right now. My life was going great; this year had taught me so much about myself and the importance of stillness.

The solo trip to the Bahamas was what had brokered the deal for me. Back in nature, I had enjoyed the stillness of life—realizing that, when God created the heaven and the earth, it was perfect. I needed to find myself, move past the hurt, and continue to learn how to forgive.

My new handbook was *The Greatest Secrets of All.* This book has literally transformed my life. The overall lesson I took from the book was that, to live a full, good, productive, and healthy life, all we needed were *love, service,* and *gratitude.* These three basic principles had brought me here; they had given me hope and allowed me to find love all over again.

Christmas came without white Santa; however, I would not be me without giving gifts. I had gotten a local company to take care of the decorations and food. We had seating for sixty-eight individuals. It was a red, white, and green type of affair. I insisted on using local flowers as much as possible. The red poinsettias were simply perfect. On one of my trips to Brussels years ago, I had seen a Christmas tree made from red poinsettias, and I wanted to replicate it in Warren's mother's backyard.

Donavan had a friend who worked at Sandals Royal, Montego Bay, and was able to convince him to get the day off to cook for us. I didn't have to ask that he was returning a long-time favor, and a happy ending was expected before this trip ended. I had now become accepting of this open relationship concept, knowing deep down that my man loved me. At the end of the day, I got to go to bed at nights with him, lying next to him and waking up to him when we choose to sleep next to each other.

The group was the right mix. The old folks were overly impressed, and the younger ones made every use of social media to showcase the gathering. My mother had a smile on her face throughout. My father flew in and surprised me; I was taken aback. My sister came with her new baby daddy. I never judged her; I just gave her an envelope with cash. This new baby daddy wouldn't last long, even if her pussy was lined with gold. My cousins were the best. I just loved the fact that they never judged me; they accepted me for me. They'd all accepted me the moment I told them I was gay. They also accepted Donavan with open arms.

My mother had built a relationship with Donavan's mother. I was simply happy that our mothers finally just accepted us for who we are as individuals and not just as gay men. All of Donavan's family members were open and liberal; and they loved him and his achievements. It was his success that they were celebrating and not his sexuality.

Donavan and I got a moment to stand at a distance and watch our families mingle and laugh with each other. If only the outside world got an opportunity to see this—to see the true Jamaica, the land of wood and water. An island paradise, Jamaica was made up of people from many different walks of life. This gathering was reflective of a true Jamaican love story—the one the media and advocacy groups never wanted to showcase. While we wouldn't want to make our lives into a reality TV series, the showcasing of this abundance of love and acceptance would be life changing.

After dinner, the sky was turning amber, and the sunset was visible on the horizon. The candles on the tables were all lit. The scenery was transformed. I had hired a local mento band. The band members, as well as the women who came as backup singers, dressed in traditional Jamaican fabric. It reminded me of old story time, somewhat nostalgic of colonial Jamaica—a party our ancestors would have organized outside the plantocracy and the bounds of the white slave owners.

This was the part of the night I had been looking forward to. I was a firm believer that, of whom much is given, much is required. I never forgot *love, service,* and *gratitude* in all that I did. I asked for the band to stop playing and motioned for Donavan and Warren to join me on the makeshift platform. I knew everyone had been wondering all day why it hadn't been put to use. Tonight was the night that dreams came true. Today was the night when we gave back to those who had shown us love.

We were all on stage just laughing with each other. Warren suggested we called our mothers up on stage, seeing that they had given us the most precious gift of all—life. With our mothers next to us, we spoke about our friendship, our bond, and what giving meant to us.

"I didn't grow up with much. I am thankful for my humble upbringing and the fact that my mother instilled the value of education in my life. I am a firm believer that, as a race, we who are

Black must remember that education is the only solid thing that will enrich our lives and the lives of our loved ones. All three of us have decided to pay the full tuition of one of one member from each of our families including their university degree."

The clapping and screaming were uncontrollable. No one knew who would be called. We felt that we should start with those in high school—two teenage boys and a girl. We had our mothers read the names—Paul, David, and Angela. All three were in high school and showed the potential to go to college. No matter the cost of the tuition for university, it would be covered in full. The only condition was that all three would get involved in some form of community service. Not only were we our brothers' keepers, but we were also firm in the belief that, to whom much is given, much is required. The only thing we asked was that those we were helping must also give back to someone else who needed help, as they would now be able to give back.

We all hugged them and wiped their tears; none of them had expected this. This was what I loved the most about giving—when the recipients had no idea or expectation of getting anything, and they were humbled by the gesture.

"So, the gift doesn't stop here." I held onto my mother's hands, and Donavan and Warren each held their mothers' hands. I motioned to the DJ to play Whitney Houston "One Wish."

There was just something about listening to Whitney Houston during the Christmas holiday. As the song was playing, I had twelve helpers all dressed like Santa's elves with gift bags in their hands.

Literally everyone was just watching in amazement, trying to figure out what was about to go down. I loved seeing the faces of people when I was giving gifts, especially when they were unaware that the gift was coming.

"Now, we cannot have a functional life in school without the right tools. I have one wish, and that is for us all to realize how important family is. No matter what, we must love each, and we all need to communicate with each other. What we need is to show our family members love and guidance. In the spirit of giving, to ensure that we are all connected to each other, everybody is getting a tablet." I had to say it in my Oprah voice for the effects of it. It wasn't a car, but it was something most of my family didn't have.

I had instructed each of the elves to stand by a table. As everyone received their gifts, I could see the excitement on their faces. The older folks were excited too, and I knew deep down they were wondering why I hadn't just given them the money, as they had no use for a tablet. I knew for sure that many of my family would be selling their tablets. If they did, I hoped they made use of the cash they would be getting.

The gift giving wasn't over. Warren and Donavan took to the microphone.

"The party isn't over yet," said Warren. "We all need to tell time. And what better way to tell the time than with Apple Watches?"

"Look under your seats," Donavan chimed in. "You get a watch, you get a watch, and you get a watch."

Just watching the two favorite men in my life help me give away gifts to those we loved was an amazingly beautiful blessing. I had always wanted to do an Oprah giveaway with my family, and this was the perfect moment.

Before the night ended, I literally greeted everyone; each personally thanked me for the gifts. Some had no clue what to do with the gifts, but they were appreciative, nonetheless. My mother gave me a huge hug and told me she was very proud of me and that the Lord would richly bless me.

The party ended after 2:00 a.m., and Warren, Donavan, and I all sat by the pool after we had finish cleaning up. We couldn't see the sea from a distance, but the view of Montego Bay at night was breathtaking. Two cruise ships in the harbor were lit up, and we saw the last flight coming in from London at the nearby airport.

Warren decided he would be spending the night in the pool house. Well, he noted that he had gotten accustomed to staying there growing up. It was the only home he knew of. Donavan and I decided to nestle together in the hammock and watch the stars as they twinkled above us.

This was all I desired for the night. Just feeling my man, lying on his chest, and smelling the sweat from his armpits was such a huge turn-on. I had grown to love Donavan, just as I had loved Nathan. There were moments when I still did think about Nathan and pondered the "what-if?"

It didn't take long before I fell asleep in Donavan's arms. He held me close to him. I told him that he might suffocate me. No matter what we had gone through over the years, what I knew for sure was this was my kind of love—a love defined by no other but us. We lay the ground rules, and we were living by our rules. I could not have asked for anything more.

I felt my safest with Donavan, and he was all the man I would ever need. I honestly didn't care who he fucked, simply because it was just a *fuckkk*—an act that doesn't last for too long. I got to cuddle next to him and build memories with him. That was all I could ask for of anyone. He just turned out to be my Jamaican guy.

Chapter 21

After the Christmas giveaway, I was ready for the real vacation. The group met up in Portland three days after Boxing Day. Donavan and I did get an opportunity to spend a full day and night at Strawberry Hills. The experience was breathtaking. The sunrise view was spectacular, and we had breakfast on the open balcony. Making love in the dead of night with tropical night creatures in the backdrop was like heaven on earth. When I say my husband fucked me, he fucked me; he had my ass creaming and he never disappointed. I woke up the next morning with his man juice dripping down my legs and him lying on my chest.

We rented a cottage in Portland, one of the few untouched sections on the island. I insisted that we hire a chef, as I didn't want to be bothered with preparing meals. After getting settled in, we spent a full day at Frenchman's Cove Beach.

Warren's minister was nowhere in sight. And sadly, Warren had to face the embarrassment that the man he had fallen in love with was too busy to spend time with him. The young man O'Neal had come with seemed to have taken a liking to Warren. I didn't want to intervene. I just felt it wasn't the right card to play. Warren and O'Neal did have a great relationship, even after all the fuckery that O'Neal had pulled. Delaney was curious to know why I was so forgiving. She also wanted to know why O'Neal hadn't uninvited himself to all the festivities.

I sat by myself with my legs pulled up to my chest just looking out at the ocean. Donavan was an avid swimmer, and I watched him as he displayed his skills and how far he could go. I was scared, well more frantic, that I could lose him. The idea of losing another lover/husband had crossed my mind.

There was nothing in this world I could ask for right now. I was in a good place financially; the house was almost where we wanted it. While the sex between Donavan and I had lessened, the level of intimacy had dramatically increased. I found myself sucking dick more, while having my hole played with to my point of climax. It was more like Netflix and chill without the nut in my ass or me flooding his ass. It wasn't s even old age, as when we did get physical, it was magical. Can I say this? Sex after thirty-five, leading into my forties was way better than the sex I'd had in my twenties.

I found myself drifting away filled with gratitude for the journey I was on now. I'd decided before the trip to get off social media completely. I had just gotten to a point where I needed to share less of me with the world. Both Donavan and I had agreed to get off the gay apps, as we no longer had a desire to share ourselves with anyone else. The reality was, we now lived outside of New York City. Most Black or Latino men wouldn't want to travel so far out just for casual sex. We did have our regular fuck boys, and Brooklyn was the hookup spot by the brownstone in Crown Heights.

After college, I found myself captivated by self-help books. Oddly enough, shortly before I decided to get off social media, I had purchased some self-motivating books. My business wasn't taking off like I'd expected it would. Money wasn't an issue, though. I had invested some of the money, and I'd started an Airbnb on the lower level of our Brooklyn apartment. Donavan made enough to pay his portion of the bills and invest in his retirement fund, as well as build a huge savings account.

Prior to my solo trip to the Bahamas, I would always say that I had a huge distrust of people. What I hadn't realized was I had a huge problem trusting myself to make the right decisions, especially when it came to letting some people in my life go. I got hooked on a book called *The Four Agreements*. Boy, let me tell you, this little book had literally transformed my life. I would be gifting it to as many friends as possible.

As I sat in stillness, thinking about life, O'Neal came over and sat next to me. At first, he mimicked my sitting position without saying a word to me. I honestly didn't know what to say to him.

"I fucked up *big*-time dude. I am so sorry for how I acted at the wedding. I really don't have an excuse for how I acted. I honestly didn't want to lose you, Akime. On the real, what you gave me—the attention, love, and affection—is my kind of love that I'm seeking. I just didn't know how good a person you were until I lost you for good. I have the utmost respect for Donavan and all. I just didn't want to see you commit yourself to another man like that ever again."

I heard him; however, I didn't know what to say. A dead silence hung between us. All we could hear was the waves hitting the sand.

"O'Neal, I had to forgive you in order for me to be in this place right now. It's not easy. Trust me, it's not. However, I still love you and will always love you. You fucked me over, dude. It wasn't just the cheating; it was how much you betrayed my love and trust in you. I gave up so much to be with you, I literally moved to London. You gave me no warning or notice. You just left me hanging." My legs lay flat on the sand, and I dug a hole with my feet.

"Akime, I feared loving you the way you were loving me. You had a plan, a great fucking plan. Your plan was coming to fruition, while everything I tried to do was crumbling around me. I love you and respect you. I just felt that I could not meet you where you wanted me to be. You reminded me constantly of how important money is to you. Your brownstone in Brooklyn was literally the center of our conversations. I felt as though you threw your success in my face. I didn't have any degrees or money set aside. It was foolish of me to have rebelled in the way I did. I just wanted my independence." He was looking out at sea as Donavan swam back to shore.

"You broke me, O'Neal. After Nathan, I felt you were the one. You accepted me with all my flaws. I feared telling you about my HIV status, yet you never rejected me. You encouraged me to live my best life. I fucking left New York to move to London to be with you. That younger guy you were seeing, we both knew he was just a fuck. He brought nothing to your life but excitement. You gave me no warning sign, dude. You said nothing. I was broken for months. I grew to love Donavan; I was never into younger guys.

"In the end, thank you for the experience. I needed it. I have no regrets about meeting you, about loving you. It was meant to be; you literally transformed my life. I forgave you. The hurt is no longer present. I realize you have regrets; your actions were yours and you have to live with them."

I saw Donavan taking his slow time walking toward us. I realized that O'Neal was getting up to walk away. I told him to stay. I reassured him that all was good with Donavan and him. O'Neal had an odd look on his face, a look that conveyed his nervousness.

"I see you two were making out while I was swimming for my life." Donavan motioned to O'Neal's hand, offering a handshake.

O'Neal held onto Donavan's hand with a firm grip and got up. "Thank you for understanding. And I apologize for my actions. I hope you can find it within yourself to forgive me. Let me leave you two alone. Enjoy the rest of the day."

As O'Neal walked off, Donavan gave me a look. I knew I was about to get a lecture. "I don't give a fuck how much forgiveness you have within you; I don't want that nigger around you, Akime. I don't trust him at all, and you shouldn't either. I was only nice to the motherfucker because of you." He sat next to me and held onto my hands. We were mindful of our environment; but he felt the need to touch me.

"I am over him, Donavan. I have forgiven him too. You know it's hard for me to hate people. In the end, I still love him, not in an intimate way though. It's not like we're going to become the best of friends. There's no reason for me to hold him up. He is pursuing someone right now." I got what Donavan was saying also, and I owed it to myself to respect him.

"I too had a past with him, one that I didn't share with you for years. I was young and immature. I was so caught up in my feelings and in thinking that being gay was all about going around and fucking. You forgave me for doing all that. I am simply happy to call you my husband, Akime. All that you have given me is my kind of love."

When we got back to the cottage, we both took a nap before dinnertime. We all decided to stay in and have dinner outside under the stars. There was something about tonight that felt odd. I was deeply at peace with myself. Seeing the stars up above and hearing the stir of the night creatures made me feel profoundly alive within myself.

There was a little secret that I hid from the small group. Two of the guys who came as a couple were, indeed, my armed security. I'd learned to take only certain chances in this life. Safety for me always came first. Warren felt I was overdoing it. But something in my spirit told me that I needed some form of security while in Jamaica.

Later that evening, Donavan and I made love like it was our last night on this earth. I hadn't felt this much passion from him in an awfully long time. I wondered if the setting we were in changed how we were interreacting with each other. The way he kissed me was like nothing he had ever done before. He licked every inch of my body; he took so much care and attention in guiding his manhood deep inside of me. He made long deep strokes. He looked me dead in my eyes while he gently bit onto my lips. I wrapped both of my legs around him while using both hands to hold onto his muscular arms. He sure wasn't fucking me tonight; he was making love to me. He was literally touching all of the right spots all over my body. I just couldn't control myself. I shot my load all over my chest, even hitting my beard. It didn't take him long before I felt his warm milk gushing deep inside of me. He lay still atop of me as I drifted off into a sleep with his soft dick inside of me.

On New Year's Eve, the group got dressed for a white party on a boat off Port Royal. The price tag wasn't cheap at all. The party catered to the upper echelon of elitist gay Jamaica. It was a given that many gay Jamaicans who lived overseas would be on the island for the holiday. At a US$100 price tag, not many local gay guys could afford to purchase a ticket.

We all dressed in our different shades of white and headed off to Port Royal where the boat was docked. This was Donavan's first time in Port Royal. Donavan and I both wore matching outfits, except for our accessories. We wore damaged white jeans with netted white jackets and went shirtless underneath, purposefully showing off our tight gym bodies. Initially, I was somewhat insecure. I felt too old to be dressing like this. Donavan convinced me to do it.

Of all the nights, Warren's partner in crime was present for this outing. Warren explained that the young, giddy-headed rich guys were all out, and his lover was on the ride just for the hunt. This was the struggle in dating an older guy. They tended to come with the level of maturity that you desire in a relationship. Yet their mindset was fucked up, as they were set in their ways. They oftentimes had nothing to lose, and manipulation was their go-to key to get younger guys to do it their way.

Warren seemed content with his current situation. I knew he wanted more commitment, but finding a man in Warren's class would be a challenge. The next best option was to date someone way beneath him—getting up every day and questioning whether your partner was actually with you for your money and privilege or just for you. In the end, I knew Warren would do the right thing.

The boat left Port Royal at around sunset. The view of the Kingston Harbor was breathtaking. I had to admit that the service on the boat was top class. It did not take long for guys to ask us where we lived. It was just a joke, as Donavan and I both knew most of the guys were just looking to fuck. This was the same group that attend the parties in the hills of Kingston. They were so far out of touch with the Jamaican gay community. It was the party for the crème de la crème in the Jamaican gay society. These were mainly the bunch from "Upper St. Andrew," who were snobbish, selfish, and arrogant. These were the pretentious gays who ostracized themselves and would do anything to ensure that gay rights weren't improved in Jamaica.

I got an opportunity to have an audience with Warren—just to check in on him. We spoke about my conversation with O'Neal and how it made me feel. Warren expressed that he was simply excited about the fact that O'Neal was not in attendance. It was indeed a good group of guys. A few known socialites were in attendance, along with some TV personalities.

We stayed on the boat until after 10:00 p.m. When we docked, we took a smaller tube boat over to the cays, where a bonfire was lit. A table filled with exotic fruits and Jamaican food delights was set out. A few opted to swim, as it was low tide. The waiters all wore Speedos—and goddamn, they had bodies with washboard abs. Some of the passengers opted not to leave the boat, as they were too scared. All of those who were in my group, expect Warren and his partner, went over to the island.

While on Lime Cay, Donavan and I got some curried goat, rice, and peas, along with fried chicken and fish. We found a secluded spot to nestle. The food was delightful; this sure as fuck was a reflection of country living. For what it was worth, it was the presentation that got us. The host spared no time supplying us with top-shelf liquor.

As the new year approached, the waiters served us all chilled glasses of imported French champagne. It was an Emeli Sandé, Tony Braxton, and Celine Dione kind of night. This was just picture-perfect. The stars were bright in the sky; the water was calm. Something about this night made me want to capture this moment for eternity. It was as though I was one with God like in the beginning when God created the heaven and the earth.

Donavan held onto my hands as we took in the festivities. I could hear my heart beating, and I brought myself closer to him. As I stood in that moment with my man, I was filled with gratitude, knowing full well that this was my kind of love. Surrounding the bonfire were drummers, drumming to the beats of our slave ancestors. As we got closer to the fire, I felt the heat from the flames warming my face. Donavan came up behind me and held me around my waist. As the clock struck midnight, we could see the fireworks from the downtown Kingston Harbor. This was a side of Jamaica that not many people got an opportunity to see.

We all shouted out "Happy New Year" in unison. I turned around to face Donavan. I held onto his face and gave him a perfect kiss—one long enough for me to feel his dick bulging from his pants. He grabbed onto my ass. And before man and God, my prince, my man, my defender gave me the sense of security found in the knowledge that I alone rocked his world.

In typical Donavan fashion, he dragged me to the darkest end of the island. I loved his spontaneous side. Who knew the fucker had brought a small packet of lube with him? I hadn't eaten much that day, as God knew I could not have a belly protruding from my shirtless outfit. No accidents were about to happen tonight. I was nervous at first, but I knew for sure that this was a safe space. By the way, can I tell you, we weren't the only ones with the same idea of fucking in the new year?

Donavan wasted no time in swallowing all of my dick as he kneeled before me in the sand. As he deep throated my dick, he used the lube to massage my anal opening, getting me fully prepared for his entry. His hands were just below my butt cheeks. Even with lube on his dick, he spat on his dickhead and gently guided his way into my manhole. As the head entered me, I gasped for air. He grabbed onto my neck as he used slow circular motions to open me up. I so wanted to make noise, but I had to be mindful of my surroundings. It was typical of us Jamaicans to fuck and make no noise at all, to avoid attention. I had my back arched and held onto both of his hands. It was as though he was fucking me to the sounds of the waves. I knew he was balls deep inside me, as I could feel his nuts hitting on my ass.

We heard other moaning sounds in the near distance. There were two other couples, a gay couple and a man and a woman. We were shocked that this straight couple was so intrigued by us gay men fucking. The lady was of medium build and attractive, and she sure was riding her man. We all made eye contact; however, it was the intrigue of being watched that made the encounter so much more enticing. Donavan held onto my arms, and he gave me short strokes.

All of us who were getting fucked were literally in a line with our backs arched. It was a competition; it was all about the egos of the men who were fucking. I was in pain, but I knew that Donavan was feeling himself, and I had to give it to him. It didn't take all three men long before they exploded and collapsed on their backs. We all laughed in unison and got dressed.

My hole was moist; I was on a real high. It had been years since I'd smoke ganja. Something about this night made me want to feel that additional high. I was on the land of the Rasta Man, the one place on earth where weed was its best. The high-grade weed from Jamaica was transformation in a one-dimensional setting. Donavan decided to not part take in the weed smoking. He wasn't against it, but he stated that he wanted to be sober just for me, as the night was all about me.

We danced all night until it was dawn. We docked back in Port Royal and headed to a house party in Stoney Hill. It was the right mix of people. The music was sweet as fuck, nothing over the top. I consciously decided not to consume any more liquor for the remainder of the night.

The party reminded me of one where I'd met O'Neal. Something strange was happening to me. Memories of my past, especially with O'Neal, were coming back. I questioned whether this was what the process of forgiveness felt like. A part of me would always love O'Neal, but I didn't even see him as a brother. His acts of betrayal had allowed me to see the real person within him. It wasn't what I was looking for in a friend.

> *We must learn to forgive all things and*
> *all people, including ourselves.*
> —Iyanla Vanzant

Happy New Year

On New Year's Day, I woke up after midday. Donavan was in a chair reading a book. He was wearing only his white Calvin Klein underwear. I lay in bed watching my husband be still, reading a book. I chose to not make any noise, as I didn't want to distract him from his reading. As I pretended to sleep, my eyes were fixated on him.

Out of nowhere, his head still in the book, I heard him say, "I know you're up watching me. Why don't you come sit in my lap and let me read to you? For some odd reason, I just couldn't sleep. I saw you looking so peaceful, and I didn't want to disturb you. I picked up this book you brought down, *The Four Agreements*. It's an interesting read, baby. I'm almost halfway through. The part about assumptions really hit hard."

I got up, embarrassingly with my dick hard. I walked over to him and sat in his lap. He put his arms around me and kissed me on the lips with my morning breath.

"It's an interesting read, mister. I'm happy you found it interesting too. I'm stuck on the impeccable words part. It's important that we choose our words carefully, ask for what we want, and be very positive in how we use our words. Not only that, promise me, no matter what, make no assumptions. If you have a question to ask, just ask it and hold me to my truth." We both sat in silence, just looking outside at nature.

The universe was telling me something. I just didn't know what it was. It might sound cliché, but three fucking birds were by the window chirping. I smiled to myself, as Bob Marley's "Three Little Birds" was now playing in my head. I remember sitting in this exact position in my grandmother's lap hearing that song playing as a child. "Every little thing is going to be all right." I only hoped that was my reality.

As I lay on Donavan's chest I whispered in his ears, "Is everything okay, baby? I'm having this odd feeling that something is out of place."

All he did was shake his head, hold onto my head, and lay it firmly on his shoulders. We both fell asleep like that. The security of knowing that he'd reassured me that all was well was all I needed.

We got up around dinnertime, and we took a shower together. I scrubbed every inch of my man's body, and he did the same to me. Night had already fallen; the night creatures were making their usual noise outside. We both stood under the shower, holding onto each other. It was a relaxing feeling; our dicks weren't hard. We just held onto each other, and we listened to each other's heartbeat. There is something about being still. It takes you to a higher level of reality. It literally brings you closer to yourself and your creator.

We got dressed and went downstairs for dinner. It was the final supper of our getaway, and everyone was patiently waiting for us. All that was going on was straight out of Leonardo da Vinci's *The Last Supper*. Something within me told me that the night was going to come with an unexpected ending.

Donavan and I sat at the center of the table, just looking at our guests. Tonight, was our last night as a group. We would return to our reality later the next evening. Later in the night, we had all agreed to check out a local New Year's dancehall session in Riverton City.

After dinner ended, we all gathered in the reading room section of the villa. Traditional Jamaican Christmas cake was served, along with Devon House butter pecan ice cream. Sorrel spiced with rum was also available as an option. Our conversations revolved around how we all could make a meaningful impact on the island. It was a progressive conversation about change and the future of the Jamaican gay identity.

The conversation was deep, yet the views were fresh and innovative. It was a given that the younger generation was the real future of the island. While some said that the JLP leadership was young, it felt like more of the same run-on political tribalism, with no significant change. It was more about the changing of the old guard. The mindset across the island was the same. There was this codependency on someone to do something for you, while the leadership within the government held everyone in political bondage until election time. Education was the means to upward mobility, yet most students who acquired a degree eventually migrated.

The conversation was deep. We went as far back as to Michael Manley, one of Jamaica's leading political activists who was tagged as a communist. Manley fought for the people and believed that the Jamaican people were the country's greatest asset. Education was the only way out of poverty. Capitalism and greed had taken control, along with the International Monetary Fund (IMF).

The conversation reminded me why I had gone to school in Jamaica at the University of the West Indies (UWI). It was my desire to give back to my people—the will to make a meaningful positive change. Back then, I had strongly believed in nationalism and nation building. I was impressed by the younger generation. Jamaica had improved a great deal; however, the international media continued to sensationalize stories. While gay rights were stalling, the Jamaican gay community was finding resources among its own members.

After midnight, we were all ready to head out to the dance. I was excited to go, simply because it would bring back memories of my college days. There was something about dancehall that pervaded the Jamaican culture. It was more than just listening to dancehall music; it was a social commentary, especially for the poorer class. After all these years, even with acclaimed international recognition, the genre was still looked down on by the Jamaican upper class.

Beyoncé and Rihanna had even imitated dancehall, not just replicating the dance routine but also capturing the beat of the music. It was only when our music and culture received international recognition, only then, that the Jamaican elite saw it as a part of who we were.

Let's not even have a conversation about soca music and all that happened during carnival time. It was hypocrisy at its highest level. Who was I to say anything? I was into neither soca nor the local new beats and rhythms. Give me my old hits reggae from the '80s and '90s, and trust me, I'm good.

When our transport arrived at the dance, we all decided to get corn soup, along with roasted yams. O'Neal seemed overly excited; we used to go to dances on some of our trips to Jamaica. As a dancer, O'Neal was in his element; and I had seen him battle local guys and win. Even though I intended to keep my distance from O'Neal, it was great seeing him in his element. The young man he was with was African, and he was clueless about what was going on. He did seem intrigued and excited to learn a couple of the dances.

Donavan stood next to me, his soup in hand, just watching the movements. To be frank, the vibes outside the dance were often more enjoyable than inside the actual dance. We all decided to stay outside just vibing with the people and getting closer to the culture. The music was popping inside. I couldn't wait to go inside.

O'Neal came over and passed Donavan a blunt to share with him. It was a form of bonding; I had no issues with them sharing a blunt.

Delaney had been quiet for most of the trip; she was trying to spend some quality time with her partner. Now she nudged me from behind and whispered in my ear, "Please keep these two far from each other, especially given that they're both drinking and now smoking."

I honestly didn't see it as an issue. I gave her my reassurance that I had this under control.

Warren had agreed to meet us inside. I was fortunate to have seen him parking and went over to his car. As always, he was alone; this time, it was expected. His partner would not be caught dead at such an establishment. While the typical dancehall wasn't a gay event, a good number of the male dancers were, indeed, gay. Typically, Jamaican gay men who were into the rude boi "bad boy" life often frequented the dancehall setting to get their fix. It was more of a suicide attempt, as these men were often closeted and would kill to conceal their sexual identity.

Warren wasted no time giving his objection to O'Neal and Donavan being so close to each other. I reassured him that all was well. Warren was adamant that it wasn't a good idea to have these two pairing up while inside of the dancehall. Italy and the wedding were too recent; the cards were stacked against both men. A voice in my head kept whispering that I needed to listen to my friends. My husband could defend himself. My ex might have a loud mouth; I just didn't see him as the kind to act out, especially in this setting.

We all got in, with eyes on us. It was a given that we were a group of foreigners. We had the right mix of women in the group, so it wasn't a suspect group of gay men. My security was with us, so I felt safe. They both had linked up with some local guys, who joined the team for the night, and I ensured that they were carrying their weapons, including my two guys. I wasn't about to take any risk; I was ensuring my safety at all costs, as well as that of the group. I had David, the taller of the two, stay as close to me as possible. He wore a jacket but I could see his gun very clearly.

The music was hype; old school dancehall was playing. I wished very much that I was in New York, specifically Langstons, Brooklyn's only Black gay club. I was not the type to let loose, however, when the beat hit me, I was ready. I always marveled at how the men would be in a corner or leaning on a wall with two or three bottles. The women were dressed more provocatively than porn stars—just for show, as they too were not dancing. I never got that shit and would never get it either.

This was where the real hype came in. The local dancers were literally lined up, waiting for the right moment to let loose. I didn't even have to question O'Neal; he would be taking part in all of this showcase of artistic skills. I honestly was hoping that Donavan would just stay in his lane. He was hyped by O'Neal, just to get the crowd going, knowing that two foreigners were going to battle the local boys.

The sound selector was hyping the crowd as always. For those who've never attended a dancehall dance, this experience is out of this world. Nothing in this world can rival what Jamaicans do with music. While hip-hop and R & B have become staples on the global market and made millions for artists, dancehall was still untapped. It was the sound selector who ran the show, setting the stage and the tone of the dance. It was rumored that the sound selector for the night was a young policeman from Mandeville.

The stage was set. The young Jamaican dancers came up, dressed in uniform as though they were coming out to war. The selector offered JMD$75,000 to the winner of the dance battle (the equivalent of about US$500). This was a lot of money in Jamaica. One after the other, the battle went on. There was even a girls' team; they did their best, but the boys were better.

O'Neal nudged Donavan to join him. I wished desperately that he wouldn't go, though I wanted him to have his fun too. My husband showed up and looked impeccable. I actually admired how in tune his body was to O'Neal's. A bit of jealousy came over me. Both Warren and Delaney came over and told me to put a stop to it. It was too late; there was nothing I could do.

The scene intensified when only three groups were left, including O'Neal and Donavan. The group that had a mixture of guys and girls seemed like the obvious winners. I overheard Donavan telling O'Neal to pull out of the competition, as they didn't need the money. Donavan kept insisting that it was a selfless act to allow the locals to battle, knowing they had proven their point.

The two other groups were hyping O'Neal to continue and keep the money if he won. A guy from the all-male group taunted O'Neal and, at one point, called Donavan a "batty boi" for wanting to pull out of the competition. Donavan had nothing to lose, so he decided to walk away. Out of nowhere, O'Neal grabbed him by the shoulder. Donavan reacted on instinct and threw the first punch.

I cannot tell you how the other group got involved, but the fight erupted among all three groups unexpectedly. Someone pulled a knife. I didn't know what to do. I instructed my two guys to step in. It was too much for them to even intervene.

I saw O'Neal with the knife. I saw with my own eyes when he stabbed Donavan multiple times in his chest. The motherfucker saw me too. He knew exactly what he was doing. He was willing to take away any love I could get from anyone.

I acted on impulse. I grabbed the gun from one of my security guys, and I aimed it at him. Before I fired my first shot, several shots were fired. Someone aimed a gun at the streetlight inside the hall.

I could see Donavan lying on the ground. I did aim my gun at O'Neal. I did aim to kill. The moment I pulled the trigger, one of my security guys restrained me and got the gun away from me. I did get a shot off. As I ran to the group, I saw O'Neal lying on the ground in a pool of his own blood. I knew I had shot him; I hoped he was dead. I no longer wanted to see him in my life, ever.

I pulled myself away from the hold my security guy had me in. I ran over to Donavan, who was holding onto his chest. There was blood everywhere. His eyes were open, filled with tears that were falling down his cheeks. His mouth was filled with blood. I used the T-shirt I was wearing to wipe his mouth. He had been stabbed at least five times in his chest. His leg was also injured.

Warren and Delaney came over, trying to see what they could do. I didn't care where I was. This was my man, and I had to give him all the love and affection I could give. Warren lifted Donavan's head into his lap, keeping him from swallowing too much of his own blood and choking. Delaney held onto his hands, as did I. I didn't so much as look over in O'Neal's direction again.

My security guys came over, lifted Donavan, and brought him to a waiting SUV. The ambulance would have taken too long. My guys had made friends with the local police. We were escorted by police with flashing lights and loud sirens to the university hospital. None of us said anything. There was a first-aid kit available. Paul, the shorter of my security team, had training as a medic, and he used a towel to apply pressure to Donavan's wounds.

The moment we got to the hospital, Donavan was rushed into surgery. I didn't know what to say or even do. I was simply happy that Warren and Delaney were both by my side. At one point, I broke down. I remembered Nathan and what I had to go through when he shot me. All I could do was keep praying, asking God to allow my husband to survive this.

After five hours, the doctor came out and asked for next of kin. I immediately replied that I was his husband. Everyone who was close by looked at me with shock and awe. I didn't give a fuck; this was my husband, and I was owning it, even if this was our end.

The doctor was a woman, and she was very polite. She asked if I wanted to speak in private with her and inquired if I had any support with me. I motioned for Warren and Delaney to stand by my side. We walked into a private room with chairs. I was nervous and told God I would give up my life to save Donavan's.

In a calm voice, she updated me. "Mr. Akime, your husband has lost a lot of blood. His left and right ribs are both broken, along with a fractured lung. While we can care for him, we don't have all the resources needed on the island. We could airlift him to Miami for emergency surgery. Our only drawback is we have no way at this hour to make travel arrangements. The hospital does not own a private jet. We no longer have a charter jet for the hospital. If you get him out of here before the end of the night, there is a stronger chance of him surviving. We will, in the interim, do as much as we can for him."

I fought hard to hold back my tears. I didn't know anyone who could get me a private jet at this hour. I had too much on my mind to think.

"There was another tourist who was at the scene of your accident who came in last night. We are unable to find any next of kin, and no one other than a young African man has come to claim his body."

The moment I heard her words I knew O'Neal's fate. I told the doctor that he was my cousin. She informed me that he'd succumbed to his injuries and had died before arriving at the hospital.

I broke down and fell to the ground; I knew I had killed him. I had never taken a life before. I was inconsolable. Warren held me up and dragged me over to a chair.

"We cannot know for sure that you killed him, Akime. Your security guy did restrain you. We heard other shots fired. Right now, we need to focus on Donavan and getting him off the island to get the best care possible."

My head hurt. I was consumed with guilt, rage, denial, and anger. Why had I allowed O'Neal to come on this trip? All the what-ifs were now in my head.

We all left to get something to eat, even though I had no appetite. Warren was busy making some phone calls. One of my security guys had a contact with the CIA, an ex-marine friend of his who was on the island. He decided to reach out to the US consulate to see if he was stationed there. The only thing we had on our side was faith in a higher power.

The news of the shooting was all over social media. The local police also got involved and were looking for me. I still had people in high places who I could ask for favors. I too made some calls to secure my safety. I had an old colleague who was on the low and sleeping with a high-ranking police officer in Kingston. He agreed to meet me to hear my side of the story. He said the video was questionable, but it seemed as though I was the actual killer.

Warren hadn't had much luck; Delaney, however, had gotten a hold of a friend, who flew in on a private jet from Milan. They were friends with her mother. She quickly asked her mother to ask for the favor. Lucky for us, it was granted. Our only obstacle was getting the hospital's approval to get Donavan on the plane to Miami. I would also have to cover the cost of the doctor who would be accompanying us.

We all chipped in and made some calls to help lessen the bureaucratic bullshit. We got everything all set and ready to go. I had some hope within me that Donavan would survive. On the way to the airport, we got a police escort.

The real issue came when we got a call that the Jamaican government was demanding that I not board the flight. They were adamant that I was a person of interest and a flight risk. Getting on the plane would mean I was fleeing the jurisdiction of Jamaican law.

When we pulled up to the airport with the waiting plane, five armed police personnel were waiting alongside three police cars lined up, barring our way. My friend's lover was adamant that I should not leave the island. They gave me only two options. I could either risk leaving the island alone without Donavan or allow Donavan to leave for medical treatment while I stayed on the island to be questioned.

As hard as the decision was, tonight I had to be selfless and think about Donavan. I knew there was no guarantee he would live. I knew how corrupt the Jamaican police force was. Warren was adamant that he wasn't leaving me alone on the island to the whims of the police officers. He insisted that my safety was just as important as Donavan living.

Delaney agreed to travel with Donavan to ensure that he get the best of care. I wrote a note, giving Delaney permission to make any medical decisions on my behalf. I had one of my security detail travel with Donavan and Delaney while the other remained with Warren and me.

As a method of protocol and a show of power and control, I was informed that I was an individual of interest and I would have to be placed in handcuffs. I asked if all of that was necessary, and the head man in charge, who seemed to be homophobic, was adamant that I had to be cuffed. I placed both hands behind my back, and I muscled the courage to hold back the tears. As I was placed in cuffs, I watched as the jet taking my husband taxied off. Warren stood next to me, and we both watched the plane as it took off in the distance.

Both of our futures were unknown. Who could have known that the honeymoon we'd planned for would turn into this? What I knew for sure was that, up to the end, if it came to that, I had given my husband, my man, my partner, my lover, my friend, and my confidante my kind of love—the only way I knew how to. I also knew for a fact that he had given me his kind of love.

I found myself sitting in the back seat of a marked police car in Jamaica contemplating my faith. A full police escort in tow, we headed to an unknown police station, while my husband flew away in the distance, struggling for his life.